What We Had

JACALYN WILSON

This is a work of fiction. Names, characters, organizations, places, events and incidents are either products of the author's imagination or are used fictitiously.

Published by:

Heaven's Mountain Publishing, LLC
5191 Columbus Road
Macon, GA 31206

Cover Design by Jacalyn Wilson

ISBN: 1539872904
ISBN-13: 978-1539872900

Dedication

For all those grandchildren out there -
(Yes, I'm talking about you, and Yes, you, too!)
You light up my life!

HOLD FAST

Life is a capricious wind, blowing us hither and yon as it will,

And we are fallen leaves, scudding and lofting with every gust.

As a bird, swept up in the gale, struggles to stay on course,

Or a tempest-tossed ship, lost in the storm, searches for guiding stars,

Just so, are we tossed about. Yet ever is God beside us.

Hold fast. He is stronger than the wind.

When I saw you I fell in love,

And you smiled because you knew.

-- Arrigo Boito

CHAPTER 1

The first time I saw Ned Parker was at the brush arbor meeting, the year I turned fourteen. Before that, I thought Jerry Johnson was the finest looking boy anywhere around, but once I set eyes on Ned, well... you'd have to have seen him back then to understand how it was.

Truth be told, I didn't even want to go to the meeting because time I got up that morning I knew it was going to be a scorcher of a day. I sure didn't want to spend all day sitting on a log bench, trying to be still while a traveling preacher did his stomping and caterwauling. I even begged to stay at home and work in the field with Pa, hard as that would be, knowing I could at least throw some cold well water on my face every once in awhile, but Momma said I had to go.

She made me wash up and put on my second-best dress and those lace-up boots that were too hot for anybody to wear in the summertime, and right after lunch we set out walking the three miles to the brush arbor site. My momma never missed a chance to go to the meetings, even when it was so hot that all the women, even the most proper ladies present, had huge circles of sweat darkening their clothes, under their arms and down the middle of their backs and even between their teats. That was how hot it was that particular day, and I might have laughed at how pitiful we all looked if I hadn't been so miserable myself. The lucky ones, including me, toted a cardboard fan from Riker's Funeral Home, and you better believe we never laid it down anywhere. Why, folks would pay as much as a dime for one of those fans on a really hot day.

I'd never seen Ned at the meetings before, and that first summer we didn't speak so much as a "Hey" to each other. But I saw him, and I knew that he took note of me, too. I could tell he was a little older than me, not quite a man yet, but getting close. Even from a distance, you could see that his eyes were a true shade of blue, and his sandy colored hair had been lightened on the top by the sun. All through that next year, I would recollect that picture of him in my mind and I would sigh, in the way young girls do, and hope that I would see him again.

When time for the brush arbor rolled around the next summer, I had reached the ripe and ready age of fifteen. I'm not saying I was ready to get married, but the idea was percolating in my brain. And the primary prospect I allowed to gain purchase rights in that dream was Ned Parker, the boy I had yet to carry on a conversation with. Momma didn't have to cajole me into getting ready that morning.

"What are you doing to your hair?" My sister Flora leaned against the doorjamb, staring at me. She was such a brat. Even worse now that she was thirteen and starting to grow some breasts.

"None of your business," I said, as I twirled a strand of my plain brown hair around my finger, squeezed it, then let it go. It hung there straight as a stick. "Foot!" I was hoping for one of those beautiful corkscrew curls. Now I wasn't one to give up, so I got hold of the strand again, wet it with a little spit, and squeezed. When I let go that time, there was a definite wave there.

Flo snorted. "It's not going to stay that way." With one last smirk, she edged away from our bedroom door and into the hall. "By the way, did somebody throw a bucket of pennies at you yesterday?"

To keep from throwing the brush at her, I clenched my fists at my side. I'd already seen the rash of new freckles across my nose, and it peeved me greatly. I'd been careless the day before, staying out in the sun too long without a bonnet, and this was my punishment. My shoulders slumped. Flo might say things for meanness, but the mirror didn't lie, not about the freckles or my hair. I twirled one more time, then put the brush down. That was the best I could do. Momma was calling from the front porch and it was time to go.

As expected, my lovely curls didn't make it from the house down to the dirt road, but I was too agitated to care, what with my stomach fluttering like a hummingbird's wings and my mind flitting from one bad outcome to another. What if he wasn't there? Maybe he would be with another girl. What if he didn't look like I remembered? He might not like me. What if I didn't like *him*?

I was walking so fast, nobody could keep up with me, especially not my five- and six-year-old brothers, Carl and Luther, who were being dragged by Momma, stumbling along on their short little legs.

"Hurry up, boys," grumbled Flora.

"Slow down, Birdie," said Momma.

But I couldn't. I almost ran through that last stretch of woods, until I stopped at the edge of the clearing. As usual, tall posts were set up to support the arbor, with chicken wire stretched between them to create a ceiling, and leafy tree branches laid thick on top, creating a room of green shadows and light. The heat was bearable this year, and there was even a slight breeze. I sucked in a deep breath and let it out slowly in a long sigh of disappointment. He wasn't there. All those daydreams gone to waste. I'd probably never see that boy again.

"Birdie?" The smooth, warm voice of a young man spoke softly from behind me.

I turned and there he was. He knew my name. I smiled at him and he smiled back at me.

That was how we began.

Ned asked Momma if he could sit with us during the preaching. I expected her to fuss and say no, but she didn't. Ned sat between me and Momma, with Flora on the other side of me. I don't know what made her so mean that day, but she kept pinching me on the leg, hard, digging in her fingernails. It was all I could do not to yell out.

Even with my sister pestering me, it was pure pleasure sitting with Ned. When it came time to sing, Ned wasn't one of those boys who just pretended to sing, moving his mouth but hardly making any sound at all. He sang out as if he truly meant it, and the sound of his voice was clear and smooth, like you'd think an angel would sound. I was the one pretending to sing, just so I wouldn't miss hearing him.

After the service, Momma surprised me again by inviting Ned to join us at our picnic spot for some tea, ham biscuits, and fried apple pies. We spread out the old quilt we'd brought with us and set the food out. Flora and Momma sat on the quilt with the boys, while Ned and I perched on a log a few feet away. Finally, we were able to talk a little. I wasn't about to waste this opportunity.

"I saw you here last year," I said.

He grinned and cast his eyes down on the ground. "Yes, ma'am, I saw you, too." Then he looked shyly up at me, as if he wanted me to like him but he wasn't sure that I would. I remember thinking that he must not know how beautiful he was, or that he could pick and choose any girl in the county. I tried to think what I should say next. There were a lot of questions to be asked, and not much time left to ask them.

"Where are you from? You don't live around here, do you?"

"No. I used to live with my granny and grandpa, near Raleigh, but they passed on almost two years ago. Then I went to live with my Uncle Arlo. It's just him and me. We do a lot of hunting and fishing, not much farming. This time of year, he always visits his friend J.D., lives about five miles from here. They've gone to the lake today, hoping to catch some bass. I told him I'd been missing church, thought I ought to attend the camp meeting." He stopped and looked at me, all serious. "My true intent was to see you again."

It felt like my breathing was hung up. My head was spinning and I couldn't think. I was still just a silly young girl, and I guess I would have swooned over him, whether he'd been a good-hearted, responsible man or a lying, no-good scoundrel. But heaven smiled on me that day. I fell head over heels in love with a good man.

CHAPTER 2

My pa was not an easy man. He worked hard, but he seemed to take no pleasure in anything. He never smiled, even when he was listening to the radio, which he did every night and heaven help the person who got in his way. Closest he came to seeming content was when he nodded his head in time to the music from the Grand Ole Opry on Saturday evening. Though it's vague in my memory, I do seem to remember one time him swinging me around in circles through the air. I was little, maybe four or five years old, and he was smiling. I can't recall another time such as that.

I asked my momma one time, why he wasn't happy anymore.

"Hush, Birdie," she said. "Things happen sometimes in life that make us unhappy or angry. Some folks are able to move on and be happy again, and some are not."

"But..." I interrupted.

"You'll understand better when you're older," she said. "Now that's that, and I don't want to hear any more about it."

"Yes'm," said I, and I knew better than to bring it up again. It would be a long time before I knew what she was talking about.

When Pa spoke, we listened and we did what he said—even Momma. Most of the time. But every once in a long while, Momma would beg to differ with him, and once she differed with him, she was not to be moved. Ned was one of those times. Momma seemed to take to Ned from the start, thank goodness, but Pa was a different story altogether. He just plain didn't like Ned.

It was the middle of that same summer, about two weeks after the brush arbor meetings. We'd worked the fields all morning, pulling weeds and hoeing, and I knew Pa would sit in the shade on the porch for about an hour after dinner, as was his habit. Back then we called the mid-day meal "dinner" and the evening meal was "supper."

The sun had been a fierce-burning blaze that morning, and the heat was still trapped inside me, needing a way out. After Flo and I helped Momma clear away the dishes, I put in to visit the creek, about a half mile from our house. It wasn't very big, as streams go, but it was usually good and cold, and I sure wanted to feel that cool water flowing over me, coaxing all the hot out.

I guess Momma could see the need in my eyes, because she just nodded, and said, "Don't stay too long."

I took off to the bedroom I shared with Flo, with her right behind me. Right quick, we grabbed a change of clothes and flew out the screen door. We didn't have bathing suits—we only knew a few girls who did, back then—so we would swim in our clothes most of the time. Every once in awhile we'd get real bold and swim in just our step-ins and a camisole. That felt good, with the cooling water right up against more of my skin, but I was always afraid we'd get caught, so I wouldn't let Flo talk me into it very often. I guess I was so darn hot that day, I didn't have the energy to fight with her about it.

So there we were in only our underclothes, sitting in the deepest part of the creek, where the water covered us almost up to the neck. We were so busy splashing each other and pushing each other's head under the water, we didn't even notice that someone was standing there, staring at us.

I reached for Flo's hair so I could yank her down again, when I saw her mouth drop open like somebody who didn't have good sense. Her gaze was off toward the rocks where we'd left our clothes. I stopped cutting up, and laid my hand across my bosom, to make sure my camisole hadn't slipped down. Satisfied that my decency was intact, I whipped my head around.

It was Ned. I gasped. "What in tarnation are you doing here?" I said, slapping my hands across my chest again. "Cover up, Flo!" I whispered to my sister.

I was glad to see he looked a little embarrassed. Lowering his head, he kicked a rock into the water. "I came to see you," he said. "Your momma told me where to find you."

"Momma said you could come down here?" said Flo, clearly amazed.

Ned nodded his head vigorously. "She did. You can ask her."

Flo looked at me as if to say, "What do we do now?"

Our reaction must have flustered him somewhat for he said, "I can see I've disturbed you. I'll come back another day." And he turned to go.

"No!" I shouted. I thought real fast. "Just go back up the path a ways, and wait till I call you to come back."

"Yes, ma'am," said he, most respectfully, and took off running the way he'd come. I heard his footfalls stop, and he called back, "Is this far enough?"

I could tell he was past the bend, so I yelled back, "Good enough. Just stay there." I grabbed Flo's hand and started pulling her toward the bank.

"D'you think he came to see us?" she asked.

"No. I think he came to see *me,*" I whispered. "Now, hurry up and get your clothes on, you little ninny, before he tries to leave again." I was so excited, I was all fumble-fingered with my clothes, and the clean ones were sticking to my wet skin, hampering my efforts to get dressed quickly.

Flo was moving slow as sorghum syrup, so when I was fully clothed, I snatched up her shirt and began pulling it over her head. "Stop it," she said. I could tell she was pouting on account of me saying Ned didn't come to see her.

"You stop it," I said. "Don't be a whiny baby." She tossed her head, but she let me help her.

"I'm not ready to go home yet," she grumbled.

"Neither am I." Putting my hands on my hips, I faced her squarely. "But if you don't act right and let me and Ned talk in peace, so help me, I'll pop your jaw the next chance I get." I raised my eyebrow in as mean a look as I could muster, and she nodded her head, sulky like.

"You can come back now," I hollered off into the woods.

"Coming." A moment later, we saw him round the trees and then he was standing in front of us. He took off his straw hat and fanned it in front of his face. His hair was plastered to his head, wet with sweat. He had on overalls and a thin cotton shirt, and over his shoulders he'd slung his boots, shoestrings tied together. He looked pretty good to me.

Ned and I could have stood there smiling at each other all day, I guess, but Flo couldn't stand it if her curiosity wasn't relieved. "What are you doing here? How'd you get here?" she demanded.

Ned turned his attention to Miss Priss, which was, of course, just what she wanted. "I walked." He wiped his forearm across his forehead. "Soon as I finished my chores this morning. Took me about four hours." He turned back to me. "I can stay until supper, that is, if your ma will let me." He looked rather uncertain about that part. I attempted to put his mind at ease, though I really wasn't sure myself, never having had a suitor come to call on me before.

"I'm sure we'd be glad to have you to supper." Then my manners kicked in. "But have you had any dinner?"

"Your ma saw about me when I got here," he assured me. He looked longingly toward the creek. "Do we need to go back right this minute? 'Cause I'd sure love to put my feet in the water for a short spell."

It was probably a good thing he had his feet cooling off in the stream, because between Flo snuggled up close on one side of him, and me on the other side, trying to maintain a circumspect one-inch distance from him, the poor boy was no doubt about to heat to death. That was the first time, but certainly not the last, that my little sister tried to act all growed-up and flirty with Ned. I guess I'd not had much to feel jealous about before, but that old green-eyed monster caught ahold of me that day and kept his talons in deep where Ned was concerned. Though we barely knew each other, my feelings were strong. The thought of losing my chance with him made me feel right anxious.

Flo was steady at it. "I bet you've had lots of girlfriends, huh, Ned?" She tilted her head and smiled up at him.

To his credit, he hardly looked at her. "Huh?" he said, merely glancing her way before turning back to me. "No. Never had much time for girls." He splashed his feet in the water. "Too much hunting and fishing to do. My Uncle Arlo isn't much for visiting or going places."

I kicked at the water, sending up a spray on all of us. "I'm glad he let you come today."

"Oh, it's not that he makes me stay there. He doesn't mind." He leaned over and rolled his pants leg back up where it was falling down. "There just wasn't anywhere I wanted to go. Before, I mean." He smiled at me.

Flo tried again. "Ned." Sliding across the rock, she got right in his line of vision. "Ned, did your uncle let you go to school? Can you read?"

Turning his head in my direction, he winked, then gave Flo his full attention. "Yes, I went to school, all eleven grades, and graduated from high school last year. And yes, I can read."

"Flo, why don't you find us some rocks to skip?" I suggested.

Her eyes squinted in aggravation as she glared at me. "Do you want to skip stones, Ned?" she asked, her expression going all sweet when she addressed him. "I'll find some good flat ones, if you'd like me to."

"Tell you what," he answered. "When you find nine good ones, we'll have a contest. The three of us, three turns each."

Flo waded into the creek, head down, searching for skipping stones. I figured we had about three minutes to talk before she'd finish her task.

"What else do you like to do, Ned? Besides hunting and fishing."

He didn't have to think long. "I like to make things. Woodworking, I mean. Arlo is a fine carpenter; he'd just rather be fishing most of the time. He's taught me a lot of what he knows, but I still have a lot to learn."

"What have you made?"

"Oh, a few tables. Kindling boxes. A rocking chair for the porch. I helped Arlo build a room onto a house last year."

"Sounds to me like you've learned a lot already." We swished our feet slowly through the water now, keeping the same rhythm, our feet almost touching. I felt I could happily stay that way forever, but my practical side won out. After all, our time together was short and limited, and I wanted to find out everything I could about this boy. "What do you do for fun? Have you ever been to a dance?"

"Sure, I've been to a few. Can't say I'm the best dancer, but it sure is fun to swing a pretty girl around in my arms." I felt a twinge of jealousy rear up, imagining the girls he'd been swinging around. "Can you dance?" he asked.

Next to his worldly experience, I felt embarrassed by my innocence. "No" I admitted. I didn't add that my pa generally had a low view of dancing, and little use for socializing in general.

"Well, I'll teach you," he said. "Sometime or another, you and I will go to a dance, and I'll swing *you* around." With that image in my mind, I couldn't help the grin that spread across my face. I just hoped my pa would agree to it.

That was all the time we had before Flo was back with her plunder. After the contest, which Ned won, I knew we'd better hightail it back to the house. Pa was probably long done with his nap, and I had to wonder what he might say about Ned coming to visit. I could only hope if Pa did say anything rude, that Ned had the fortitude to keep coming back to visit me.

As a matter of fact, Pa was rude. To the point of being hateful, I'd have to say. If it hadn't been for my momma, smoothing things over and overruling whatever meanness Pa hurled out, I don't think Ned would have stayed for supper.

It started before we even sat down to the table.

"Who are you, boy?" said Pa.

Ned smiled and held out his hand. "Name's Ned Parker, sir." Pa ignored his hand and sat down. Momma showed Ned to a place between me and Carl, while Flo and I put the rest of the bowls on the table. Then we all took our seats.

"Hmmf. Well, I reckon there'll be enough for all of us." Then he proceeded to ask the blessing. The irony of it was not lost on any of us that were old enough to understand.

A few peaceful moments ensued while the food was passed around and we all began to eat.

Momma tried to start a conversation. "Ned, did you say you live in Trapperton County?"

'Yes, ma'am," he said.

Pa tossed his hat in the ring. "Nothing good ever came out of Trapperton County." My head shot up and I glared at him. I didn't care if he saw me do it or not.

Momma waited a minute and tried again. "You live with your uncle?"

"Yes, ma'am. Before that, I lived with my grandpa and granny. My mother died when I was born and my father died when I was ten, of tuberculosis."

"Oh, I'm sorry to hear that, Ned. Any brothers or sisters?" said Momma.

"No, ma'am."

"World's better off without any more orphans. Too many of 'em on the streets now," said Pa.

Momma and I exchanged glances. Ned kept his head down and continued to eat.

"These beans have too much salt, and the biscuits are hard as a rock," groused Pa, flinging his fork and knife down on the plate, making a loud clatter. He pushed his chair back and stomped into the front room, from where we heard the sound of the radio starting up.

Momma sighed with relief. "Ned, would you care for another biscuit?"

"Yes, ma'am, I would. They're delicious. Best I've ever eaten."

Now, wasn't that a gentlemanly thing for him to say, especially after Pa had tried to put Momma to shame about the biscuits. I was right impressed, not that it made any difference, since Pa had already so thoroughly humiliated me.

Not surprisingly, Ned didn't linger after supper. He thanked Momma for the meal, said goodbye to the rest of us, and left. I ran off from the house, because I wanted to be alone. We had some apple and cherry trees on the other side of the garden; that's where I went and hid myself, leaning on the far side of a cherry tree trunk. Flo called me from the porch. I heard her, but I didn't answer. I stayed there pondering things until the stars came out. I just knew that this was the end of us, before we even got started good. What boy would come back, after a girl's pa was so dang hateful?

Two weeks later, Ned came to call again.

CHAPTER 3

For the rest of that summer, Ned called on me almost every week. The third time he came, he wasn't on foot. He whirred in on a rusty old blue bicycle. Over time, he kept working on that old bike, and by the end of the summer, it was halfway presentable looking. At least he didn't have to spend his whole day walking when he came to visit.

We sure had a lot of fun with that bike. I know it wore him out, pedaling from his house to mine and then back again, but he never complained about that. Instead, he gave me and Flo ride after ride on the handlebars, up and down the farm roads and the county dirt roads. Ned even talked Momma into going for a ride one time. I could tell she was nervous, but once she got past that, she couldn't stop grinning. That's one memory of my momma I've always liked.

After a while, Pa must have gotten used to Ned, or maybe he realized he had a free farmhand whenever Ned visited. At any rate, he stopped being so rude, but he never did stop being harsh and unfriendly. Ned took it in stride, however, and managed to bring a sweet lightness to the rest of us whenever he was there. Luther and

Carl followed him around like two puppies chasing their mama's milk, and they loved it when he would tussle with them, rolling all over the ground, giggling, which he did almost every time he came.

Toward the end of July, on the day that Ned came the air was strange and heavy. The sun was out in the early part of the day, but by midmorning the clouds hung low and gray. We picked purple hull peas that day, I remember. When dinnertime came around eleven, Momma was up at the house with the boys, and Flo, Ned, and I were with Pa in the field, trying to fill our bushel baskets the rest of the way before stopping to eat. A huge clap of thunder made us all jump, then stand stock still. With large plops, only a few at first, followed by more and more, the rain began, turning quickly into a deluge. Almost immediately, the breeze grew chilly as the downpour cooled the hot earth and the wind poured in from someplace else, maybe from the mountains, because it was almost cold. Ned picked up Pa's basket and stacked it on top of his, motioning Pa to go on to the house. I did the same for Flo, who was more than happy to oblige.

We couldn't run, not with two bushel baskets each, but we set a brisk pace to the barn. By the time we got there, we couldn't see ten feet in front of us, there was so much water coming down. We were soaked clear through, of course.

Now, don't think I wasn't keenly aware that Ned and I were alone. We'd not been truly alone before that, for there was always some member of my family around, wanting to enjoy the pleasure of Ned's company. Oh, I'd walk with him a little ways when he was leaving, but even then, the boys were apt to follow us, or I'd know that Pa was watching us from the front porch.

When I put my baskets down, I couldn't look at him. I felt awkward. I began to swipe my arms, swishing the excess water off.

Then, a hand appeared in front of my face, and Ned gently pushed my wet hair to the side. I stopped my fidgeting and waited to see what he was going to do next.

"Birdie, can I kiss you?" His eyes were big and serious.

I nodded. I'd never been kissed before. Well, except for Jerry Johnson, in the second grade, and that shouldn't count, because he had taken a dare from his friends at the time and because I bloodied his nose as soon as he let me go. So, as I see it, this was my first real kiss.

Ned leaned in toward me, and I got to thinking that since he was six inches taller than me, I really ought to help him out by raising my head and meeting him halfway. So I lifted my face to his.

Unfortunately, I went a little too far, and the top of my head rammed into his nose.

"Mmmmf," was all he said, but he grabbed his nose and took a step back.

"Oh, no. Oh, no," I said, realizing what had just happened. "I'm so sorry, Ned. Are you hurt? Let me see…"

He had his eyes closed, his hands covered his nose, and he was trembling. Everybody knows how bad it hurts when you hit your elbow or your big toe, or your nose, so I was more than mortified that I had caused him so much pain that he was crying.

Reaching for him, I slowly pulled his hands away. At least his nose wasn't bleeding. Then his eyes opened and his mouth turned up in a grin. He started laughing.

He was playing with me! "You oaf," said I, pretending to be miffed. I swatted him several times with my hand. Then he caught my hand, and pulled it to his chest. With his other hand covering my cheek, he kissed me. A simple kiss, as first kisses ought to be.

He pulled back far enough to look into my eyes. "Birdie, you are something special," he whispered. That brought a lump to my throat, so I couldn't speak. Which was just as well, because I didn't want to talk, I wanted him to kiss me again.

He did. The second kiss was longer, deeper. Just right for a second kiss.

The third kiss... I don't know how to describe the third kiss. It seemed as if part of me became part of him, and part of him became part of me. It wasn't just a physical touching of lips, it was a merging of souls.

After we kissed like that, I got kind of carried away, making plans in my head for a grand future with Ned. I guess girls tend to do that sometimes, and I was definitely a silly young thing. It didn't take long for me to get all wound up about how we were going to live and put food on the table for all the children we were going to have.

We pulled corn one morning, and spent most of the afternoon shucking it in the shade inside the barn. We had both sides opened up so the breeze could flow through. Momma and Flo had gone on in the house, to begin the work of scraping the ears to put up cream corn. Pa had taken the boys over to the garden to dig potatoes, and only Ned and I were left in the barn to finish shucking the last bushel of corn.

"Ned?"

"Hmm?"

"Why do you like me?" I watched him closely. Clearly, he was considering how best to answer me.

He was perched on an overturned bucket, and he shifted it around so that he faced me. He cocked his head and seemed to be giving it a great deal of thought. "Hmmm. One reason I like you is because nobody but you would ask that question." He picked up another ear of corn and started stripping the husks down. "You're not full of yourself like some people are, so you're not aware of all the fine qualities you have. Qualities like kindness and generosity." His hands stilled, and he looked at me. "You're always fair, and you stand up for what's right." He began shucking again. "You're smart. And you're not a quitter."

"But how can you know those things are true about me? You've not known me long enough..."

"Yes, I have. I've known you long enough. I've seen how you are in the little things. You're firm but kind with Flo. You make the boys play fair. You're thoughtful of your mother. You work hard at everything your pa asks you to do, without complaining. I know what you're made of, Birdie." He reached up and pulled a little curl from my hair and tugged on it. "I like your hair, too."

"Oh, stop. You're being silly now." I straightened my hair back up.

"I like being silly, and so do you," he teased.

I raised an eyebrow. "Sometimes, yes, I do," I admitted. "But today, I just want to talk. Can we do that?"

Instantly he quieted. "Something wrong?"

"No. It's just that... Questions occur to me sometimes. Questions I never get to ask, because we're either working or my family is always right here with us. I just want us to talk about, you know, important things."

"Well, all right then. What did you want to talk about?"

I hesitated.

"Go ahead," he said.

"I've been wanting to ask you... Ned, what do you want to do with your life? Do you want to be a farmer? Do you want to hunt and fish and be a woodworker on the side? You could even be a singer. Do you have any plans for your life?" I hoped he didn't feel threatened by these questions, but I wanted some reassurance that he took seriously his responsibility to provide for a wife and children someday. The woman couldn't be expected to do it. He'd graduated from high school over a year ago, so he was of an age to think of these things. Yet I'd never heard him mention any dreams or goals for the future.

"These things are important to you?" he asked quietly.

"Somewhat. Yes." I knew I didn't want to be poor, and I didn't want to live on a farm. And if I wanted those things, I had to have a man who would work alongside me, not wander off in just any old direction.

"I admit I haven't given it a lot of thought. I'm happy right now. I have a place to live, food to eat, the pleasure of a beautiful girl's company." At that, he gave me a big smile. "It's enough for me."

This wasn't the kind of answer I wanted. I tried to explain. "It's enough for now, but what about later, a few years from now? If we were to get married and have children, how would you support me and our children?"

Ned didn't answer for a minute. Then he cleared his throat. "I can see that the situation would be different then. I guess I haven't thought it out like I should have." He laid his ear of corn back in the basket and stood up. "I think I'll head on home. Arlo said something about doing a little night fishing, so I better go."

The tone of his voice and the look on his face, well, it made me afraid I had just made a big mistake. I jumped up too. "I'll go with you to the road," I said.

He gave a backward wave and said, "No need." I watched him as he trudged the worn path to the house, picked up his bicycle, and pedaled away.

Maybe I had pushed too hard. Maybe eighteen-year-old boys weren't supposed to be thinking about such as this. But I was thinking about it and I wanted to know what his plans were, doggone it.

If this otherwise fine and good-hearted fellow only cared about being happy, and didn't have a sense of responsibility for the family he might have in the future, that was something I wanted to know sooner rather than later. If Ned couldn't think past the blessings of today and do a little planning for the scarcity of tomorrow... well, then, maybe he wasn't the right fella for me.

CHAPTER 4

"Birdie, when's Ned coming back?" whined little Carl, pulling at the hem of my shirt. I shook his hand loose and tried to ignore him. All four of us were sitting on the back porch snapping beans. Tonight, when it cooled off, Momma and Flo and I would be up late canning.

"Yeah, Birdie. Where's your beau?" Flo sat in the rocker across from me, swinging her leg back and forth, kicking me in the shin. "Huh?" Kick. "Huh?" Kick.

"Stop kicking me, or I'll turn you over backwards in that rocker," I threatened. I didn't need the third degree from my younger siblings, not when I felt blue enough on my own. Three weeks had passed since our talk and Ned still hadn't come back.

Momma stuck her head out the door. "Birdie, come and help me with supper."

I handed my bowl of snapped beans over to Luther.

"Can I help, too?" asked Flo, clearly eager to leave off snapping beans.

"No, I need you and the boys to finish those beans. You can help me can them tonight." Momma said no more, just let the screen door slam shut behind us.

It was even hotter inside the house, with all the heat of the day still trapped inside, and little or no breeze to move it along. Momma motioned to the box of potatoes on the floor. "Pick out some little ones, and scrape the skin off. We'll be having new potatoes in butter and milk tonight."

She'd have no quarrel with me over that. I didn't much care for the work of scraping, but nothing could beat the smooth, tender taste of new potatoes. I crouched down by the box and loaded up my apron.

When Momma finished silking the corn, she set it aside, then took her biscuit bowl out from the cupboard and filled it half full of flour, to begin the task of making the biscuits for supper.

Generally, my momma didn't do a whole lot of talking. I guess she was too busy working to think about carrying on a conversation. But I liked it when she talked to me.

"Birdie?" said Momma, squishing the flour and lard and milk between her fingers, gently.

"Yes'm?"

"Did you and Ned have a disagreement?"

I wasn't sure how to answer. We didn't actually have a disagreement, it was more like we just didn't resolve the question. "Well…"

Momma didn't push. She kept mixing the dough and patting out the biscuits.

I finally huffed, "Sort of. Maybe. I don't know."

Momma still didn't say anything, just kept forming biscuits from the dough. When she had the pan full, she opened the oven and popped them in. Then she put the corn on to boil and started slicing tomatoes. "Birdie, you're a smart girl. I'm sure you'll figure it out, however it's supposed to be."

I stopped scraping. "But I don't know if I'm doing this right, all this with Ned," I fretted. "How do you know, if you've never done something before?"

"Don't worry so over it," Momma soothed. "You're only fifteen, and I don't want you even thinking about getting married until you finish the eleventh grade and have your high school diploma in hand." Momma sounded quite stern, so I watched her carefully to see what else was going to come out of her mouth.

"I guess maybe before you die, you'll see whether I'm right or not..." Momma stopped cutting tomatoes and stared out the kitchen window as if she was seeing a vision of some sort out there. "I have a strong feeling that the world is sitting on the edge of change. Maybe not in my lifetime, but for sure in yours."

This didn't sound like my mother, talking about the world changing. "What are you talking about, Momma?"

"Things have already changed because of the Great War. We lost so many of our young men—God rest their souls—but the change is in the ones who came back. They'd gone and seen something of the world, something other than the farm they grew up on or the factory they worked in. They'd seen some awful things, but they'd also seen some beautiful things." I'd never heard my momma talk like this, about these kinds of things. I realized, I guess for the first time in my life, that my mother was a person with thoughts and ideas and an identity beyond being my mother. She wasn't through talking, either.

"I can feel it, inside of me, that things are going to be different for you than they were for me. Girls are going to have more choices in the future. Birdie, you're going to have choices, if you want them, about what to do with your life." Momma turned away from the window to look right at me. "I want you and Flo to be able to choose. If you want to be a farm wife, that's wonderful and fine. But if you have a yearning to do something different, I want my girls to have that chance."

She came over to me and gently shook my shoulders. "There's forks in the road just ahead of you, Birdie. The first fork is whether to get married or to finish high school first. I've told you what I want and expect from you. I hope you'll respect my wishes, but you'll have to make the choice yourself. Choose carefully. Choose wisely."

She started slicing tomatoes again. "You're a smart girl. You'll figure it out." Then she was done talking.

That evening after supper, Flo was still all pouty about Momma letting me help with supper, while she, Flo, had to finish snapping beans. Nothing seemed to suit her, and Pa was even worse than Flo. It had entered my mind on more than one occasion that Pa appeared to pick on Flo, singling her out more often than the rest of us for tongue lashings and whoopings. But he was harsh toward all of us, so it was hard to judge.

As long as I could remember, we'd always kept two pigs at a time. Every winter, we'd slaughter the older of the two, and the following spring, we'd buy a piglet to take its place. All of our leftovers went in a slop jar we kept beside the stove, and most days after supper it was Luther's and Carl's job to carry it to the pigpen. Momma always walked down there with them, though, because she said you couldn't trust a pig not to get mean.

While they were gone, Pa went out to the front porch. Flo and I were washing the supper dishes and getting the kitchen set up for canning the snap beans. She was digging around in the bottom of the cabinets, looking for empty mason jars, when I heard Pa calling her to bring him his tobacco. I guess she didn't hear him, with her head stuck inside the cabinet, and she'd been so ornery with me that I wasn't of a mind to do her any favors. So I didn't tell her. He called again, and she still didn't hear him. I should have told her then, but I didn't.

When I heard the screen door slam, I nudged Flo with my foot, and said, "Pa's calling you." But it was too late. He came into the kitchen and, bending down, he snatched her arm and pulled her straight up into the air, plumb off of her feet. Then he proceeded to slap her on the jaw, three times, until Momma flew through the door and grabbed his arm and yelled at him to stop.

He let go of Flo then, and I pulled her against me before she could slide to the floor. Pa whirled on Momma with a glare of pure hatred in his eyes, and drew his hand back as if to strike her, too, but he didn't. Shaking his head, he put his arm down and went out the back door, making the screen door shudder.

Flo sobbed, "Why'd he do that? I didn't hear him. He hates me..." she wailed, and pulled away from me, falling into Momma's arms.

"Birdie, take the boys to your bedroom and play with them," said Momma.

"Yes'm." I pulled the two boys loose from where they were hiding behind Momma's skirt and drug them down the hall with me. I felt like the lowest of the low. This had happened because of me, because I had the devil in me. I could have told Flo sooner that Pa was calling her, but I was selfish and mean-spirited. Hateful, just like my Pa.

A few minutes later, Flo slipped into the bedroom, subdued and sniffling. The boys and I rallied together to try to make her feel better, and help her forget what had happened.

Flo said she wanted some water, so I went to the kitchen to get a glassful for her. Looking out the window toward the barn, I saw Momma and Pa arguing, yelling at each other. They weren't hitting, but their fists were clenched and ready. Momma was stomping her foot, and getting right up in Pa's face, and Pa looked ready to blow a gasket. I couldn't stop watching. I must have been gone too long, because I felt the other three come up behind me and gather round me, to watch the spectacle. Finally, Momma threw up her hands, hollered one more time, then trudged back toward the house.

Water forgotten, the four of us high-tailed it back to the bedroom, where we didn't say a word, just sat there looking at one another. We'd never seen anything like that before, and didn't quite know what to make of it. As the oldest, I suggested it was probably best to keep our mouths shut and act like we hadn't seen nothin', so that's what we did.

Gloria was my best friend. When school was in session, we were always together, but during summer vacation, we saw each other only rarely, so I was thrilled when I got a letter from her.

"Momma, look." I held out the letter to show her. It was early afternoon, hot as the dickens in the kitchen where Momma was baking pies.

"I've got flour on my hands, Birdie. What is it?"

"Gloria wants me to come spend the night with her this Saturday night. It's her birthday. Can I please, please, please, go?" I begged.

"That was nice of her to ask," she said. "Scratch my back, Birdie, right in the middle. The sweat is tickling me, running down." She stood still, holding her floury hands above the biscuit bowl.

I would have done just about anything she asked at that particular moment, so I hurried to scratch her back most willingly. "Can I go?"

"*May* I go."

"May I go? Please?"

"That's enough. Thank you," she sighed. "Will you be going to church on Sunday morning?" Momma was a stickler about not missing church.

"Yes'm. She said we'd go to church, then have dinner at her grandma's house, and they'll bring me home in the middle of the afternoon." I held my breath, waiting.

"Well, I don't see anything wrong with that," she said. "The Robertsons always stop by on Saturday morning to see if we want to ride into town with them. You can ask them to drop you off at Gloria's road."

I felt a little bad, leaving Flo after the rough week she'd had, but I simply couldn't deprive myself of seeing my best friend. There was so much I had to tell her.

My gift to Gloria for her birthday was a hand-embroidered handkerchief that I'd worked myself. Momma said I had a talent for needlework. The hanky had a bluebird stitched in one corner, and Gloria's initials, *GS*, in another corner. Everyone complimented me on it, and though I knew it was not as perfect as a professional seamstress might have done, still it was neat and even and the bluebird made it sweet and cheerful. Gloria said it was nifty, so I guess she liked it.

Most of Gloria's very large family had come for the birthday celebration, so the house was overflowing with people. It wasn't until bedtime that we two girls had more than a minute to ourselves.

"Have you seen Harry this summer?" I asked her. Harry and she had been an item most of the last school year.

"Oh, no, not at all. We had a big fight at the Independence Day picnic."

"What happened?"

"I caught him making goo-goo eyes at Myrtle Slocumb. And what's more, he didn't even deny that he'd been carrying a torch for her."

"You don't say... Gee, I'm sorry, Gloria."

"Don't be sorry on my account, honey, If Harry and I hadn't broken up, I wouldn't have given Evan Spencer the time of day," She snickered. "He's the bee's knees, Birdie. I swear I think I'm in love."

"Don't swear, Gloria. So, it's Evan now, huh?"

"Uh-huh. And what's this I've been hearing about you and that hotsy-totsy fella from over the way? I hear tell he's been riding a bike all that way to see you every other day."

"That's Ned. And it's more like once a week. We met at the brush arbor, first of the summer."

"Is he a looker?"

"Straight out of the moving pictures. But I think I scared him off."

We sat cross-legged on the bed, and Gloria leaned in close to me. "Well, you know, Jerry Johnson has been asking me about you all summer. He's still got a crush on you."

I rolled my eyes at her. Jerry was an immature little boy compared to my Ned. "Jerry's sweet, in his own goofy way, but I'm not interested..."

"Well, he goes to my church, so you'll most likely see him tomorrow. Won't hurt to take a second look."

"Hmmm. I don't know..."

From outside the door, Gloria's father shushed us. "Time to sleep, girls. I don't want to hear any more talking."

"Yes, sir."

Giggle.

"Yes, sir."

I'm not exaggerating when I say that Jerry Johnson stuck to us like glue at Sunday School and preaching the next morning. Gloria kept arching one eyebrow at me, which made me want to laugh, but I managed to behave myself. Then Jerry ingeniously maneuvered himself so that he sat beside me during the service. He shouldn't have done that.

Jerry's voice was like fingernails down a blackboard. Or a tomcat howling in the night. All I could think about was how beautiful my Ned's voice was, and how much I missed him. As much as I enjoyed visiting Gloria, I was ready to go home, to wait for Ned. Who knew? Maybe he would be able to forget my impatience and the premature demands I'd made. Maybe he would come back to me.

The summer would be ending soon; the end of August was almost upon us. It had been a month since our disagreement, and I was slowly coming to accept that I should have let Ned set the pace for our relationship instead of trying to rush things along. I knew I loved that boy, but my practical side, that part of me that wanted to keep things going in the direction that best suited me, kept rearing up, trying to make things happen a certain way. Or maybe it wasn't practicality at work, maybe it was something else. I knew what I wanted, and that was to get off of this farm, and to do that I needed a husband who could provide a comfortable life for us. That it happened to be Ned, the best and kindest of men, could have been my great good fortune, had I not driven him away with my needling demands. Where would I ever find another one such as he?

At least Flo and I were getting along better. For one thing, Ned wasn't there, so she wasn't constantly trying to insert herself between me and him, to get his attention. And now that I knew Pa was actually treating her unfairly, I watched for it, and diffused the situation whenever I could. Flo saw what I was doing, and it changed her attitude toward me. We grew closer and didn't fight as much.

The final week of summer vacation arrived. School was to start back next week, the day after Labor Day. For the most part, the crops had been harvested, sold and put up for the winter, so on the last Saturday of summer vacation, Momma said all four of us could go to the creek and spend the whole afternoon.

After splashing around with the boys for an hour or so, Flo and I scooted over into the deep part and let ourselves float in the water. It was a lovely lazy way to spend a hot afternoon. So pleasant, I could almost forget about Ned.

I felt the water move around me as Flo sat up, but I didn't budge or open my eyes. Then I heard one of the boys slosh through the water toward us, stopping right by my feet. I cracked open one eye.

"Is there room for me?" said Ned.

I grinned up at my fair-haired beau. "Always."

CHAPTER 5

In summers past when we were out of school, our farm was like a quiet island, uninhabited except for the natives, which would be us, the Calhouns. Except for Sundays when we went to church, the only folks we ever saw were the extra hands who helped Pa harvest the cash crop. With all the chores and gardening, there wasn't much time left to socialize, anyway. It was usually just Flo and me, splashing around down at the creek, or sewing, or reading. Every once in a while, after listening to them beg and beg and beg, we'd give in and play ball or go fishing with Luther and Carl. Still, I missed my friends, so I always looked forward to school starting back up after Labor Day. But this summer had been different, because of Ned. This time, I hated to see the summer come to an end.

I needn't have worried. At Momma's suggestion, Ned started coming on Sundays. He would meet us at the church after Sunday School, in time for the preaching service. The best part was listening to him sing. His voice stood out over all the rest, not because it was the loudest, but because it was the clearest and purest. It wasn't long before folks put in to have him sing for us during preaching. He'd just get up and sing, never seemed to feel the least bit nervous. We'd never seen anything like it before. Everybody commented on it. Even Miz Layson and Miz Dalrymple, the oldest ladies in the church, widows who were always gossiping and complaining and were never happy about anything, even they couldn't find anything to say against Ned's singing. They did have a few things to say about his old blue bicycle and the length of his hair, however, but they couldn't rustle up anyone who seemed to give a hoot about it.

After church we'd go on back to the house, have our dinner, and then, because it was Sunday and laboring was kept to only the essentials, we had all afternoon to talk, take a walk, or listen to the radio. Usually, Ned and I would either take a walk through the woods—accompanied by Flo, Luther, and Carl, or some combination of their company—or we'd settle on the front porch swing and talk.

It was a day in mid-fall, and starting to get a little nip in the air. The leaves had already changed colors, and most had fallen. Only a few stragglers still clung to the branches. The boys were around the side yard, which was thick with hardwoods, raking up mounds of leaves and then jumping in the piles, over and over. We could hear them giggling. Flo was in the front room listening to the radio with Momma and Pa. I thought it was too cold to go for a walk, so we decided to settle on the swing for a while.

To keep us warm, I brought out a quilt to lay across our legs and we held hands underneath the covers. We were still tippy-toeing around each other since our disagreement. He hadn't brought it up, and I sure wasn't going to bring it up either, at least not right now. I knew it would have to be dealt with sooner or later. But later would do just fine, I thought.

Ned was swinging and humming, swinging and humming. I'd noticed that he oftentimes hummed when he was nervous or had something on his mind. I just waited. I figured he would get to it soon enough, and he did.

"Birdie?"

"Huh?"

"Have you heard anything about a barn dance over at Holloway's farm?"

I perked up. "It's supposed to be the first Saturday in November, I hear. And there'll be a fiddler, a guitar, a banjo player, and an upright bass. It ought to be a real wingding."

"You're gonna go with me, aren't you?" he asked, as if it was a foregone conclusion what my answer would be.

I decided a little teasing was in order. "Well, are you asking me, Mr. Parker?" I simpered and turned my head away. "Because I may have had some other offers coming my way, you know." And I cut my eyes back toward him, looking from under my eyelashes, trying to look serious.

He sputtered and spat out, "Well, I just thought... I've been coming to see you since the first of summer...did you already accept somebody else?" he demanded.

I tried to keep a stern face, but I started giggling instead. I nudged him with my shoulder. "No, you goon-faced nincompoop."

He gave me a befuddled look, then shook his head.

I decided to show a little mercy. "I'm going to the dance with you, Ned."

He smiled with relief. "Okay."

"I'll ask Momma about it."

"Good enough." He pushed off with his feet and got the swing going again.

"There's something else I want to talk to you about," he said. I twisted my head to look at him. I was usually the only one who wanted to talk about things. What could Ned possibly want to talk about?

"I'm listening," I said.

It took him a minute to gather his thoughts, then he began. "I've been thinking about what I want to say. Bear with me, Birdie." He grinned. "And pay attention. 'Cause it may be a long time before I talk serious like this again."

Oh, me. Ned wanted to talk serious. I sat very still, and barely took in a breath.

"I'm, uh…well, you asked me some questions…I hadn't thought much about those things before. You know, about doing something with my life, and having a family, and taking care of 'em all. It's just—living with Arlo—we sort of live however we feel like it, we get up every morning and figure out what we want to do that day. And there's not a thing wrong with that," he hastened to add. "We're happy, and we're not beholden to anybody."

"But I just think…"

"No, Birdie. Whoa. Let me finish saying what I have to say." I shut my mouth and nodded.

"If I chose to live the rest of my life with Arlo, I expect we'd continue on as we have been, and we'd be fairly happy fellows." Ned picked up my hand and rubbed it gently. "But last summer at the camp meeting, I saw the most beautiful girl and I watched her. I saw how she held herself and how she smiled. And then this summer I got to know her, and she's everything I thought she would be."

Now he was making me cry; I could feel the tears coming. I sniffled and he dug down in his pocket, drawing out his handkerchief and handing it to me.

"Birdie, I want to spend my life with you. I want to have a family with you. And I promise you, I will do everything in my power to take care of you and our children."

"Oh, Ned." I wiped my eyes again.

"I haven't figured it all out yet. I'm not really sure how I want to earn my living…"

I sniffed. "We've got plenty of time. Momma said I have to finish school." I laughed in relief.

Ned looked around, to make sure we were still alone, then he gave me a quick kiss. That wasn't enough for me. Grabbing his hand, I put my finger to my lips, and we tiptoed off the porch, finding that it wasn't too cold after all to go for a nice long walk down toward the orchard.

Later that month, we heard about the stock market crash, but it didn't mean diddly to us at the time, just something that happened way off in New York City. I had my own eggs to fry, what with high school and Ned and making plans for our life together. Eventually, over the span of the next several years, the depression got our attention, as it trickled down to folks all over the country. Some were hit hard, and for others, life went on as usual. We were somewhere in the middle, not as bad as some, worse than others. But that all came a little later.

Right then, I was more worried about what to wear to the barn dance, and of course, I still had to get permission to go. Momma was not easy to persuade, but Pa would have been impossible. I don't believe she ever told Pa about the dancing part, only that it was a get-together. At any rate, I couldn't wait to get out of the house that evening, I was so afraid they would change their minds. The Robertsons picked us up at the road, me and Ned and Flo. It was crowded in their Model T, but we all squeezed in. I wouldn't have cared if they'd drug me along behind, I was that keen on finally getting to go dancing.

It was just like I'd thought it would be. It took me a dance or two to get the hang of it, but Ned had the rhythm in his feet, and it came through his arms and up mine, so all I had to do was hang on to him and feel the music. The fiddler was masterful, from the quick and lively square dancing to the slow, twirling ballads. I didn't ever want to let go of Ned, but I did make him dance with Flo a time or two. After the other fellows saw her dancing, it wasn't long before she had to turn down dance partners.

When the musicians took a break, I strolled outside and sat down on a bale of hay while I waited for Ned to bring me some apple cider. For November, it was right warm, but then, I was already fanning myself from all the dancing. I'd just begun to cool off, when I heard Flo's voice carrying across the way, from the side of the barn.

"I wouldn't have him even if he looked like Rudy V," said Flo, her disdain clear from the tone of her voice.

Another girl's voice answered, "Then why'd you sneak off behind the barn to meet him? Huh?"

"I did no such thing," Flo replied.

In the meantime, Tommy Shumaker ambled out of the barn from the same door I'd used. I guess he couldn't see me in the shadows, because he glanced around as if to make sure no one was looking, then he scooted around the corner of the barn.

The other girl, probably Glenda Richards, Tommy's current girlfriend, must have spied him then. "Here he comes now, the man in question. Let's just ask him. Shall we?"

Tommy must have tried to turn around and run, but he was too late. "Uh-uh," admonished Glenda. "Come back here, you louse. You came out here to meet Flora, didn't you, Tommy?"

"No, Glenda, I swear. Just a coincidence, that's all it is." His voice quivered. Good grief, what a scaredy-cat he was.

Glenda wasn't satisfied. "Then why were you and this hussy huddled up in the corner talking for so long?"

Jumping off the hay bale, I decided that was enough. As I went around the corner, I saw Glenda grab a handful of Flo's hair and pull, while that sap Tommy just stood there with his yapper wide open. Running up to Glenda, I got hold of a great big handful of her hair and gave it a fearsome yank. She let go of Flo like she was a hot poker, so I turned her hair loose.

"You stay out of this, Birdie," she hollered, loud enough that I just knew everyone would be coming out of the barn before long to gawk at us.

"Whatever's going on between you and your flame, you need to take it up with him." I spoke low, but serious. Then I told a lie. "My sister came out here to meet me, not your genius boyfriend. So the two of you just need to scram."

Tommy finally came to life. "Come on, Glenda, honey," he purred. "Let's go back in and find something to drink." Flouncing her dress and tossing her nose high in the air, Glenda took the arm he offered and left. I was wickedly happy to note that her hair was still sticking up all over the place, giving her the appearance of two devil horns.

Flo tried without success to rearrange her hair back like it was. I pushed her hands aside. "Here, let me." I tucked and twisted and got it looking respectable again.

"Thank you for lying for me, Birdie," she whispered. "I thought she was gonna kill me."

"What are sisters for?" I answered, and hugged her, good and hard.

We had our garden and chickens and pigs, and Pa had forty acres of good farmland for growing a cash crop to sell. He'd always planted tobacco, up until the year I met Ned, when he switched to corn and wheat. I asked him why. He said two sentences, which was a lot for him. He said, "Ten years ago, tobacco brought eighty-six cents a pound. Last year I got nine cents a pound." I was old enough to understand what that meant, and I have to say it shocked me. Now, it made sense, the increasing scarcity of money in our household.

Regardless of how poor we'd become, for the rest of that school year and the next one, my feet didn't touch the ground when Ned was around. The stories about how you feel when you're in love for the first time are true. It's heady and wondrous and it fills your heart to bursting. I didn't want to wait to get married, but Momma's words rang in my head and I didn't want to go against her. You wouldn't have thought, by looking at my momma, that she had such forward-looking ideas about girls, and she did mostly keep it to herself, except when she was talking to me and Flo. Looking back now, with the advantage of history and experience, I'd have to say my momma had never been more right about anything.

One time during that year, Ned's uncle Arlo came to Deckler Springs and I got to meet him. They were a lot alike, Arlo and Ned. Mostly gentle and easy to get along with. Head up in the clouds sometimes so that you had to pull them back down to earth, like reeling in the string on a kite. And once they settled on anything they were hard to budge. In other words, stubborn. So far, I hadn't had a need to test that tendency of Ned's, but with the optimism of youth, I was certain we could manage whatever came along.

He still hadn't settled on a vocation, but from working with Arlo, he did become proficient at carpentering and furniture making. The spring before our wedding, I think he realized he needed to do something, so he took a job at the furniture factory in Deckler Springs.

What time I wasn't spending with Ned or going to school, I did what I could to prepare for having my own home. Momma always bought the flour that came in the cloth sacks, which she would use to make quilts and curtains and sometimes even our dresses. While I waited to get married, she let me use most of the flour sacks to make two nice size quilts, which I put up for myself and Ned. I always did have a hand for sewing and embroidery, so I scraped up the money to buy two pairs of pillowcases, and I did the embroidery on them. Those I didn't keep for me. I sold them, and bought four more pairs, embroidered them and sold them. My little nest egg was growing, but more slowly than I would have liked.

Then I learned that some of the well-to-do ladies in town liked to have smocked outfits for their babies and younger children, so I taught myself how to smock, with the help of a book from the library. I used my pillowcase money to buy fine lawn fabric for the little dresses and gowns, and Momma helped me with the sewing.

The results were quite lovely, and I had high hopes for my nest egg.

The first time I went to one of the big houses in town, I was so nervous and scared that I let the old biddy talk me way down on the price. She kept saying she could buy the same thing from the Sears & Roebuck catalog for much less than what I was asking, which I found out later was a bald-faced lie. I barely covered the cost of my materials on that sale, but I learned a valuable lesson and I never let it happen again.

CHAPTER 6

And so time passed. I received my diploma on a Friday and on Saturday afternoon Ned and I got married. Flora was my maid of honor and Ned had Arlo to stand up with him. Our wedding was very simple, with just the flowers out of our garden for the bouquets. We couldn't afford to buy new garments for the ceremony, so Momma and I sewed the dresses for myself and Flora, who was my maid of honor.

The dresses were almost finished when Flo put her two cents worth in. "Why'd you make me wear pink? It makes me look like the inside of a pig's ear." My sister could always find something to complain about.

"Why didn't you say something sooner?" I replied, to which she huffed and walked out of the room. I only picked pink because it was the fabric that was on sale, and besides, I thought she liked pink. Mine was white eyelet with tiny pink rosebuds, and I borrowed a pair of white shoes from my best friend, Gloria. On our wedding day, Ned said I was beautiful beyond words. That was exactly how he said it.

Pa did not attend my wedding. I don't think I'll ever be able to completely forgive him for that, or for the row he caused on the morning of my marriage. He had everyone in the house crying and upset, and all over the fact that the chickens got out of the hen house the night before. It was Luther's and Carl's job to fasten the door to the coop, and they had been known to occasionally get distracted from their task. The chickens would generally take to the trees and the next day someone would have to coax them back into their house. On my wedding day morning, the chickens had indeed all roosted up in the branches, and nothing would do Pa but to have all of us out in the yard, poking and prodding at those pesky birds. Still, we could have endured the delay that caused in the wedding preparations, had it not been for the tantrum-snit-conniption fit my father threw when the most persnickety chicken we owned, known as Sister Cackleberries, dumped a pint of poop on Pa's freshly shampooed head from her perch way high up in the tree. Oh, Lordy, mercy. It was awful.

Carl and Luther went and hid under their bed. Flo and my momma suffered from sudden attacks of nausea and sore throats, because they couldn't seem to stop gagging and coughing. I knew they were laughing, though. They finally gave up and went back in the house. Pa and I were left with the chickens. He was mad, and I was bawling my eyes out, as quietly as I could, afraid that this three-ring disaster was going to ruin the most special day of my life. He finally yelled at me, "Get the hell on to the house!" so I deserted him and the chickens and didn't look back.

The second part of the day was not like the first part of the day. Right before the wedding, Ned and I had a photograph made, under the big oak tree in the churchyard, next to the white camellia bushes. Ned had his hair slicked down with some kind of pomade. He didn't really look like himself, but he was still the most attractive man of my acquaintance. We made a handsome couple, and I don't think I'm bragging when I say that.

After the ceremony, we greeted our guests on the steps of the church. I had a bag packed, so when all the formalities had been observed, I kissed my momma and sister, hugged the boys, and Ned and I joined Arlo in the cab of the truck Arlo had borrowed from a friend. The truck sputtered to life and we were off. It was a beautiful day to start our new life together.

"Will you tell me now?" I asked, poking Ned in the ribs. He'd told me he had something special planned for our wedding night, but so far he'd refused to tell me about it.

"Not yet," he said, casting a warning glance toward Arlo.

Oh, ho. So Arlo was in on it, too. "Arlo?" I said. I'd only been around Ned's uncle that one time, but from everything Ned had told me about him, he was a good joe.

"I don't know nothin' from nothin'," Arlo said. "Mum's the word," he assured Ned.

"Birdie, you're gonna like it," said Ned.

"I guess I'll know soon enough, anyway, won't I?" I saw that we were heading into the foothills. It didn't matter, really. This was my wedding day, and Ned and I were now husband and wife. We would remember tonight, no matter where we were.

Graduation on Friday, loose chickens this morning, and a wedding this afternoon. I hadn't realized how exhausted I was. After a half hour of winding around the curves, I fell asleep leaning against Ned's shoulder.

"Wake up." Ned patted my head and moved his shoulder. With my eyes still closed, I could hear water lapping against something. Where was I?

I opened my eyes. Filtered through the trees, the afternoon sun was still bright, but beginning to wane. We were in a clearing, and I could see a tiny house—actually "shack" would be a more apt description—and a small lake with a rough-looking dock. Ned was watching me, apparently to gauge my reaction. "Where are we?" I asked.

He grinned. "Do you like it? This place belongs to Arlo's friend, Roger. He said we could stay as long as we like."

"It's beautiful," I said. And it was. A list of questions scrolled through my mind, but I decided to not spoil this moment with the mundane. Ned had gone to some trouble to plan this romantic tryst, and I would trust my new husband with the details.

Arlo agreed to come back for us on Monday afternoon. Then he was gone, and we were alone.

I wasn't prepared for the beauty of it. I understood the mechanics, and I knew that it was supposed to feel incredibly good, finally yielding to the desires we'd held at bay for months on end. As the Good Book says, "And the twain shall become one flesh." But, Oh, great God almighty, wasn't God brilliant?

I couldn't keep my hands off of my beloved. It was a good thing Ned's chosen honeymoon spot gave us complete privacy, with no one else on the little lake except us, for I'm sure I became quite the brazen hussy. Over those two days, we enjoyed relations several times in the bed, on the floor, and in various positions. We even braved the mosquitoes Sunday night and consummated our love on a blanket on the dock. By the next morning, the red bites were itching us to death, but we just laughed and decided it would be our little secret as to how we got bitten in all those strange places.

Dreaming of happiness, feeling that at last they have each found the one who will give eternal understanding and tenderness, the young man and maiden marry.

-- Marie Stopes

CHAPTER 7

Ned and I were in complete agreement that we should not live at the farm with my parents after we were married. Momma had offered it to us, just until we could "get on our feet," but we declined. We both knew there was no way we could live under the same roof as my Pa.

Arlo had offered, too, but though I liked Arlo, living at his place would be like living on the frontier. It so lacked in amenities, plus I feared that Ned would fall back in with Arlo's relaxed lifestyle. That wouldn't do, for my husband had a wife to support now. I wasn't one to hanker after all the finest things in life, but there are certain minimum standards a woman wants to maintain for her family, electricity and facilities better than an outhouse being two that should be non-negotiable.

So we found us some rooms to rent near Ned's job in Deckler Springs. It was two small rooms, and a bath that we had to share with two other apartments. The bed was a twin size, which we found to be no inconvenience at all, being in our newly married state as we were. In the other room was a table and two chairs, and a small wood burning stove to serve for both cooking and heating. We didn't plan to stay there long.

At the end of that first week, Ned came in with his pay and handed it to me, his eyes shining. "All right, then, wife, here's the money for this week."

I laid the envelope aside on the table and threw my arms around his neck. He was warm and sweaty, but I didn't mind. I was much more excited about spending the next two days with my darling than I was about the money he'd earned. "What shall we do with the weekend?" I kissed him before he could answer, then kissed him again.

He ran his hands over my back and pulled me closer. "We could make an early night of it. How does that sound?"

"That's a wonderful thought, sweetheart." I kissed him again. "But could we get out of here for a while? Please? We don't even have to spend any money. We could just take a walk through town, look in the shop windows and such."

"Sure, baby. Give me a few minutes to clean up, and we'll go." He walked through to the bedroom, taking off his shirt. "We can get a sandwich at the diner, if you want."

I clasped my hands together under my chin and whispered, "Thank you, Jesus." To Ned, I answered, "That'd be swell, sugar." I picked up my fan and waved it under my arms, then around the back of my neck. There was no cross ventilation in our place, so the heat of the day lingered until deep into the night. Ned was lucky to be out every day, staying busy.

By the end of the second week, I had come to the conclusion that I needed to look for a job. Staying cooped up in two rooms or taking aimless walks through the streets of Deckler Springs, with my only activities being preparing Ned's meals and washing our clothes, was driving me batty. I couldn't even do any smocking or sewing because the lighting inside our little rooms was so poor. I needed a job.

When he came home that Friday, I was sitting in one of our two chairs. He leaned over and kissed me, then sat down in the other chair and tossed his pay envelope on the table. I guess he could tell I had something on my mind. "What's the matter?" He held his hand out to me and I took it.

I had planned what I was going to say, to convince him that it would make sense for me to get a job, just temporarily. Those plans were forgotten, and I blurted out, "I have to get a job."

Taken aback, he replied, "I thought we agreed that it would be best for you to take care of the home, and I would take care of earning the money."

I pulled my hands from his and covered my face, elbows resting on the table. "I know. I know we did." I peeked out from behind my hands. "But I have nothing to do all day. It doesn't take much time to cook and clean for just the two of us." I didn't want to sound like a whiner, but I was definitely whining now. "I'm stuck in these two little rooms the rest of the day, all day, every day."

"Why don't you visit your friends from school? Meet some neighbors. Have coffee with them," he suggested.

"Ned, I'm bored out of my gourd. I don't want to sit around and drink coffee with the neighbors," I argued.

Leaning back in his chair, Ned folded his arms across his chest. "I thought since you'd always had to work so hard on the farm, that you'd be happy to have all this time to yourself, and not have to work so hard." He wasn't angry with me, he just looked surprised, that's all.

Relief swept over me. As always, this sweet boy only wanted to make me happy and give me good things. "You'd think so, wouldn't you? But I want something to do. I *need* something to do. And I might as well be doing something to earn some money for us. We can save the money for our future."

Leaning on the table, his chin in his hands, he thought about it, then nodded. "That sounds smart. But what if we have a baby?" His eyes sparkled at the thought of that.

"Then I'll quit the job," I grinned. "I never heard tell of a baby that wasn't a lot of work. I'll have plenty to keep me busy then." Sliding from my chair, I went around the table and hugged him from the back. "Thank you, darling, for understanding." I squeezed harder and whispered, "I love you so much."

He reached around and, pulling me into his lap, he began to kiss me.

By mutual agreement, we decided to stay at home for the evening.

When Gloria told me they were hiring at the hosiery mill, I applied and was hired straight away. I was no stranger to hard work, so the effort required for my job at the mill seemed rather trifling by comparison to picking beans in the hot sun. Plus, I enjoyed the camaraderie with the other women. The extra money was nice, too. Ned and I were able to buy a radio, which made our evenings more pleasant, and we even splurged every few weeks with a night on the town, usually dinner and a movie, but occasionally we went dancing. I tell you, we thought we were pretty hot stuff in those days.

Then we found our little house. One of the men Ned worked with had a house he wanted to rent, right here in town. The rent wasn't much more than we were paying for our rooms, so we didn't hesitate to grab that little gem before someone else did.

It was heaven to me. We had a bit of a yard, and I filled the front walkway with flowers. Around back, over time, we built ourselves a small patio and found some secondhand metal furniture to put out there. There were two bedrooms, a front room, and a kitchen with plenty of room for a dining table. And, most important of all, a bathroom, complete with toilet, sink, and a claw foot tub. Did I mention it was like heaven?

All of that first summer, whenever I could arrange a ride there and back, I'd spend Saturday at the farm. Besides wanting to see my family, it was beneficial to them, and to me, whenever I could go help Momma and Flora with the vegetable garden. It gave them an extra hand with the work, and they always gave me a generous share of the fresh and canned vegetables.

It was different, going there after I was married. Momma treated me more like an equal, and I felt very grown-up asking her about the best way to get a stain out, or the trick to making my fried chicken moist and tender. Flora, on the other hand, was hard to figure. She seemed almost angry with me, and I could tell she'd been giving Momma a hard time, too.

"What's got Flo's panties in a wad?" I asked.

"You know better than to talk that way," said Momma.

"Sorry," I murmured. "But what's wrong with her? Why is she acting that way?"

Momma sighed as she placed the dinner dishes in the sink. "I wish I knew. I'm used to your Pa being in a bad mood all the time, but Flo's never been this bad before. Between the two of them, there's little peace in this house." She handed me a wet rag to wipe the table. "I sure do miss you, Birdie."

Flo came through the screen door just then. "I guess you wouldn't miss me if I were gone, would you, Momma?" She got a drink of water and went back out.

I looked at Momma. "Is she like this all the time?"

Momma shrugged. "Just about."

I loved visiting the farm and spending time with Momma, but sometimes it was a relief to get back to our little house, where the disagreements were few, and happiness was the order of the day.

Those first two years after Ned and I were married, we sometimes felt like we were living like the stars of the moving pictures. We weren't, of course, but neither one of us had ever had so much money to call our own. I wouldn't say we went crazy or anything. But having a bit of money in our pockets made us a little cocky sometimes. A little arrogant. A little less grateful than we should have been.

"Birdie, I thought you might could use this quilt to wrap up in, when you're sitting in your front room." Momma pulled the small quilt out of the cabinet and offered it to me. I could see that she had used some of the prettier flour sack material in a nice diamond pattern. Knowing that Momma didn't enjoy sewing as much as I did, I should have been appreciative of her taking the time from her chores to make something pretty for me. But I wasn't. I thought it looked old-fashioned and homemade, not at all a proper fit for my modern way of life.

I hesitated. "This is real nice, Momma, but I just bought a coverlet from the mill store to keep in the front room. It matches those curtains I got the other day." I felt a moment's guilt that my life had become so rich while Momma's remained spare, but I quickly brushed it away. Ned and I were simply enjoying the fruits of our labor. We deserved everything we had.

"Oh. Well, if you don't need it, I'll just keep it for another day." She folded up the quilt and tucked it away.

There was one other time in particular that I now look back on with shame. Flo and Momma had made a batch of bread-and-butter pickles from a recipe that I had always been partial to. Those pickles were especially good with pinto beans or mustard greens. The thing was, Ned and I hardly ever ate dried beans anymore, not pintos or white navy beans, and I never cooked greens. Those were staples for people who had to pinch pennies and couldn't afford better. Ned and I didn't fall into that category anymore.

Momma proudly set out half a dozen jars of those pickles on the kitchen table. "Here's you some of your favorite pickles, honey."

I stared at the jars, and they seemed lacking compared to the grocery store goods I'd gotten used to. I wanted the pickles, but I didn't want to be a person who could only afford homemade. I picked up a jar. "I'll only take the one. We just don't eat beans like we used to."

The look Momma gave me was strange. "That's fine. The Millers up the road are having a hard time right now. I'll take them a few jars."

Flo had been sitting there listening. "Birdie thinks she's all hoity-toity now, with her own job and plenty of money." It was too close to the truth, and I despised Flo for figuring it out so easily. "She's too good to eat beans now. Better not stay to supper, Birdie. We might be having pintos and cornbread this evening." I glared at her. Satisfied that she'd gotten a rise out of me, she flounced out of the room.

Much as I adored my husband, it must be said that, of the two of us, I was the one with the head for money. Not that I didn't enjoy splurging just a bit, or allowing us each our little pleasures. But it was me that put some money aside every week. There'd been so much hullaballoo over the banks closing around the time of the stock market crash that we decided against putting our money in the bank. We had a secret hiding place for it, and no, we didn't put it under the mattress. I always thought that was a right foolish thing to do, considering that a house could easily catch fire and burn up all your money. So we dug a hole in the corner of the shed in the backyard. We stashed our Mason jar down in the hole and covered it with a box of dirt mixed with manure, figuring no one would be wanting to steal dirt.

Thieves never did get into it. But Ned did.

CHAPTER 8

We had a terrible fight when Ned bought the automobile. Before that, I guess I'd never been truly angry with him, but when he went behind my back and took our money without so much as a word to me, let me tell you, I flung a fit that could be heard over in the next county. After growing up with my Pa, you better believe I knew how to throw a good one.

It was on a Saturday. I was in the backyard, digging in the flower bed when I heard the most gosh-awful noise coming from down the street. It kept getting closer until it seemed to be right on top of our house, and then it rumbled and stopped. I got off my knees and brushed some of the dirt off my hands, because I wanted to take a gander at whatever was making such a ruckus. Before I could get around the side of the house, here came Ned, kind of bouncy-like, with the biggest grin I'd ever seen on his face.

He grabbed me and swung me around through the air. I couldn't help but smile back at all his joy. "Birdie, you're gonna love it," he said. Then he set me down and took my hand, and started dragging me toward the front of the house.

"What is it?"

"You'll see. It's fantastic."

He hadn't been this excited on our wedding day, I thought. When we came around to the front of the house, I saw it, pulled into our yard at an angle.

"Whose is it?" I asked. It never entered my mind that it could be ours. I thought maybe he had borrowed it from someone. Maybe we were going to take a ride somewhere. Now wouldn't that be grand?

Ned laughed. "You never thought we'd have one, did you?" He pulled me right up next to it and opened the door. "Climb in. We'll go for a ride."

I made no move to get in. In a calm and quiet voice, I clarified, "This automobile belongs to us?"

Ned leaned against the hood and kept on grinning. He had no idea of the fury that was about to be raining down on him. "Yeah. Isn't it great? You can learn to drive it, too. You can go see your momma whenever..." He finally noticed that my fists were balled-up and I was glaring at him. "Wh... What's the matter?"

"I'll tell you what's the matter, mister." My voice grew louder as I stuck my finger in his chest and poked it hard, over and over. "Where'd you get the money, huh? You wanna tell me that?"

"I thought you'd like..." The light was just beginning to dawn on him, that maybe he'd made a mistake.

"Shut up." I'd never spoken this way to him. I didn't like it, but I couldn't stop. He'd betrayed my trust, and I was heartbroken and furious at the same time. He was going to hear what I had to say. The neighbors were, too, but I didn't care.

"That was my money, too," I yelled. "Mine. Not just yours, mine. Ours, remember? And it's not just a matter of whose money it was. I thought we agreed to keep everything out in the open, no secrets. Well, what do you call this? I call it a secret. You went behind my back, and spent all this money without even talking to me about it." By the end of that tirade, I was screeching and shaking.

Ned had his arms stretched out toward me, trying to find a spot that wasn't hostile, but every single bit of me was angry. I wouldn't let him touch me. Against my will, tears were filling my eyes.

Gritting my teeth, I ground out, "Do we have any money left? Did you use it all? What are we going to do when the baby comes?"

Ned put his hands in the pockets of his overalls and kicked the grass. He wouldn't look at me. "There's a little bit left in the jar," he mumbled.

"How much?"

His voice got even lower. "About twenty dollars." He was hanging his head now in shame. Good enough for him, I thought. He should be ashamed.

"Well, you can take this thing right back where you got it from, and get our money back." Stumbling in my haste, I ran across the yard to the front door, slamming the screen as hard as I could behind me.

Standing in the front room, I watched through the window as he got the automobile cranked and circled back on to the street. Then I sat down on the floor and cried. We had a baby coming in about eight months. I hadn't told him yet, because I wanted to be sure. I was a little ticked off that he didn't even catch it, when I'd said, "when the baby comes." But then I had to be fair. We said things like that all the time, when we talked about having a baby at some point in the future. That part really wasn't his fault. But the money and the auto, that *was* his fault and I wouldn't soon forget it.

He stayed gone all day. I figured he might be afraid I'd scream at him some more or throw something at him if he came home too soon. I might have done it, too. All the rest of the day, I worked a little, moped a little, kicked a few things and muttered a lot. I didn't fix any supper. He didn't deserve any and my stomach was still in knots.

When it got dark, I tried to read, but my mind kept wandering. I never thought Ned would do me this way. He was a dreamer, for sure, and could bring a smile to my face faster than a lightning bug could glow then disappear. He was kind and generous, a man to love forever. But was he always going to sneak and go behind my back? Could I count on him? In the yellow lamplight, with the book lying open on my lap, all kinds of bad thoughts went through my head.

When Ned got home that night, I was already in the bed, but not asleep. There was no loud engine noise, so I assumed he had gotten our money back. He was extra quiet as he undressed and got ready for bed. I didn't make a sound, just waited.

After he lay down beside me, I asked, "Did you get our money back?" My voice sounded hard, even to me, but I didn't care.

He didn't answer right away. Then, "No. The sale was final. They wouldn't take it back." I didn't ask why I didn't hear it chugging back into the yard. He admitted later he'd gotten out and pushed it the last four blocks home, so it wouldn't wake me up.

He tried to sell it himself, but nobody wanted to buy it. Not many people had that much money. I could tell it cost him some pride to do it, but from that point on, he made sure he discussed all of it, every little thing, with me. Though I started out from a place of doubt, as the week wore on and he slunk around like a whipped puppy, my anger began to melt. He'd just made a mistake, as we all do. I couldn't stay angry with him forever.

On the following Friday, after we got paid, the idea of going out for the evening was not brought up by either of us. We knew those days were gone, at least for the time being, while we tried to rebuild our savings. Supper was sandwiches, plus the last of a pound cake. After listening to the radio for an hour or two, I asked Ned if he was ready to go to bed. He must have recognized that tone in my voice. He smiled at me. "Are you?"

I smiled back at him and nodded. He followed me to the bedroom.

I'd heard a few of the older married women at the mill talk about the particular pleasure of "making up" after an argument with their husbands. Since Ned and I had never had a serious argument before, I didn't pay too much attention to them.

Turns out they couldn't have been more right. Ned couldn't do enough to please me that night. And please me he did. More than once, as a matter of fact.

That 1928 Model A Ford Tudor was a wonder. If it hadn't been for the way he'd gone about it, and if we'd had plenty of money to throw away, I'd have wanted it just as much as Ned did. Anyway, it looked like we were stuck with it, for a while at least. Stuck with the Model A and stuck with the additional obligation of ten dollars a month, which Ned had forgotten to mention, because since he had only enough cash to pay half of the total cost of three hundred sixty dollars, he had signed his name to pay the rest on time. Good thing he settled for the four-year-old used model. A new one would have cost us five hundred, and we'd have had to make payments for almost four years. At that time, that was beyond my imagining.

When Ned taught me how to drive, I was surprised. It wasn't that hard. The biggest challenge was getting it cranked up, for it could be a bit cantankerous sometimes. We used it mostly on weekends. After all, we were used to walking to work every day, so we kept right on.

Two weeks after he bought the Model A, I was sure about the baby. I hadn't told anyone else, not even my momma. I wanted it to be special when I shared the news with Ned, so that Saturday afternoon I got all dolled up and I fixed Ned's favorite meal, fried cubed steak with mashed potatoes and gravy. Everything was ready by five o'clock, but Ned wasn't there. I guess I should have told him we were having cubed steak so he wouldn't be late, but I wanted to surprise him.

The gravy was thick and lumpy by the time he got home, and when he came through the door, he was streaked with black grease. "Where have you been?" I asked. "And what in the world have you been doing?"

When he grinned, his teeth stood out white against all that black gunk. "Joe was showing me how to work on the Tudor. You won't believe what's inside that thing."

My aggravation slipped away, to be replaced by desire. He was a looker, all right, this husband of mine, and instead of being repulsed by all that filth on him, I found myself enchanted by the manliness of it, and the contrast of his smile and his eyes against the rest of his face. I leaned in toward him, careful not to touch the greasy parts, and kissed his soft lips. "Go get cleaned up," I murmured. Instantly he caught my mood. Holding his hands up and away from me, he kissed me again, and though only our lips touched, I could feel the warmth and the craving spread all over my body.

Pulling back, I pressed his chest with the tips of my fingers. "Go." As he walked away, there was a promise in his eyes.

I got to thinking about it, about what would come later, and I found I couldn't wait that long. I could hear the water running in the tub. I turned the stove off and waited. The water sloshed against the tub when he got in. Slipping down the hall, I opened the bathroom door and stepped into the doorway.

"That's an awful lot of grease you have on you, sir. I thought you might need some help scrubbing it off."

Ned raised an eyebrow at me and grinned. "Come in, Birdie, and close the door."

CHAPTER 9

Not long after Ned bought the Model A, I began to notice a change in my sister.

We'd been invited out to the farm for Carl's birthday, not that we Calhouns made a lot over birthdays. Momma did always manage to produce a cake, but there had been a few years, when times were lean, when there was no birthday present.

When we'd finished eating cake, Carl and Luther went outside to play with the whirligig Ned and I had bought for Carl's birthday. Flo and I were helping Momma with the dishes when Pa got up from the table. "Flo," he said. "Throw that last bag of fertilizer in the wheelbarrow and bring it to me down at the apple trees." He made to leave.

"I'm helping Momma right now," said Flo, never sparing him a glance. "Maybe Ned would do that for you."

Ned and I caught each other's eyes. What the heck was going on here? Trying to diffuse the situation, Ned spoke up, "I can go get the fertilizer."

Pa said, "I told Flo to do it." It was a challenge. We all knew it, and we all waited to see what was going to happen next.

Flo turned away from the sink to look at Pa, soapy water dripping from her fingertips. "I said I'm busy." She didn't move, just kept staring at him.

Pa tilted his head and his lips thinned with anger as he glared at her.

The look she gave him back as good as said, "I dare you to do anything about it." Several seconds passed.

When Pa was the first to yield, you could have knocked me over with a feather. He kicked his chair back under the table and went out the back door, slamming the screen. We could hear his boots stomping down the steps leading off of the porch.

Ned said, "You think I should go get the fertilizer for him?"

I shrugged. "I wouldn't." As soon as the dishes were done, Ned and I hopped in the Model A and drove back to town. Try as we might, we couldn't come up with anything to explain that scene back at the house.

Whatever it was, it certainly improved my sister's disposition. From that time on, she didn't seem angry with me and Momma anymore, but that's not to say that she was an angel. She was a little bit lazy and a little bit arrogant, I thought, but then again, she had always been that way. For whatever reason, she wasn't letting Pa pick on her, and albeit reluctantly, he was allowing the change. If you asked me, that was a good thing.

Back then, even though some babies were born in a hospital, they were just as often birthed at home by a midwife or a family member. It wasn't a hard choice for us to make, since money made the choice for us. We decided that when the time came, Ned would drive me to the farm, where I'd deliver our firstborn with

Momma's expert help, stay a few days and then come back to our little house. Sounds simple, but of course few things go as planned.

First of all, my baby decided to come early. My plan was to stop working two weeks before delivery, but that didn't happen. The night before my last day at the mill, around about midnight, with Ned dead to the world and me wishing I were, too, things started moving along.

"Ned." I shook him by the shoulder.

"Mmmff. Wha...?"

"Oooh." I felt my water break, wetting the sheets beneath me. "Ned, you need to take me out to Momma's."

That woke him up. His head shot up off the pillow. "The baby?"

"Uh-huh," I said, holding onto my belly as I rolled out of bed. "My bag is by the chair. I'll be ready in just a minute." I went down the hall to the bathroom.

While I got myself freshened up, I heard him stumbling around all over the house—and humming, so I knew he was nervous and excited—but I couldn't imagine what he could be doing. Come to find out, he was making me a bed in the back seat of the Model A, complete with every pillow in the house, quilts, and blankets. It was only a fifteen-minute ride, but bless his heart for doing it anyway. He also managed to make a pot of coffee and put it in his thermos to take with us.

All his excessive preparations caused me to have to sit in the chair by the front door and wait on him. By the time he helped me out of the chair, almost thirty minutes had passed, and I was fit to be tied. "Are you *ready*? *Finally*?"

"Yeah. Oh, yeah. Sorry, Birdie." In his excitement, he was all fumbly and awkward in his attention to me. "You want me to carry you?"

I closed my eyes and shook my head, trying to make my voice sweet so I wouldn't have to look back on this night and feel bad about chewing my husband up and spitting him out like an old piece of bubblegum. All this birthing discomfort was making me unlike my normal patient self. "No, sugar, just help me to the car, and let's go."

He insisted I get in the back seat so I could stretch out. I gave in without a fight. He got us cranked, and we were on our way. I had had several contractions before we left the house, but the first one I had in the car was different, grabbing my belly with a mean vengeance. It took my breath, but I tried not to make any noise, so as not to worry Ned. He probably couldn't hear me over the humming anyway.

We were halfway there—five miles from town and about an equal distance from the farm—when the second one hit me. It caught me by surprise, and before I could stop myself, I half-moaned, half-gasped. He heard me then.

Ned's face in the mirror as he looked back at me was fearful. "Don't worry, Birdie, I'll get you there," he promised. He put his foot down harder on the gas, and I felt us speed up.

Then I felt us slow down again. I heard Ned pumping the gas pedal, over and over, as we gradually came to a stop.

"What's the matter with it?" I asked.

"Don't know." Then he got out of the car and raised the hood. I don't know what he was looking for, and I doubt he did, either.

"Does it need gas?" I yelled to him. Silence. *Oh, Lord, say it isn't so.*

"Ned?"

"Yeah?"

"Is that gas can still in here somewhere? In the boot, maybe?"

Silence again. I could feel another contraction starting, the strongest one yet. As I rode it out, not even trying to be quiet anymore, Ned opened the back door behind my head and climbed in on the floorboard so he was facing me. Head bowed in shame, he took my hand and rubbed it gently.

"I'm so sorry. I meant to keep the tank full..." Even in the scarce moonlight, I could see the embarrassment in his eyes. I put myself in his place, and knew how awful I would feel if I were in his shoes. I had to forgive him.

"It's okay, Ned." I pulled him toward me and hugged him and kissed him. "Got any ideas about what we should do?"

"If there was somebody close by, I could get help, maybe borrow a wagon?"

"No houses between here and the farm. Back toward town about a mile, there's a couple of farms, but they're a good distance from the road."

"I could carry you the rest of the way," he offered.

"That's four miles, honey, and it's cold tonight. You'd have to carry me and my blankets. If we have to stop and deliver this baby..." That didn't bear thinking about.

"I could stay here. You and I could deliver the baby." Even though I knew we both had plenty of experience watching the animal births on the farm, I was afraid we wouldn't know what to do if there was a problem.

"Well, there probably won't be a soul coming down this road until daylight," I commented. "It's barely one o'clock now." We retreated into our own thoughts for a moment. Then I asked him, "How fast and how far can you run?"

"Run?"

"Yes. I was just thinking you could get there a lot faster on your own."

Ned thought a minute. "I'm in pretty good shape. Best possible time might be a little over thirty minutes." He considered it some more. "If I'm walking and carrying you, it might be possible in an hour and a half, but it could take more than two hours. What would you rather do?"

I knew what I wanted. It wasn't being stuck on a cold night in the middle of nowhere, on the verge of becoming a momma. I chose what I thought would be the least uncomfortable for me. "I want you to run. And hurry!" At least I'd be relatively snug with all these quilts and pillows.

"I'll come back with the wagon as fast as I can," he said.

"No," I corrected him. "You come back with the wagon *and my momma*." I felt the clenching feeling that would precede another contraction, and I gritted my teeth.

"I will." Ned handed me the thermos, tucked the blankets up around me, and kissed me. Then he was gone, swallowed by the darkness, leaving just the sound of his footfalls racing away until even that was no more.

I sang every song I knew while he was gone. My voice was nowhere as sweet as Ned's; still, I could carry a tune. I'd have to stop singing when the contractions were at their worst, but the rest of the time, I sang. Reuben, Reuben, Sweet Betsy from Pike, Oh, Susanna, Comin' Thru the Rye, Loch Lomond. And then I started on the hymns. By the time they got back, I was plumb hoarse, and I could feel the baby, ready to come out and hear the music.

And then Sally was born, right there in that 1928 Ford Model A Tudor.

CHAPTER 10

I read later that 1933 was the year that the Great Depression hit its lowest point. For Ned and me, it didn't seem so bad, at least not yet. We had our Sally, like warm, bright sunshine, keeping out the cold and dark, so we were happy. Without my wages from the mill, though, we had to watch every penny. I no longer had any hesitation about accepting help from anyone, mostly my momma, and more than that, I was truly grateful for it. Beans and greens, as well as potatoes, became staples at our house again. We didn't mind it; we had each other, and we had our Sally.

Our lives shifted that year. Instead of going out, we were content to stay in our cozy home at night, passing Sally back and forth between us. You might think, being an only child as he was, that Ned wouldn't know the first thing about caring for a baby, but he was a natural from the very beginning. When she began to smile and laugh, he knew just how to coax her into it, better than anyone else, even me.

I'd never seen anyone be a daddy before, except Pa, and I'd certainly never seen my pa do things for my momma the way Ned did things for me. He worked so hard to make things easier for me, sometimes it made me cry. I'd come back to the kitchen to wash the dishes after feeding the baby and he'd already have them done. Or I'd take a nap with the baby on Saturday after lunch, and when I woke up, he'd tell me to take the car and go visit Gloria while he watched Sally. I don't guess he knew it was making me love him more and more, and wrapping my heart round and round with strong bindings made of love and respect. He was a good man, my Ned.

Sally's first Thanksgiving, we spent most of the day at the farm. While Flo and I helped Momma with the dinner, Ned and the boys played with Sally, who was queen bee on her pallet on the floor. Until it was time to eat, Pa mostly stayed out in the barn by himself. In the past few months, I had caught him a couple of times, when he thought no one else was around, picking up Sally and holding her, patting her head and her hands. It made me wonder what had happened to him. He was a hard man, but there was still some gentleness in there.

During dinner, Flo insisted on having her turn holding Sally. I could see it in her eyes, that she couldn't wait to have one of her own.

"Let us keep her one night, Birdie," she begged. "Momma, you want her to, don't you?"

"Fine by me. I haven't gotten to hold that baby near enough. Luther, that's enough gravy," said Momma.

"Oh, please, Birdie," said Flora.

I exchanged a look with Ned, who gave a slight nod. "All right. Ned and I were wanting to go to the Christmas party at the factory in a few weeks." I reached over and let Sally wrap her little hand around my finger. "Little Miss Priss, what do you think about that?

Auntie Flora will be your babysitter for the evening." Sally bubbled and cooed her approval.

When the day arrived to drive off and leave that sweet thing for the first time, I had trouble letting Flo take her out of my arms. But the thought of a whole night alone with Ned, an uninterrupted night of slumber, and sleeping late on Sunday morning was a strong motivator, and I finally let her go. Ned, on the other hand, almost balked, but I pulled on his arm and he finally walked with me back to the car.

I wanted Ned to pay attention to me that night, so I climbed in and scooted right up next to him. "It's just you and me tonight, sweetheart." I reached up and ran my hand through his hair. "Remember before we had Sally, sometimes we'd be up half the night, making love?"

He put his arm around me then and pulled me even closer. "Are you thinkin'...?"

"Mmm, yes." I rubbed my hand across his chest. I caught a whiff of his aftershave and the smell was seductive, evoking sensations of remembered touch and taste. "Do we even have to go to the party?"

"You know I have to go." Ned pulled my hand down and held it. "They laid off two fellows last week. Rumors are there's more to come."

"You're right. I forgot." That sobering thought was enough to kill the mood. We couldn't afford for Ned to be laid off. We were barely getting by as it was. I stuffed my desires down. Delay would only make it sweeter.

Ned's company employed more than seventy people, so the party was big and loud. I made a point of speaking to not only

Ned's supervisor and the owner, but also to their wives. After I had paid all my dues, I looked for Ned. He was in the middle of a group of guys, talking automobiles. Since Ned was one of the few lower level employees who owned one, they looked on him as an expert, and he was obviously enjoying the attention.

I took a moment to watch him. His buddies loved him. You could see it by the eager way they gathered around him. They respected him, of course, as a true man's man, for he could hunt and fish and carry his share of any load, but they loved him because he was kind to them and treated them with respect. They knew they could count on him. I loved him for those reasons, too, but there was more. When he looked at me, I knew he saw into my soul. He didn't just look at me, he looked inside me. For a second, all but the center of my vision clouded over, and all I could see was my husband. He looked up and smiled at me. There it was. That was all I wanted.

I moseyed over to the refreshment table and fixed myself a plate. The party was in the packaging and shipping area, with the loading docks just beyond, and some folks were slipping out the big double doors to the docks to smoke or cool off. Inside, the air had grown hot and stuffy, so I followed along.

For the middle of December, the weather was mild, which meant it was cold and crisp, but bearable without a coat for a little while. I found a stack of pallets and set my plate and my drink on it. Beyond the gravel parking lot, the woods were thick and dark. I was glad to be somewhere quiet for a minute, away from the roar of a hundred people talking at once.

"Birdie? Birdie Calhoun?" There was Jerry Johnson standing beside me.

"It's Birdie Parker now, Jerry."

"Of course. Old habits." He took a draw on his cigarette. "How's married life, sugar?"

How could I have ever thought this guy was cute? "Things are great. Ned's a wonderful father."

Jerry blew out the smoke in perfect little donut shapes. "You know, you and me... Once upon a time..."

What a creep. "No, Jerry, not really." I picked up my things to go back inside.

"Oh, yeah, there was something there all right." He drew closer, and I could smell the liquor on his breath.

I looked around, and no one else was out on the docks any longer. I tried to move around to the left, and he blocked me. He took the plate and the cup out of my hand and set them back down on the pallets. Then his arms were around me, and he tried to kiss me. I could feel my lipstick smearing.

I had on those clunky heel shoes that I'd bought myself back when I was working at the mill, so I hauled off and stomped him good on the top of his right foot. He jumped back, yelling, "What'd you do that for?"

I ignored him and hurried back inside.

Still surrounded by his pals, Ned saw me come in and lifted his glass in greeting. Then his gaze slipped past me as the door reopened and Jerry came in. Ned's brow furrowed. Surely he didn't think...? With sudden clarity, I knew what he was thinking. I wanted to go snatch him out of that circle and set him straight, but I didn't want to cause a scene, not here in front of his bosses and coworkers.

Then I saw Jerry pull Ned to the side, giving him an earful. If I'd been able to get to them, I'd have tried to knock sense into both of them. Into Jerry for being such a womanizing disrespectful jerk, and into my husband for doubting my fidelity. As it was, I was pushed back toward the door by Santa Claus and a couple of females sporting reindeer antlers. Fuming and not trusting myself to keep quiet, I decided to go wait in the Tudor.

Ten minutes later, Ned got in, slamming his door.

"What is the matter with you?" I asked. I knew what the matter was, but I wanted him to say it, so we could go ahead and get it out in the open. Then I could pick his accusation apart and maybe save the rest of our night. I knew I hadn't done anything wrong and I wasn't going to let him say I did.

He cranked the car, but didn't put it in gear. Staring straight ahead, he began. "You were outside with Jerry, and don't try to tell me you weren't ga-ga over him just a few years ago." He turned his head away from me, toward the window. I could barely hear the next part. "And I saw your lipstick, Birdie. You kissed him."

Ooh, how stupid could he be? "No, Ned. It didn't happen that way. He came up to me and started talking. When I was moving away, he *tried* to kiss me. I pushed him away and went back inside. That's the sum total of what happened." This was not right, having to defend myself when I hadn't done anything. I waited to see what else he had to say.

"Well..." He seemed a little less certain, but plowed on. "That's not what Jerry said happened..."

"Oh, really?" My anger bubbled up now like the grease on cracklin's. "So, it's my word against Jerry's now?" I'd had enough. I grabbed the door handle. "Go on home, Ned. I'm walking." With that, I got out, pulled my coat collar closer, and started walking in those clunky heeled shoes.

I walked about a half a mile with the Model A right by my side, Ned waving the two cars that chugged by to go around us. He was steady talking, apologizing for being such a sap, and asking me to please to get in.

My legs were cold, and I could feel some blisters where those shoes were rubbing. Stopping in my tracks, I thought a minute, then walked over to the car and leaned in the window.

"I didn't do anything wrong." My words were curt as I asked him, "You believe me?"

"Of course, I believe you." He reached over and opened the door. "Get in, Birdie."

I hesitated, but only for a second because my feet were killing me. I hopped in. Then I took my shoes off and threw them at him, one at a time. He held his hands up and ducked. I crossed my arms and leaned against my door. I'd been purely angry up to that point, but now my feelings were hurt, too. How could he doubt my faithfulness with so little cause? Tears began to pool in my eyes, then run down my face. I swiped them away, and sniffed.

He motioned with his hand for me to come closer.

Still not looking at him, I scooted to the middle of the seat. He put his arm around me and drew me in closer.

"It's just... I'm so afraid of losing you," he said. The anger seeped out of me then, like water through a sieve. He was just afraid, that's all. I was torn between punishing him with some more self-righteous anger, which he completely deserved to have raining down upon his head, or letting his outburst slide by this time, with little consequence to him for not trusting me and for assuming the worst. I admit that the thought of losing our first precious night alone in months was the deciding factor for me. I didn't want to spend time fighting or talking that night, so I chose the easier route. I let it slide.

Scooching up closer to him, I leaned my head against his shoulder, sighing. "It's only you, honey. Always you, and nobody else." Reaching up, I placed my hand on his cheek, rubbing gently. "Never doubt it."

Taking my hand, he turned it over and kissed the palm. "You're mine. I won't have anyone else touching you, or loving you like I do."

We had no disagreement there; that was just how I wanted it, too.

So we had our evening alone and it was long and it was sweet and it was intense. It wiped all those doubts away until they were only silly memories.

CHAPTER II

E very once in a while, Arlo would show up on our doorstep and stay a few days, and we were always glad to see him. Though he was a little rough around the edges, you couldn't find a kinder heart than his. That fellow could tell a story, too, so we knew we were in for some good entertainment when he came to visit.

In between visits, I'd write him about once a month, but Arlo wasn't much of a correspondent, so it was a rare thing indeed to receive a letter from him. I believe it was in the late spring of 1934 when the post brought a missive from him, and it was full of surprises. I was more than halfway through the carrying of our second child, who was almost certainly conceived on the night of the Christmas party, and little Sally was running me ragged now that she was walking on her own. When I lived on the farm, I'd had to corner plenty of chickens and piglets, but chasing Sally around all day plumb wore me out. That day she was particularly rambunctious, to the point that I'd had to set Arlo's letter aside to be read later.

When he got home from work, Ned was busy with our little garden until suppertime, so it was after supper before he opened Arlo's letter. We knew something was up, because it was two whole pages long, and Arlo never wrote more than a few sentences.

"What does he say?" I asked, bouncing Sally on my knee.

You couldn't just read Arlo's letters. You had to decipher them and interpret them, filling in the meaning with the few words he provided. Ned studied it for a minute. "Okay, he says his friend's brother died out in Texas, and the friend wanted Arlo to drive out there with him. It took them four days to get there." Ned read some more. "Holy Toledo." He looked up at me with the strangest expression. "Arlo's gone and gotten married."

"What?"

Ned waved his hand to shush me. He studied the letter again, moving on to the second page. "A widow lady, a rancher. Lives on the spread next to Arlo's friend. Love at first sight, he says." Ned looked at me and grinned. "Can you believe this?"

I clasped my hands under my chin. "It's so romantic. Will she come here to live?"

A frown crossed Ned's face. "He's moving out there. He's selling his place to a neighbor, and wants me to come get all his tools and machinery."

"Oh," I grumbled. "We'll never get to see him now. And he's the only family you've got."

"Yeah, but.... Arlo in love?" Ned smiled wistfully. "He deserves to be happy. And who knows? Maybe someday, we'll take a trip out there to see him. When money's not so tight."

"Yeah, maybe." It seemed like an unlikely pipe dream to me. We would miss Arlo, that was for sure.

About that time, Ned's hours were cut back to four days a week. Not just his, but all the factory workers. Then both of the textile mills in town announced temporary layoffs, due to a decrease in orders received. We thought it was a hard blow to all of us and to Deckler Springs. We didn't know that was only the beginning.

Through necessity, we devised other ways to earn money. I oiled up my Singer and sewed and smocked and embroidered whenever I could, mostly in the evenings when Sally was down for the night. Ned added on to the shed in the back to make room for the woodworking machinery he got from Arlo. A new sign in our yard read: Custom Furniture and Carpentry Work. The problem was, not many folks had the wherewithal to purchase our wares and services. Still, a little bit here, a little bit there. It was enough to make up the difference. For a while, anyway.

Susan was born in September, and of course, we called her Susie. Sally and Susie. I loved the sound of that. We still drove to the farm most Saturdays, but things were different now. Used to be, we went to help them, and now we went so they could help us. Momma usually sent us home with some kind of foodstuff, and Flo would always take over with Sally and Susie whenever we were there, giving me a much-appreciated break.

That winter, Flora got herself a beau. His name was Gerald. A nice looking man, several years older than Flo, with black hair and eyes so dark they looked like two pieces of coal. It was hard to tell if Pa liked him, but he didn't seem to mind him being around. That is to say, he wasn't hateful, like he was towards Ned at the beginning. It wasn't anything I could put my finger on, but there was just something about Gerald that I didn't trust; he had a sneaky way about him. I don't think Ned cared for him either, though he made an effort to be friendly, one young man to another, and they got on all right.

Once, while they were still courting, the four of us went to a barn dance together. When the fiddler announced a break, I motioned to Flo. "I'm going to get my sweater from the Tudor. Do you want yours?"

She was laughing and having such a good time that night. With a little squeeze to Gerald's arm, she said to him, "I'll be right back, sugar. Don't go anywhere." Then she laced her arm through mine, and we walked outside, across the field to where the wagons and automobiles were parked. Once we had our sweaters on, she went back to the barn and I went inside the house. As I turned a corner into a dark hallway, I saw two figures up against the wall. It was Gerald with a young woman of my acquaintance. They broke apart when they saw me.

"Gerald?" I couldn't keep the disgust out of my voice.

Even in the shadows, his insolence was clear enough. "None of your concern, Birdie. If you know what's good for you, you'll tell no tales tonight."

I started to bow up at him, but realized that my sister was the one who needed an earful from me right then. I said nothing else to him, but went outside, took Flo to the side and proceeded to tell her what I'd just witnessed. Instead of being angry with him, she got mad at me. I finally gave up trying to reason with her.

The next spring, in 1935, Flo and Gerald tied the knot, and he moved in at the farm.

Over the next two years, we never knew from one week to the next how many hours Ned would get to work, or whether he would get to work at all. On the radio and in the newspaper, reports came from all parts of the country, saying how the bottom had dropped out of the economy and how people were out of work and starving.

I thought more than once that if I had to live through times like these, I was the luckiest girl of them all to have Ned by my side. He could find the happiness in the most dismal of situations.

Over the summer months, when he was laid off and couldn't find any extra work to do, my husband somehow knew when I needed a shot of fun to keep my despair at bay. One bright summer morning, he sprang up out of bed and said, "Let's pack a lunch and go spend the day at the creek." So we gathered up both girls and all the necessaries, and off we went. We slipped in by the back way to the creek, where we spent the whole day in and out of the water, swimming, fishing, and playing with our babies. Then we went home and fried up some fresh fish for supper.

Other times, Ned helped me work in the yard, or I'd help him finish up a woodworking job. I liked watching him work in his shop. Sometimes I'd put the girls down for their afternoon nap and spend their whole nap time watching him. It was like an orchestra playing a song, only the instruments were his tools, and each one had its own sound and its own rhythm. Ned was the conductor and I was the lone audience member, sitting up on his waist-high workbench, swinging my legs back and forth. Watching him move forward and back, plane in hand, leveling a piece of lumber until it was polished smooth as a baby's bottom, his muscles showing through his shirt, rippling with every pass, it made the manual labor become a sensual thing. I guess it was that season in my life, when I was eager and ready, for I couldn't stop myself. I'd have to reach for him and touch him. I admit it—sometimes I slowed down the work instead of helping it along.

Every couple of weeks, we walked to the library and borrowed books for us and the children, knowing that in the evening we would sit together on the sofa and read to our girls until bedtime. Then we'd lie in the quiet together, Ned on his side of the bed and I on mine, until one of us would tire of reading and reach out, pulling the other one into an even more intimate diversion. When it was cold outside, we had our own party inside, just me and Ned. We'd put the girls to bed, and share a bottle of "giggle juice" as we called it then, cuddled up on a quilt in front of the fireplace. For us, the walls of our little house held at bay the troubles of the world, financial or otherwise.

Every month or so, on a Friday or Saturday night, we would invite friends over for a get-together, friends who knew what our hardships were, because they were their hardships, too. They all brought some little tidbit of food to share, and if the Opry or some other dance music was on the radio, we sometimes rolled back the rug and danced for a few hours. Or the men would stand around outside, smoking and telling lies, while the ladies engaged in girl talk around the kitchen table. Maybe it was because we were young, but on the whole, those were some happy times. Money, or the lack of it, couldn't alter that.

Not that we were immune to disagreements, particularly over finances. We had our share. After all, we were only human. Most of the time, Ned was steadfastly optimistic, but occasionally he would fall into a dark hole, and it would take both of us to dig him out. It scared me, the first time that happened, because I thought it was for good.

What drug him down most often was feeling that he wasn't able to provide for his family as a man should. He took that responsibility most seriously, which was mildly surprising considering a few years earlier, when we were courting, he'd hardly given it any thought at all. But he'd changed in that respect, probably due to the girls, who were the light of his world. Thankfully, the darkness only lasted for a while. He'd shake it off and have another go. We always knew it was over when he woke up smiling again.

The biggest blow of those years, second only to leaving our little house, was when we had to give up the Model A Tudor. Ned and I both loved that automobile. The freedom and convenience it gave us, the prestige that came with owning a car, the exhilaration of breezing along, with the wind lifting our hair and the sun heating our skin when our arms were cradling the outside of the door through the lowered window—there was nothing like it. But the time came when we had to let it go to pay our rent and put food on the table.

Ned was laid off again, and the rumor mill was strongly on the side of it being either a very long layoff or a permanent closing. He applied at numerous other places, and the response was always the same: no work was available, and if work did become available, it would go to their own laid-off workers.

Still, we chose to believe that things had to start getting better and that Ned would be back at work within a few months, at the most. We would sell the Tudor, make do until next spring, and then, when business was back to normal, we would reclaim all of the ground we'd lost.

The problem was, no one wanted to buy the Tudor. Most people didn't have any money, and the few that did were holding on tight to what they had. Even the car dealers wouldn't buy it back. We became desperate. We kept going down on the price until we were at half of what we'd paid for it. Just below half, the brother of one of the mill managers, who lived in Raleigh, came for a visit, and snapped it up at two hundred twenty-five dollars. Ned was heartbroken, but there was nothing else to be done.

Christmas that year was lean. I tried not to be bitter, for we'd had some lovely, abundant Christmases in earlier years. Then, we'd been able to buy gifts for each other, and a small mountain of gifts for each girl. This year there were no gifts for the two of us, and we spent no money on the girls. Instead, we used our ingenuity and all that free time we had. I made each girl a darling little rag doll, and Ned made doll cradles for both of them. Of course, the girls were so young, they didn't realize there was anything different about this Christmas. But Ned and I knew.

The New Year of 1938 gave us little cause to celebrate. Ned wasn't called back to work, and in March, the factory gave up any pretense of re-opening. We were devastated. We had done all we knew to do. We even thought of writing to Arlo to ask for help, but then, a letter from his new wife gave us to understand that they were struggling, too, and might even lose their ranch. Momma and Pa helped us some with food, but they had no cold hard cash, such as we needed to pay our rent and electricity. When the factory closed its doors in March, we had used almost all of the money from selling the car.

We dug in our heels to avoid asking Pa if we could stay at the farm, just for a little while, until business picked back up, but finally the day came when we had no other choice. Reluctantly, we asked, and begrudgingly, he agreed.

While we were selling our furniture and packing up our belongings, I did have one memorable pleasure, completely unrelated to our financial troubles. I'd had my name on the waiting list at the library for over six months, biding my time to get my hands on a copy of Margaret Mitchell's *Gone With The Wind*.

Finally, it was my turn and somehow, mostly at night, I managed to devour that weighty tome. The scenes from the war were graphic and harsh, and changed my view of the reality of war and its human consequences. It was the longest and most heart-wrenching book I'd ever read. I didn't understand how Mrs. Mitchell could let the book end that way. Just when Scarlet was coming to her senses, Rhett gave up and took off. I cried for two days. In truth, I wasn't sure if I was crying for the young girl Scarlett or crying for us. I was just crying, that's all I know.

CHAPTER 12

Shutting that door for the last time was hard. We sold everything we could, and one of Ned's friends, who had a truck, took the few remaining pieces of furniture, along with most of the boxes I'd packed up, out to the farm the day before. While I did a final walk through, Ned and the girls waited outside at the end of the driveway. Honestly, it wasn't really about checking to see if we'd left anything; it was me, needing a few minutes alone to say goodbye to this place where I'd spent the happiest years of my life. First, there was the kitchen, where we'd run the gamut from fancy to plain, but always sufficient and always with love and laughter. Then the girls' bedroom, where memories of cribs, cradles, toys, puzzles and milestones filled my eyes with tears. Next, my treasure of a bathroom, with its claw foot tub, a luxury I truly hated to give up. And then there was our bedroom, with private intimacies I'd cherish forever, a place that was for the two of us alone, where work and friends and finances were not allowed to spill over and ruin what we had.

Walking on through the front room, I opened the door and turned back around. In the far corner, that's where Ned's favorite chair used to be. He'd sit there with the lamp on when he wanted to read. When I asked him, he would make room for me, too, in that chair. I remember sitting on his lap one Christmas Eve after the children were abed, gazing through partly closed eyes that made the lights on the tree all blurry in a multi-colored dreamy glow. It was so beautiful that year. That was back when Ned was working, and we'd had the money to buy lights for the tree. Sally and I had made paper chains, while toddler Susie watched in fascination. I'd cut snowflakes out of cardboard, then painted them white.

There were so many presents from Santa Claus that year that they spilled out beyond the tree. I remember thinking that I wanted to hold on to that moment forever, because I was so very happy. I'm glad I didn't know that this was coming, that Ned would lose his job, and that we'd be going back to the farm. Sometimes it's better not to know.

I locked the front door and dropped the key in the mailbox hanging next to it. Before I turned to join them, I swiped my eyes and pulled myself together. I didn't want the girls to see me cry. Sally was five now and Susie almost four, old enough to remember this day.

Ned's friend was supposed to pick us up at ten that morning and give us a ride to the farm, but he never showed up. At noon, I fed the girls some crackers and water, and Ned and I decided we would start walking. We felt sure someone would come along and pick us up once we reached the main road.

We all had an armload. Even the girls had a little bag to carry. Ned pushed the wheelbarrow, loaded up way over the top with the last of our belongings, including the quilts and pillows we used to sleep on the floor the night before.

I felt a wave of anger for our landlord, old man Bartow. We had always paid our house rent regular as clockwork until just a few weeks ago, when our money had dwindled to dust. And Bartow must have known about the cut hours, and the lay-offs, and the factory closing. Didn't he have any kindness in his heart for the hard times we were going through? Even the last few months, when all we had was the money from the Tudor, the rent was always first on the list to be paid. Then, before we'd missed the second week, he told us to get out.

Reluctantly, I admitted to myself that times were hard for everyone. Maybe Mr. Bartow had reached the same point we had, where he had no choice but to do things he'd rather not do.

Lordy, it was hot that day. By the time we reached the end of the block, little rivulets of sweat were running down my back. The girls' bangs were plastered to their foreheads. The boxes I carried were awkward; I tried to swap them around a bit, but it wasn't working.

Ned saw my predicament and he stopped. He smiled at me, plucked two of the boxes from my arms and settled them on top of the wheelbarrow. "Better?" he asked.

I nodded my thanks. He was wearing his raggedy old straw hat, which gave him a little relief from the sun glaring down on us. Taking it off, he plopped it on my head. "It'll keep the sun out of your eyes," he said.

"Now, my little curtain-climbers," he said, turning his attention to the girls. "Let's see if we can't find a royal carriage for you to ride in." That said, he shoved and lodged the boxes tightly in the front of the wheelbarrow, hollowed a bowl shape into the quilts and set the girls on the very top. "Sit still and hold on, girlies."

We set off again, all of us in much better spirits. I gave Ned a quick hug around the waist, and quickened my step, pulling up even with the girls, so I could keep my eye on them. I looked back at Ned, who winked at me, as if to say, "We'll get through this. You'll see."

Though we were generally very shy about sharing our feelings in front of others, I couldn't help myself. "I love you, baby," I said.

Our little peeps joined in.

"I love you, Daddy."

"Wuv you, Daddy."

Yes, we would make it through this. We had each other, and we were together.

Finding our place in the scheme of things at the farm was not easy. There were only three bedrooms, and they were taken. Momma and Pa, Flo and Gerald, and Luther and Carl. The room that was to be ours was really only a storage room off the kitchen. Since we weren't in a position to be choosy, we took what was offered and tried to be grateful. We didn't plan to be there very long, anyway.

In our room, the twin beds which we'd brought from our house were already made up, one to be shared by Sally and Susie, and one for Ned and me. *It's only for a few months*, we kept saying. *Just for a little while, until Ned finds another job.*

Luther and Carl, big strapping boys now, had hired themselves out for the summer, since Gerald was there now to work the fields with Pa. So Ned and I were free to use their bedroom most of the summer, until they came back for the start of school. After that, back to the twin bed for us.

Besides the two twin beds, we'd managed to put a chest of drawers in the storage room, and there were boxes under the beds and stacked high along the walls. Carl and Luther made room for a second chest of ours in their bedroom. Ned's favorite chair was squeezed into the front room. A few more items of furniture were stored in the barn. Everything else was gone, sold over the last few weeks.

As we sat down to supper, there was a little flapping about who was to sit where. When Ned accidentally sat in Gerald's place, Flo got a little snippy, but Ned apologized and we shifted around a bit until everyone seemed satisfied.

"Momma, how's your vegetable garden?" I asked. "The girls and I could pull some weeds in the morning, if you like."

"Well, now, I just did that today," Flo broke in, before Momma could answer. I could see that she was getting back to her old, angry days again.

I made light of it and said, "In a day or two, then. Those old weeds grow fast, don't they, Sally?"

"Mmm-hmm," she mumbled, her mouth full of Momma's gravy biscuits.

"I think she likes your biscuits even better than mine, Momma," I said.

Flo snorted. "I made the biscuits tonight, Sister."

Ned jumped in then. "They're real good, Flo. Did you make the gravy, too?"

Mollified, Flo conceded that point. "No, Momma did the gravy."

"It's all good, Momma," I said, then added, speaking to the grownups at the table, "I know our being here is going to put a strain on all of you. But we'll do whatever we can to not be a burden. We'll do our share of the work around here," I assured them.

Momma nodded, looked at me, then Ned. "I know y'all will."

I turned to Pa. I wanted us to start off on the right foot all around. "Pa?"

"It'll all come out in the wash," said he, never even looking up from his plate.

What the heck was that supposed to mean? Closing my eyelids, I rolled my eyes underneath, safe from anyone seeing my aggravation. That mean old coot. Despite our willingness to get along, this was going to be a long sojourn, be it ever so brief. Between Pa's orneriness and Flo's self-centered ways, we'd be lucky to make it through a single day without harsh words being said.

I kept quiet for the rest of the meal, except for helping Sally and Susie a bit with their food. After excusing himself, Ned went to the barn to get some of our things. Nobody else had much to say, except Gerald, who'd been holding a running conversation with himself, interrupted only by occasional grunts from Pa. When he started in on the view he'd had of the neighbor's pigs coupling, I hurriedly got the girls up and went out on the porch so they wouldn't have to hear the coarse details that were spilling out of his mouth. I wasn't afraid of dressing Gerald down for talking like that in front of the girls, but I decided to save that fuss for another day. For today, what with uprooting my family and moving us to a place filled with discord, I'd had enough.

Who, being loved, is poor?

-- Oscar Wilde

CHAPTER 13

The next morning, I woke to the sound of Momma moving around in the kitchen. It was still dark outside. Seeing as how our new sleeping quarters were right by the kitchen, I guessed this would be the way of things from now on. I sighed. I'd just have to get used to it.

Careful not to disturb Ned, who had slept on the outside while I lay next to the wall, I eased down to the bottom of the mattress, then felt for my clothes. I was buttoning up my shirt when he whispered, "Come here."

I tiptoed over and sat down on the edge of the bed. "What?" I whispered.

His hand was on my shoulder, fingering my hair. He knew I liked that. He wiggled to make room, then pulled me down until I was lying beside him, facing him. We kissed several times, and I felt a familiar warmth building. He felt it, too. He pulled me even closer, cupping my bottom and pressing me against him.

"Momma?" Susie's voice trembled, so soft I almost didn't hear it. She probably didn't know where she was, waking up in a strange, dark place like this.

"Shhh, baby. I'm coming." Reluctantly, I untwined myself from Ned and went to her.

The sky was lightening up; the sun would rise soon. While I comforted Susie, Ned dressed. As I watched him, I could still feel his hands on me. I reminded myself this was just a man putting on his clothes, but I couldn't deny the yearning just the sight of him gave me. This particular man stirred my body and my heart. He had a way about him, this man did, a sweetness in his soul, that kept sad thoughts and darkness in their place, that brought out the joy and the laughter in the most mundane of things. A fear of losing him clutched at me. The thought was unbearable, and I rejected it as impossible. I shivered. Mercy, what deep thoughts to have before breakfast.

Ned leaned over and kissed Susie, then Sally, who was now awake, and then me. "I'm going to look for work," he said. By the time I got the girls dressed and out to the kitchen, he was gone.

Sipping my cup of chicory coffee, I leaned against the sink while Momma fixed soppy eggs for Sally and Susie. "Where's Flora?" I asked.

"She'll be up directly," said Momma, sliding the gently cooked eggs onto their plates. Using a fork, she carefully laid open the yolks and handed each girl a piece of toast to sop her egg with. "Flora goes to the Jamison's house three days a week now, cleaning, cooking, working in the garden, whatever Mrs. Jamison needs help with."

"I didn't know she had a job. They pay her for that?"

"They pay her good for it. Mrs. Jamison is right poorly with the arthritis now and she needs the help. She can't do it all on her own anymore."

"I'm sorry to hear that. Wish I was so lucky, to have a way to earn some extra money."

"I don't know, Birdie," Momma shook her head. "She spends it on herself, mostly. A new dress, a hat. A movie magazine."

I got a damp rag and wiped each girl's face and hands. "Scoot. Get your dollies and go out to the porch to play." Clearing the table, I said, "That doesn't sound too smart, not with money hard to come by and so many folks out of work."

"It's my money. I'll do what I like with it," said Flo as she entered the kitchen, making me wonder if she'd been standing just beyond the kitchen door, listening to us. Guess it wouldn't hurt to be careful what I said from now on.

Regardless, I didn't want to start the day with an argument. "You're right. It's yours, to do with as you please." I tried to smooth things over. "I guess I just wish we'd been smart and saved more when we had the chance."

Flo shrugged and said nothing further while she gathered her breakfast. Then, with a mug of chicory in one hand and a fatback biscuit in the other, she left the house, the screen flapping closed behind her.

Hurrying after her, Momma stuck her head out the door. "Bring that coffee cup back with you this afternoon, and the one you left there the other day, too."

In the cool of the morning, we worked in the vegetable garden, Momma and the girls and I. The girls were more hindrance than help, but that was to be expected. They stuck with us for almost twenty minutes before starting to whine that they were thirsty. I told Momma to take them to the house while I finished the weeding. I didn't mind working by myself. It gave me time to think in the quietness.

Propping my arm on the top of the hoe handle, I watched them walking between the rows, stirring up little clouds of dust. Sally talked a blue streak to her grandma, who nodded every once in a while. Susie wanted to stop and look at every little bug or weed blossom, so Sally had to give her hand a tug every other step. She was a good big sister. Our two girls were getting so big and it had happened so fast. Sally was like me—practical, a little bossy—while Susie was all kindness and dreams, like her daddy.

I finished up the second row and started on the third. Not even ten o'clock yet, and it was already hot. Now I remembered why I didn't want to spend my whole life as a farmer's wife. The hair next to my scalp was wet, and there were trickles of sweat tickling down my back. I had worked my way back to the edge of the garden nearest the house, so I decided to walk up to the house to get a drink.

It was cooler on the porch, because of the shade, of course, but also because of the well. Pa's daddy, my grandpa, had built the back porch around the well, which made it especially handy back when I was a little girl, before we had indoor plumbing. Loosening the tie-rope from around the pulley handle, I slid the wooden cover off the hole and leaned my head in so I could enjoy the waft of cold air rising from the depths. I let the bucket down. When I felt it hit the water, I gave it time to fill up, then rewound the pulley. Pushing the half-full bucket to the side, I closed the cover and took the dipper off the bent nail where it had always hung. I may not have missed working in the field, but I did miss our well water. Ice cold, with the flavor of the minerals from the earth below, combined with the taste of the tin dipper. No better drink in the world on a hot day.

Before I went back to the garden, I got one of Momma's bonnets from the house. I knew if I didn't, my scalp would be sunburned by the end of the day, not to mention my face. Coming down the steps of the porch, I saw Gerald loping across the yard from the direction of the corn field. Before heading into the barn, he turned his eyes toward me. I couldn't say why—after all, it was only a look—but it made me feel uncomfortable, and I wished Ned was close by, instead of away from the farm.

Midday dinner was quiet and quick. Pa and Gerald didn't have much to say. Even the girls were quiet, so I suspected they were tuckered out and ready for their nap. I took them to our room and laid down with them, but with only one window, there was no breeze at all and it was too stuffy to sleep. So I moved them to Carl and Luther's room, which was on the shady side of the house. The flutter of the curtains at the window showed the air was moving, at least a little.

The boys were working with a farm crew and wouldn't be home for another week. Ned and I had stayed in our own bedroom with the girls last night, just so they wouldn't be scared in a new place and all, but I thought, if the girls went to sleep all right tonight, my husband and I might take advantage of the privacy of the boys' bedroom. I wanted to finish what we had started in the dark that morning.

Soon as the girls were down for their nap, I slipped out the door. I wanted to go put my feet in the water for a bit, down at the creek, but when I walked out on the porch, I saw Gerald between me and the path to the creek. I didn't feel like fooling with his slick self, so I went back in and laid myself down with the girls.

Pa had us between a rock and a hard place, all right. I knew it, and Ned knew it, too, because he and I had talked about it. Until we had prospects of some sort, we had to do what Pa said. Like I said, my pa was a mean man. A hard worker, but an unhappy, mean man.

When Ned finally came in that first night, I could tell he'd spent the day working hard. He looked like his legs couldn't have carried him much further. My heart ached for him, having to put in a full day and then walk back from wherever he'd been. Pa didn't own a tractor, and he wouldn't let Ned take the wagon and mules, for he said he might need them during the day while Ned was gone. So Ned walked.

I hurried to get his feet under the table so I could serve him his supper, which I'd kept warm in the oven. The girls wanted to climb on him, but I made them go play in the front room until he finished eating. While Ned and I sat alone at the kitchen table, all the other grownups were on the back porch, catching the slight breeze that was blowing through the trees, easing off the heat of the day.

"That was good, honey," he said, wiping his mouth with the damp towel I'd given him. "Thank you."

"Did you get enough? There's some more mashed potatoes, and a little bit of fried okra…"

Ned shook his head. "That's enough." He twirled his glass of milk, then chugged the last swallow down. "If you'd rinse this out and get me some well water, though…"

When I walked out on the porch to get his water, Pa said, "Where'd he work today?"

"I didn't ask him," I answered, and went on with my task.

Pushing out of his rocker, Pa went inside to the kitchen. I ground my teeth, wishing I could spare Ned from whatever inquisition Pa had decided to start in on.

Meantime, I got the water drawn and the cover back in place and hurried back in with the glass of water. Pa was already getting up from his chair and walking down the hall. I placed the water in front of Ned and began clearing the table. "What did he want?" I asked.

Ned continued to stare down at the table. He looked like a beaten man. "Wanted to know who I worked for today and how much they paid me."

I pulled out a chair and sat down, waiting for him to go on.

A minute passed. "I stopped at the Daley's, then the Rowell's, then the McDaniel's farm. They needed a little fencework done. I got a dollar and a half."

"For all day?"

Ned nodded. "Didn't get to their place until nine this morning. And they fed me a passable lunch." He looked at me sadly. "We didn't know how good we had it, did we?"

I leaned over and put my arms around him. "Me and the girls have still got it good, baby. We've got you and you're the best thing that's ever happened to us."

He kissed me and hugged me back.

Then I remembered Pa. "What did Pa want?"

Ned took a deep breath, then let it out. "The money."

I sat up straight then. "What?"

"He took it all. For room and board."

I couldn't believe my ears. My pa had sunk to a new low. "Yeah, and he's gonna give it back," I threatened, and pushed away from the table.

Ned grabbed my arm. "No. Leave it be."

"But…"

"Leave it be, Birdie. He's right. We owe him something for taking us in and feeding all four of us."

"Huh? No, Ned," my voice started to rise.

"Shush, now. Shhh, listen to me. It's just for a little while, until I find something permanent. We've got the girls to think about. We can't risk being thrown out, and there's nowhere else to go. We have no other family here, and most of our friends are worse off than us."

I was crying softly now, shaking my head back and forth. Ever since Ned lost his job at the factory, I'd been having visions of us walking the roads all day, sleeping in a stranger's barn, the girls starving and thin. I couldn't bear it, couldn't ever let that happen. "It's not fair. It's just not fair."

"Who said life was fair, sweetheart?" He used his thumbs to wipe away my tears. "Like you said, we've got each other, so we've still got it good."

"Daddy! Daddy!" The girls couldn't wait any longer. They were up in his lap before you could say "Jack Sprat." Then he hugged all three of us, the girls giggled, and I smiled. Things weren't so bad, I guessed. After all, we had each other.

CHAPTER 14

Something happened that night that had never happened before. Ned fell asleep while we were making love. We paused for just a moment and he laid his head on my chest, and then he was out. That told me, more than anything he could have said, just how exhausted he was. He'd been trying so hard to keep me and the girls happy and calm, all while spending himself to provide for us in whatever way he could. I felt ashamed that he had to use his energy on me. I should be taking better care of my husband, and I resolved to do just that.

In spite of my good intentions, he was up and gone before I woke up the next morning. When I went to the kitchen, Flo was feeding the girls their breakfast. Whatever tension there was between the two of us, Flo loved my daughters and she treated them with kindness and love. I wished again that she could have a baby of her own, it was so obvious that she wanted to be a mother.

"Where's Momma?" I asked, kissing Sally and Susie on the tops of their heads.

"She's out on the porch, washing clothes. Her arthritis has flared up again. I told her you and I would do the garden this morning, then help Pa and Gerald in the field this afternoon."

"That's fine, and I don't mind. But why doesn't Pa let Ned help him? He could do as much as you and me put together."

"You're a ninny, aren't you?" Flo whispered, leaning over the table so the girls wouldn't hear. "He wants the money Ned can earn working somewhere else. He'll get the same amount of money from the cotton no matter who's working the field."

I pondered that thought. It made sense, in a warped kind of way. "What about your money? Ma said you spend it on yourself, so why doesn't Pa get your money?"

Flo turned away from me, pouring herself another cup of chicory. "We have an understanding, Pa and I."

"What kind of understanding?"

"That's between him and me, although I expect you have a good idea what I'm referring to." With that, Flo took her cup and her bonnet and went outside.

What my sister meant by that cryptic remark was a mystery to me. But I reminded myself yet another time that these arrangements were temporary, and that I just needed to keep my mouth shut and take care of my family. That's exactly what I planned to do.

So the days of that summer sped by. The vegetables began coming in, which meant we ate well, but it also meant grueling days of picking, snapping, shucking, and slicing, followed by late nights of canning and putting up. It would have been unbearable to have the stove going all day in the kitchen, so we waited until after supper to get started.

Momma was in her element here. She knew how to can and preserve with the best of them. Flo and I were just the hired help and we knew it. In the midst of the work, we seemed to forget all our differences and enjoy the pleasure of a job well done. That is, until the night of the accident.

Momma's part was done, and her hip was hurting, so we sent her out to the porch to get off her feet and cool off. We were on the last dozen jars of the evening, and tired and hot, both of us. Flo moved the clean, hot jars from the drying area by the sink to the kitchen table, where I would fill them with several ladles full of blanched squash and add enough liquid to cover the squash. Then Flo would lay the lid on top, screw on the band, and move the jar to the other end of the table.

I had filled the jars nearest me, and was moving to the last few, a little further out. The pot was almost empty, so low I couldn't fill the ladle any more. So I got the pot off the stove and held it with one hand, tilting it so I could fill the ladle with my other hand. Flo was moving the filled jars, and our arms accidentally collided. I lost my grip on the pot, and all the rest of the hot squash and broth fell on Flo's forearm. She screamed bloody murder. I threw the pot down and tried to get Flo over to the sink, but she was hard to handle, all the while blessing me out for doing that to her. Momma, Gerald, and Pa all came bursting in, wanting to know what the devil had happened.

"Gerald, get a bucket of well water and bring it in here," I ordered. He rushed out the door.

"Come on, Flo, we've got to get this washed off of you," said Momma, who was on Flo's other side now, pulling her toward the sink. Poor Flo was struggling.

"Mommy?" Susie and Sally were standing in the doorway to the storage room. I was about to tell them to go back to bed when

Flo herself said, "It's all right. Aunt Flo just got some squash on her arm, and it burns a little bit." Amazed, I watched Flo's face, which was now peaceful, in spite of the fact that her whole forearm was still covered in steaming squash. "You go on back to bed now, and I'll show it to you in the morning." The girls did what she said.

By that time, we got her to the sink, and Gerald was back with the cold water. Momma held Flo's arm in the sink while we slowly poured the water, washing everything away. Taking a clean kitchen towel, I put it under her arm, and sat her down. "I'm so sorry, Flo."

"My fault, too," she said, sniffing.

"Here. Let me put this butter on it." Momma took the cool butter and gently smoothed it over the burn. When she was finished, she said, "You'd best put on a thin cotton shirt tonight, long-sleeved."

"Yes, Momma," she answered.

I said, "Go on to bed, Flo. You, too, Momma. I'll clean up in here."

The next day, Flora went on to the Jamison's house, since it was one of her days to work. When she got home, just at supper time, she was a bit snippy, but really no more than usual. After we'd finished eating, she went right on back to her bedroom. Momma and I got supper cleaned up, then I heard Momma knocking on Flo's bedroom door. "Are you all right?"

"I'm fine. Just a little tired after working all day."

"Oh. All right then."

From then on, if it was one of her days to work at the Jamison's, Flo didn't do any work at the farm. She'd get home right when supper was about to be on the table, then after supper she'd either go to her room or she'd go sit on the porch until time to go to bed. At first, she used her arm as an excuse, but before long, she just acted like it wasn't her place to have to do anything. It was one of those things that kind of sneaks up on a body, comes on so gradual you don't think about it. I just kept reminding myself that we'd be out of here before long. No need to start a ruckus.

Most days, Ned continued to go off and try to find some work. Sometimes, he got hired for several days in a row. Most of the time it was only for a few hours, if he was lucky. Some days, he found no work at all. He even tried to get on with the seasonal farm crew, to work with Luther and Carl, but they had a waiting list of willing workers and he was at the bottom of the list. The thing was, summer would soon be over, and so would the summertime work. Ned stayed in touch with friends from town, hoping to hear that the factory would reopen, or that the mills were hiring again, or just anything, but there was nothing. No news, no improvement, no jobs to be had. I could tell it was weighing on him, pulling him under.

It was toward the end of August. Most of the corn had already been harvested and sold, but there was one field Pa had planted late and was just now coming in. Flo was at the Jamison's and Ned had a two-day job, which was good, except it was five miles away. He told me the day before that he would probably spend the night there and get home a little after supper today.

Early that morning, while he was busy dusting cotton, Pa sent me and Gerald to the corn field, along with the wagon, to pull the rest of the corn. If you wanted to preserve the sweetness, it had to be picked in the cool of the morning, and since Pa had a buyer lined up for today's pick, he wanted to be sure it didn't turn.

Momma was cutting up apples to dry, while keeping an eye on the girls.

The field was one of the furthest from the house, hidden by a low rise, so despite my aversion to Gerald, I rode in the wagon with him. Once there, I purposely kept things all business, and made a point of staying a few rows away from him. He was behaving like a gentleman, or at least as close to a gentleman as Gerald was ever going to get. I began to relax. It was a beautiful morning, cooler than usual, and I found myself humming.

"What's the name of that song?" Gerald asked. I cringed. I must have been humming louder than I thought. This was the last thing I wanted, to carry on a conversation with Gerald. Still, he was married to my sister, and he seemed to be making an effort to behave, so I tried to answer pleasantly.

"Down in the Valley," I answered. "You've heard it before?"

"Naw." He stepped through the two rows separating us, and started pulling corn on my row. "I never listen to music much."

I didn't reply.

"But that sounded nice."

What should I say? "Thanks."

When my bushel basket was full, I headed to the wagon with it. He stopped me and held out his arms. "I'll take it."

Startled, I let him take the basket. Wasn't this a strange thing, I thought. Even the vilest of folks I'd come across in my life seemed to have a bit of goodness in them. Well, maybe not goodness. Maybe loneliness. Maybe wanting to feel normal. It was hard to believe Gerald was acting this way for the sake of being good. Still, I could be polite, and I could be grateful for the consideration, no matter with what intention it was given.

The morning continued in that vein, until we finished harvesting the corn. Gerald hitched up the mule, and we rode the now-overflowing wagon back to the barn.

After dinner, Pa took the corn to the buyer. I put the girls down for their nap, then walked out on the back porch to talk to Momma.

"How's your hip feeling?"

"Hurts a little." She was still busy as always, doing something with her hands since she couldn't be on her feet. At the moment, she was working on a rag rug.

"Should I pick the green beans again, do you think? There's probably enough of them ready to fill a couple dozen jars."

"You probably better. No need to let good food go to waste, and there'll be more of us to feed than usual this winter."

She didn't say that to hurt me, but it did make me feel badly. I was always feeling sorry for us, for having to stay at the farm, and didn't spare many thoughts for how it made things harder for Momma and Pa. I'd just have to try harder to make our presence less burdensome.

"I'll get started then."

The cool of the morning was no more. Picking beans wasn't the hardest thing to do, but it was hard on the back, all that leaning over. I'd been picking for almost an hour when I became uncomfortably aware of someone watching me. I straightened up slowly, bracing my back with one hand. Using my handkerchief to wipe the sweat from my face and neck, I glanced left and right. Sure enough, there was Gerald, beyond the garden, over in one of the cotton fields with a hoe in his hand, staring at me with those coal black eyes of his, as if he had every right to look.

He was such a cad. That was what they called a slick, no-good fellow in one of the movies I'd seen. So much for any good intentions this morning. He wouldn't be staring at me like that if Ned were here. I decided I would ignore him and go on picking the beans.

Another hour passed and I'd gotten all the beans that were ready. I didn't have a watch, but I knew it was time to go in and help Momma with supper. Not for the first time, I thought that if it were my house, we'd be having leftovers at suppertime, not heating up that old wood stove, turning the house into a miserable, sweltering oven. But as I'd been told a couple of times lately, it was not my house and not my choice. Pa didn't want leftovers every night, so Momma gave him what he wanted.

I'd already taken one full bushel basket of beans to the back porch so we could snap them after supper. I took this second full basket to the barn, along with a hoe and an empty pail. Leaving the basket just inside the door, I entered the relative darkness of the barn. Even before my eyes could adjust, I had no trouble making my way to the side wall to hang up the hoe. I was putting the pail in its place, hanging it on a hook from a cross beam in the ceiling, when I felt his hands close around my upper arms from behind.

Disgust coursed through me, then anger, pure and hot. I knew dang good and well who it was. I unhooked the pail, and whirled around to smash it against the side of Gerald's head. In disbelief, he clutched his ear with one hand and with the other reached out to grab me. I sidestepped around him and ran out the door, calling back, "You touch me again and I'll tell Ned." I took a few more steps, then whipped around to add, "And Flora, too." Breathing hard, I stomped toward the house, whispering to myself, "That cad."

Lucky for me, Momma was no longer on the porch, else she would have seen me telling Gerald off. She did hear me stomping up the back porch steps. When I flung open the screen door, she was standing there with a potato half peeled, watching me. "Birdie?" she said.

I couldn't bother her with this. There was already enough tension in the house. "I stubbed my toe," I lied. "I'm going to see about it." I left her standing in the kitchen and went to the boys' bedroom to get calmed down. Of course, the girls heard me come in, and quickly followed me.

While I pretended to listen to them, I came to a decision. Ned and Flora must never know about what happened. If I told Ned, he would fight Gerald, and that would be a mess. If I told Flora, she would take Gerald's side and my sister would hate me forever. The way I saw it, I had no choice. I would have to handle this myself.

CHAPTER 15

Hot, dusty, and tired, Ned shuffled into the yard in the late afternoon and went straight to the well, drawing up a fresh pail. Taking the dipper from the nail, he drank his fill, then carried the pail over to the wide top porch railing that was used as a shelf of sorts. An enamel basin hung nearby, and he poured it full of the fresh water. After washing the dirt from his face and hands, he tossed out the dirty water and washed again. Finally, he sat down on the bench and took off his boots. Carrying them to the side of the porch, he emptied the dirt and pebbles onto the ground.

I saw him from the kitchen window, but I was elbow deep in flour and buttermilk, so I took my satisfaction in the mere sight of him. There were so few things I could call my own these days, but this man was mine. Our little house was gone, the Tudor was gone, our financial stability was gone... If Ned were gone, too, how would I live?

I knew I had become a clinging, needy wife, the likes of which I'd formerly despised, but I couldn't help it. When I tried to imagine our family's future, the picture was blank and that made me afraid for us. After living under this roof again for several months, I felt more and more hopeless and less and less like myself. The episode with Gerald added to my frustration.

We had a good supper that night, with plenty of fresh vegetables. Green beans, cream corn, sliced tomatoes, stewed squash, pepper gravy, and buttermilk biscuits. As usual, Flo came in just in time to sit down at the table with us. I think she did that on purpose, though how she could know precisely when we sat down, I couldn't figure. I guess it didn't really matter anyway, because on the days she worked, she refused to lift a hand to help with anything. She said she'd been "working all day," and went right on to the front room and put her feet up. It made my blood boil. What did she think Momma and I had been doing all day?

While we were at the table, Momma said, "I got a letter from the boys today."

"They all right?" Flo asked.

"They're fine," she said. "Their boss man, Mr. Bruce, asked them to stay on through the fall and winter. Carl says they'll go to school there and work on the farm after school and weekends."

"Boss man must really like them," I commented.

Momma raised an eyebrow. "Mr. Bruce doesn't have any sons to help him, you know. But he does happen to have three or four girls, same age as our boys."

I laughed. "Well, that puts things in a whole new light."

"Ought to be here," said Pa. "Not off gallivanting."

No one said anything in reply, until a few moments later when Flo said, "All I know is, I miss 'em."

When supper was over, I told Momma to go rest and I sent Susie with her daddy to pick any tomatoes and squash that were ready. Sally helped me clear the table and wash the dishes. "Momma, when we get done, will you and Daddy take us down to the creek?" she pleaded. "Please, Momma?"

I was tired from working outside all day, and I knew Ned had to be tuckered, too, but the idea of being together, just the four of us, was so appealing that I gave in without a fight. I nodded and said, "Let's see what your Daddy says." When he and Susie came back, we asked him, and he agreed.

The path to the creek was familiar, so the girls ran on ahead of us. Ned and I held hands, just like we used to do back when we were courting, and the world felt right again. We all waded barefoot in the cold water, splashing playfully. It was refreshing and relaxing, and I felt at peace for the first time in a long while.

While the girls played in the creek, Ned and I sat on the bank, leaning against a log. Ned was quiet. He was that way a lot lately, but I accepted that he might be tired, or discouraged, or doing some figuring on how he could provide for us. Tonight, it seemed as if he might have something else on his mind, so I waited. Finally, he spoke.

"Birdie, I've done everything I know to do, gone every place I know to go. There's not any work to be had in these parts. Not any more than a few hours here and there. Not enough for us to live on, or have any hope of moving back into our own place. The summer's almost over, and farm work's gonna slow down." He took my hand in his calloused one and went on. "I can't sit here at the farm all winter and do nothing. Your pa and Gerald have it covered, and I'm just another mouth to feed."

"Just say whatever it is you've got to say," I urged him, as fear filled my heart.

"Well, it's just this. I wrote a letter to my cousin Bart today. I asked him to keep an eye out for me a job up there in the coal mines, in West Virginia."

Oh, Lordy, I couldn't go on, if he wasn't here with me. I buried my face in my hands, and tried not to make a sound, so the girls wouldn't know I was crying.

"Come on, now." He gently pulled my hands away and wiped the tears from my cheeks. "You've got to be strong for Sally and Sue. If I can get a job up there, I'll work for a while, and send you some money. You can save it, and if things don't get better here, you and the girls can come up to West Virginia, too. We'll get us a place up there." He paused. "I've got to work, Birdie. A man's supposed to support his own family. I've tried hereabouts long enough. It's time to try something else."

A few weeks passed and nothing happened, so I began to hope that this idea of his would be completely forgotten. But just before the trees began to turn orange and gold, he got a letter from Bart, saying there was a job waiting for him, if he wanted it. Two days later, my husband was gone.

September was over. October passed, then November. I didn't think I could survive without Ned, but I did. I wasn't happy, but I had the girls to think of, so I took one day, one hour, one moment at a time, and dealt with it. I wrote Ned faithfully every week, and he never missed a week of sending me a letter, either, not at the beginning. He sent money, too, just as he promised. It wasn't much, but I saved every penny of it.

I was afraid to leave it in the house. I wrote Ned early on and told him never to mention the money in his letters, in case someone snuck into my room and read them. I didn't trust Pa or Gerald, either one of them, to be anything but sneaky and mean, so I always took the money straight out of the envelope and kept it on my person for a day or two, until I felt sure they weren't watching me. Then I took the girls to the swing that hung from a big limb on the hickory tree behind the barn. I pushed them on the swing for a while, then I sat down next to the tree and used a stick to dig down between the roots, always keeping an eye out for any snoopers. The money went into a jar, and I filled in the hole and covered the ground with little sticks and leaves.

When Pa asked me if Ned had sent any money, I lied. I said, no, it was costing him so much to live up there, he didn't have anything left over to send me. I never liked to lie, but I decided when you're dealing with someone who's going to steal from you or hurt you, there might be times when lying was justified.

The first Friday in December was hog-killing day. The heavy work was handled by Pa and Gerald, but the rest of the dirty job fell to the womenfolk, namely me and Momma, as this happened to be one of Flora's days at the Jamison's house. In spite of the harshness of the work, almost all of which had to be done outside in the wintry cold, I looked forward to this day. For one thing, it was something different in the midst of days that were always the same. All other chores were put on hold, unless absolutely necessary. And Momma made it plain that I was in charge of the women's work this year, and I liked that.

Sawhorse tables were set up, and a tarp stretched overhead and down one side to provide a bit of shelter. I was thankful for it, for a misting rain set in about mid-morning, and with the bite of a light but icy breeze, I sometimes couldn't feel the large, sharp knife I wielded. Whenever I noticed the numbness becoming dangerous, I stopped and warmed my hands by the fire, where the pork skins were already cooking in a big cast iron pot.

I saw that all the standing and the cold were bothering Momma's hip, so when she went inside to fix us some dinner, I told her to not come back out, that I would handle the rest of it on my own. It would take until long past supper time to finish it by myself, but I couldn't ask my momma, with her painful arthritic joints, to suffer any longer in the cold and dampness.

When we finished our dinner, Pa stayed inside with Momma, while Gerald and I bundled back up. Out in the cold, we worked without speaking for the most part, and three hours later, Gerald had finished the men's part of the work. He laid more wood on the fire and went inside.

By myself now, I worked on, taking even more breaks by the fire, as the wind rose slightly and the rain turned to sleet, then snow. I was considering going back on my word and asking my mother to come help me, when Gerald reappeared, picked up a knife and started working alongside me. I wondered if he'd come out here on his own, or whether he'd been shamed into coming by my momma, but I didn't really care at this point. I gave him a grateful look, said "Thank you," and kept working.

With Gerald to help me, everything was finished and put away by suppertime. Shivering, we climbed the steps to the back porch as Flora came around the corner of the house. Inside, I sat down in the straight back chair close to the woodstove. Even when the others sat down at the table, I couldn't bring myself to leave the warmth of the stove. Sally brought me a plate and I tried to eat a little, but I couldn't swallow it. My throat was starting to hurt and I couldn't stop shaking. Finally, I gave up, and calling the girls to come with me, I went to our little room and took myself to bed.

CHAPTER 16

Through that night and straight on through the next, I wasn't aware of anything real, except that I was first hot with fever, then freezing with chills. Momma and Flora came in every few hours to give me aspirin and make me drink some water, but aside from that, all I knew were my fever dreams. Strange. Powerful. Full of wild colors and weird people.

Finally, at daybreak Sunday, I came to myself for a little while. I was still feverish, but not as much. I lay in the bed and listened to the house come to life. First, Momma in the kitchen, getting breakfast started. Then she came in to our room and woke the girls. I could hear the whole family in the kitchen now. All I could do was lie in the bed and listen.

Everyone was getting ready to go to church when Momma came in to check on me. She put her hand on my forehead and I opened my eyes. "Good," she said. "Your fever's gone down some. Usually does in the morning. There's biscuits and eggs in the warming oven if you feel up to it. I'll check on you when we get back from church." Nodding, I turned over on my side and went back to sleep.

When I woke again, I realized I was hungry. The house was quiet. I shuffled slowly into the kitchen, surprised at how weak I was. Opening the warming oven, I passed over the eggs and picked up a biscuit, then poured myself a cup of chicory from the kettle on the stove. It was still hot, and very strong. Taking tiny nibbles on the biscuit, I wandered through the house, ending up in the front room, where Gerald was looking at the Farmer's Almanac. I had forgotten he would be home. He had established himself from the very beginning as a non-churchgoer, and with Pa's support, had so far managed to circumvent Momma's rule that all who stayed under her roof would have their hineys in the pew on Sunday morning. She must have trained Pa right in that respect, or maybe he really didn't mind going to church, because he always went with her.

Gerald had the coal-burning heater going strong, and the warmth felt luxurious. Pa would have a fit if he knew Gerald had put that much coal on at one time, but I decided he wouldn't hear of it from me. It felt too good, after being in our always chilly bedroom off of the kitchen.

He was sitting in the only comfortable chair in the room, Ma's rocking chair, so I perched on one of the straight back chairs, blissfully close to the heater, and ate my biscuit in unfamiliar comfort. My mind was still fuzzy, as if I could go back to sleep any moment, as if I might topple off that chair if I closed my eyes. But even in my stupor, I was very aware of Gerald. I still didn't trust him, but I remembered the way he had helped me with my part of the work on the hog, and I couldn't help but wonder why.

I was picking a few crumbs off my sweater and popping them into my mouth when I sensed him staring at me. Suddenly afraid, I was careful not to look in his direction. Instead, I bent down to retrieve my cup from the floor and rose to leave the room.

"You still sick?" he inquired in an amazingly decent voice.

Curiosity got the better of me then, and I looked to see if his face would reveal any ulterior intentions. My reading of his countenance gave no indication of anything other than genuine concern. Carefully I replied, "I'm some better today, I think."

He nodded his head at me and went back to the Almanac. Still standing there, I ventured another comment. "I wanted to thank you for helping me with the hog. It was awful cold…"

He looked at me again with those dark, brooding eyes of his, and it unnerved me so that I couldn't think what to say next. "Anyway, thank you," was all I could manage.

His only reply was another nod, then he returned to his reading. An overwhelming tiredness struck me, and I recognized the signs of an unbeaten illness demanding that I pay my due. Feeling woozy, I put my hand against the wall to keep my balance. I drug myself back to the bedroom, borrowed an extra quilt from the girls' bed, and pulled the covers up tight around me. I could feel my fever spiking again. The strange dreams started up once more and I was sucked under.

This time, I dreamed of Ned. He was back, and it was nighttime, and we were wild for each other. We fell onto the bed, tearing our clothes away in our eagerness. His hands touched me, and I could feel the weight of him pressing me down into the mattress. He gently pushed my hair away from my face, then kissed me. I kissed him back, so glad he was home that I was smiling through tears of joy. The fever tumbled through my dreams in irrational directions, and I began to feel that something wasn't right. I knew I should wake up, but I wanted to stay with Ned in my dream. I was torn. Finally, I opened my arms to him, pulling him ever closer, pulling him into me. Then I opened my eyes.

Through the fever, I tried to reconcile the man in my dreams with what my eyes were seeing. It was Gerald looming over me. I couldn't get a firm hold of that thought; it kept slipping away, for reality didn't exist in this fever dream.

I tried to speak, to tell him to stop, to leave me alone, to get out of my room, but he touched my lips softly with the tips of his fingers, and the unexpectedness of it made me pause. It reminded me too much of Ned's tenderness. Ned. Oh, how I missed him. At all times, of course, but oh, how intensely I missed him at night, in my bed. My mind swirled with the effects of the fever as I tried to rally my better reasoning. Then Gerald touched me, gently kneading and caressing my skin, and the fever would allow only one overriding thought to exist—the aching need for fulfillment.

The fever dragged me under again and I was lost.

They said I had a seizure that evening. That my fever got so high that they were bathing me with alcohol. I have few memories of that night, except hearing my momma cry over me, when she thought I was gone.

CHAPTER 17

Come Monday evening, the fever was almost gone but I was very weak. I laid in the bed, my face to the wall, thinking. My thoughts were jumbled, like a kaleidoscope. Was it real? Did Gerald come in to me and have me, or was it a dark dream? I knew I needed to think, but the fever had addled my brain. I couldn't separate the dreams from reality. It wasn't until Flo and Momma walked me into the kitchen the next morning and I saw the insolent look in Gerald's eyes that I knew for sure. My soul was in anguish as I took myself back to the bed.

If Ned were here, I'd tell him what Gerald had done, and Ned would most likely kill him. When I played it out in my head, I could hear Gerald's defense. "She wanted it as much as I did. If you're gonna kill me, better kill her, too." My stomach turned at the truth there.

It was a moot point anyway, for Ned was gone. There was no one but me. Pa would only say something nasty and mean. Momma could do...what? I didn't know that she could do anything. And Flo? Flo would most certainly take Gerald's side and place the blame squarely on me.

I decided there was nothing for it but to wait. First, I had to get my strength back, then I would watch for an opportune time. Someway, somehow, Gerald would pay for what he'd done to me.

After lunch, when the men had cleared out of the house, I rejoined the living. Fortunately, my quietness was attributed to a slow recovery, so I was able to avoid any unnecessary conversation, and even more important, any probing questions. As much as possible, I stayed close to Momma and the girls.

Thankfully, Gerald stayed away from the house for the rest of the day, and when he did come in for supper, he paid unusual attention to Flora, which had her preening and gushing like a young bride. They retired to their room at an uncommonly early hour.

One week later, Gerald had a high fever which raged for days, ravaging and weakening his body. Pneumonia set in and he succumbed suddenly, going to meet his Maker early on Christmas morning, the tenth day after falling ill.

I should have felt sympathy for Flora, but all I could feel was relief. Relief that I would never again have to look at him and be reminded of what he'd done. What I'd done. I didn't know whether to blame myself or not. After all, I was sick, feverish, and he was the one who came into my room and took advantage of the situation. On the other hand, in the midst of it all, I'd known he wasn't Ned, and though I'd tried to get him off of me, in the end I gave in, because I wanted someone to touch me. I was weak, giving in to my desires, knowing in my heart it was wrong.

But it was over now. Just two days before Gerald passed, Ned surprised us by coming home for Christmas. He seemed different somehow, older, less the young boy and more the battle-weary man. But he was still Ned, kind and loving. He spoke of us coming to live with him in a few months. I didn't relish the thought of moving so far away from my family, but I would have moved to the other side of the world to be with him. I knew that now more than ever, and I saw no reason, now that Gerald was gone, for telling him what had happened with my sister's husband.

The funeral was held the day after Christmas at Momma's little church down the road. It was a cold, damp, miserable day, just the sort of day Gerald deserved. Flora asked Ned to sing at the funeral, and he was happy to oblige. I finally cried then, not for sorrow from Gerald's death, but because I hadn't heard Ned sing in such a long time. At the graveside, the preacher was blessedly brief, perhaps seeking to spare the mourners extended exposure to the weather. The few friends and family in attendance gave their condolences and departed quickly.

Even Pa seemed to be feeling the cold more than usual or, heaven help us, maybe he felt a little compassion for Flora losing her husband. For whatever reason, he bordered on generous when he loaded up the heater with coal that day. There was an abundance of food in the house, supplied by thoughtful neighbors and church members, so except for the fact that a dearly departed loved one was being mourned, the mood in the house was almost festive.

In the late afternoon, Ned and I sat on our bed, sharing all the news and stories of the past months, things we hadn't had time to write about, when Pa came to the door of the bedroom. "Another month, it'll be time to plow again," he stated flatly. "I s'pect you need to stay here and help, instead of going back up yonder." Thinking that was all that needed to be said, he started to walk away.

"Pa, I don't think I can do that right now," Ned replied. "They just gave me a promotion, and a full-time permanent job. I was just telling Birdie, in a couple of months, maybe three, I'll have enough saved to send for her and the girls." He shared an understanding look with me and continued. "Don't you think Luther or Carl could come home and help you just as good as me?"

Pa smacked his lips, a sure sign of his disfavor. "Yep. We can handle it just fine without you. You can just go on back up there."

Now uncomfortable, just as Pa had intended, Ned offered, "I know you've been having to feed and shelter my family, Pa. And I've got some money I set aside to pay you for that." Rising, he fumbled around in the bureau drawer and drew out a five-dollar bill. "I know this isn't much, but I'll send you some more when I start making more money, with my promotion and all."

Pa took the money, tucked it far down in his front overall pocket and walked away. Never said another word.

The next day, Flora and I were in the washhouse, doing the laundry. I noticed my sister was unusually quiet, but I chalked it up to her grieving state and paid it no mind. She and I never seemed to be as close as other sisters when we were growing up, and even now that we were grown, there was not much sisterly bonding and sharing between us. I did my best to put my time with Gerald in a dark, secret place in my mind, and I hoped I could leave it there forever, never to think of it again. Still, my guilt made me go out of my way to make things easy for Flora, to try to make it up to her in some way, even though it was doubtful she would ever know what had happened between her husband and me.

The weather being too uncertain to risk hanging the wash outside, I snapped out the sheets, and with the help of a step stool, hung them across the lines, strung up every which way in the ceiling of the washhouse. Flo poured more hot water into the wash tub, grabbed a pair of overalls and the bar of soap, and scrubbed everything across the washboard. Staying in rhythm, she spoke in a hateful tone to me, saying, "He told me what you did, *dear sister*."

My heart seemed to stop beating, and I couldn't move. My mind raced. Could I just lie about it? Gerald couldn't contradict my story, not from where he was. Maybe I should simply deny it all. Not just for my sake, but for Flora's and Ned's sake. "What are you talking about?" I said, using the most innocent voice I could muster.

Flo answered bitterly, "My husband." She spat out the word with disgust. "My husband told me on his deathbed, when he wanted to clear his conscience and confess all his sins. He told me about your little meeting that Sunday morning, when I was at *church!*" Flo gave up any pretense of scrubbing the clothes now and concentrated on impaling me with her eyes.

I got down from the step stool and faced my accuser. Keeping my voice calm, I attempted to make my face look open and honest as I lied, "Flora, I haven't done anything. Gerald must have been out of his head with fever."

Flo stood with her fists clenched and her face twisted in a grimace. "*No,... he... wasn't!* He was clear as a bell, and he knew exactly what he was saying." She started toward me with blood in her eyes. "He told me how you came out in your nightgown after we were gone to Sunday School, and how you invited him to come to your bed."

Flo grew closer, and I was afraid. I backed away, but there was nowhere to go; Flora was between me and the door. "I didn't do it, Flo. Nothing happened." She reached for my throat, but I slapped her hand away. Enraged, Flo began to slap and hit me, wherever she could find an opening. I held off hitting her back until I realized she wasn't going to stop and I'd better defend myself. Screaming now, I hit her, over and over again.

The bigger of the two of us, Flo had the advantage. She got her arms around me and then wrestled me to the floor, with me shrieking and denying everything all the while. Sitting on top of me, she pulled my head back by the hair with one hand, and pressed down on my throat with the other hand, cutting off my air. Gasping for breath, and knowing beyond a doubt that Flo was about to kill me, I wheezed out, "I swear it wasn't me, Flora. I was asleep when he came in my room. I tried to make him stop…"

Flora let go then, grimly satisfied that she had gotten the truth out of me. She stood up over me, feet straddled on either side. "I always knew you were a slut, flouncing around like you were better than me." The words from Flora's mouth never registered with me at all, for the only things I was aware of at that moment were the pain in my side and the look on the face of my husband as he stood at the open door of the washhouse.

Staggering outside, I saw Ned walk determinedly down the dirt road toward town. I knew there was no need to go after him. The truth was out. I'd just have to wait on him to calm down, and pray that he could find enough love in his heart to forgive me. I didn't know if that was even possible anymore, though, because the time for my monthly issue had come and gone a week ago.

Ned never came home at all that night, or the next night, either. Flo and I steered clear of each other and spoke only when necessary. Momma inquired about the reason for our fuss, but never received an answer from either of us. My girls were smart enough to know that the safest course for them was to stay out of the grownups' way and be as quiet as the mice that sometimes got in the flour bin. And that's exactly what they did. Of course, Pa couldn't have cared less about a squabble between two females, just as long as his meals were on the table and the radio signal was strong enough to pick up the Grand Ole Opry on Saturday nights.

Late Sunday afternoon, I was in the smokehouse, cutting off a piece of streak o'lean to season some beans, when I was startled by the sudden appearance of Ned, who had come quietly up behind me. I turned to face him. I couldn't tell by the look of him what conclusion he had reached about our situation, but I could tell by the smell of him what he'd been doing. He reeked of liquor and sweat, and I couldn't be sure, but maybe a little whiff of perfume was on him, too.

"I'm back," he said, keeping his gaze steady on me with a look that was part contempt and part compassion. I didn't know which direction he was going, and I couldn't speak anyway, because my chest was heaving with sobs that I couldn't turn loose. Not yet.

"I'm mad as hell at you. And I'm even madder at Gerald, may he rot in hell forever. I'm mad at you if you did it willingly, and I'm mad at you if you didn't, because you didn't tell me about it." He slammed his hand against the wall, and his anger seemed to settle into place inside of him.

"I wasn't here. This wouldn't have happened if I'd been here." His lips trembled. "I'm mad at myself for not being here."

I threw myself against him, and his arms came around me, crushing me so hard I could barely breathe. The hot tears were cleansing and we wiped them from each other's cheeks, smiling tentatively. The emotional release quickly turned to a hunger for each other. We were young and strong and needy at that moment, so we rolled a heavy barrel against the smokehouse door and came together on the dirt floor.

Ned wanted to stay with me, but I talked him into going back to West Virginia, where there was at least a glimmer of hope for our family's future. He left on New Year's Eve.

I couldn't admit it to myself at the time, but I had another reason, even more compelling, for wanting him to go. I hadn't told him about being with child, and though I wouldn't admit it, even to myself, I was hoping that if enough time passed before I had to tell him, then maybe he would believe the child was his.

CHAPTER 18

By the first of February, there was no doubt in my mind that I was pregnant. I hadn't confided it to anyone, but Momma suspected as much, I could tell. On Valentine's Day, Flora proudly announced that she was expecting Gerald's offspring. Though there had been no reconciliation between us, I was still happy for Flo, who had ached for a child of her own for so long. I dreaded making my own announcement, and feared that Flo would immediately make my adultery known in some ugly way. So I kept putting it off, as long as I possibly could. When Momma began making pointed looks directly at my belly, I figured it was time.

I decided to tell Flora first, alone, so that if there were some scathing remarks to be made, perhaps they could all be said in private. I had also made up my mind that this child was to be Ned's, even though I knew otherwise. I didn't want Ned to ever feel that people were looking at our child and wondering if he was really the father. I would deny anything else until the bitter end.

It was Flora's day to go to the Jamison's house. That morning, I waited until she crossed through the yard and started down the dirt road, then I ran to catch up with her. Hearing my footsteps, she stopped and turned around. "What do you want?" she asked.

"I want to talk to you." I kept walking down the road and Flo fell into step beside me. "Flora, I... uh... I'm pregnant. With Ned's baby." I cut my eyes over toward Flora to gauge her reaction. "It's his, Flo. You don't have to worry about that. But... I just thought I should tell you first. You know, in private. So you could hear me say it. In private."

Flo rolled her eyes. "All right. So, you're pregnant. Whoopee for you. I don't care. All I care about is that I'm having Gerald's baby. Me. Not you. Me."

"And I'm happy for you," I hurried to say. "Really, I am. I know you've been wanting a baby for a long time." Hesitantly, I patted her shoulder. "You'll be a wonderful mother, Flo."

She seemed to swell a little, with pride or happiness or both. "Thank you, Birdie."

Not wanting to press my luck, I decided to let well enough alone, so I hugged my sister and ran back to the house.

After that, things got better between me and Flo. She was so excited and happy about the baby that her grieving and anger took second place. She even asked my advice about a lot of things—the layette, teething, pacifiers, schedules, nursing. I was flattered that my sister considered me a source of information. In a way, both of us expecting at the same time made it easier to talk about such things. By unspoken agreement, we avoided anything that would break the fragile peace between us, though there was always a lingering doubt hovering like a shadow in the background.

One blustery day in March, we were enjoying a quiet afternoon of sewing baby clothes. Momma and the girls had taken the wagon down the road to visit a friend of Momma's who was sick. Pa was out plowing the fields, getting ready for spring planting.

"Are you going to keep working for Mrs. Jamison after the baby's born, Flo?" I inquired.

She answered, "I don't think I have much choice, do I? With Gerald gone and Pa as stingy as he ever was, I'll have to work if I want to have any money to buy things my baby needs."

"Hmm. I hadn't thought about it that way. But don't you have some money saved?"

"No. Well, just a little. I spent the money I earned on things that I needed. It was Gerald, mostly, that handled the rest of the money, the little bit that Pa paid him. He wasn't very good at handling money. Always seemed to slip through his fingers as soon as he got it."

"Well, I wouldn't know about those things. Ned does send me a little money along, now that he's working." I tried to be careful what I said about my money. I wanted them all to think I had almost none. "He's saving what he makes so he can get us a place up there in West Virginia. Every time I get a letter, that night Pa comes to my door wanting his share. I tell him I need it for the girls, which is true."

Flora got a conspiratorial look in her eye. "I can't believe you don't know how to get around that. How to handle Pa?"

That got my attention. I put my sewing down. "No. How?"

"You just threaten to tell Momma what he did to us when we were growing up."

"What are you talking about?"

Flo stared at me in disbelief. "You know. The things he made us do." She prodded. "You remember, don't you, Birdie?"

I pondered on it, then said, "No. What did he do, Flo?"

Flo squinched up her face, like she didn't really want to talk about it. "He would catch me off by myself sometimes, and... make me do things for him. Touch him, you know, his man business, and things like that." She opened her eyes then and looked at me. "He did it to you, too, didn't he?"

I was horrified. With my hand over my open mouth, I shook my head *no*. Why had he done this unforgivable thing to Flo and not to me? Surely she wasn't lying? Somehow, I didn't think so.

"I hate him," Flora said coldly, keeping her eyes focused on her sewing. "Anyway, that's how I got him to leave me alone and stop picking on me all the time."

I was boiling inside, like a pressure cooker with the lid clamped down. "But... why didn't Momma do something? You told her, didn't you?"

"I tried. Several times. But I couldn't get the words out, it was so nasty. I was afraid she wouldn't believe me." She looked at me then with the most pitiful face, and my heart broke for what my sister had been through. Putting my sewing aside, I went and hugged her, and rocked her back and forth in my arms while she wept the pain away.

I didn't know how I would face my Pa again without trying to kill him. As furious as I was, I might just do it. This was pure, righteous anger I was feeling. Those who were strong were supposed to protect the weak, not molest them. This explained a lot, but it still didn't explain why. As I saw it, "why" didn't really matter anyway. There was absolutely no reason that would excuse his actions.

For two days, I let it simmer. And I made a plan.

I wanted him to know that someone besides Flo knew the truth about him, and I wanted to give him just a taste of pain, to make him remember the occasion. Right or wrong, I don't know, but I couldn't let anyone, not even my own father, get by with no consequences for hurting an innocent child.

So I watched for the right time, and then I waited for him in the barn with a two-by-four. I should have been nervous or agitated, but I wasn't. Sometimes before a storm hits, there's a stillness in the air, you know?

He was alone; I made sure everyone was either occupied elsewhere or in the house, far enough away that they wouldn't hear anything.

He came in from the sunshine into the dark of the barn. I called to him from one of the stalls, "Pa, come here a minute."

Never suspecting, he came around the corner into the stall, and I knocked him upside the head just as hard as I could with that two-by-four. He tumbled into the hay, and I could see a knot forming already. He wasn't knocked out, but he was dazed. The first time I swung, I didn't have to think about it at all. The second time, I had to remind myself of what he'd done to Flo.

I waited until he started to rise, then I hit him the second time. He fell back, whimpering, "What the hell are you doing?"

Hitting a man with a board was not as simple as I'd thought it would be, even if he did deserve it, and on top of that, I began to be afraid of what he might do to me later. I was breathing hard by then. In between gasps, I answered him. "Remember what... you did... to Flo?" My gasps for air were turning into sobs.

Groaning, he got up on his hands and knees. "You don't know it all."

I looked at him on the floor. He was a pitiful, mean man. He deserved this. I had to take the third swing. The third swing was for my girls, as a warning, so he would never, ever think of touching them.

Swiping tears and runny snot from my face, I leaned down and I talked fast. "Doesn't matter why you did it, only that you did. You deserve to die, but I'm not God, and I won't take His vengeance from Him. The next time I swing, it's to make sure you remember this: If you ever lay a hand on my girls, I will kill you, that is, if Ned doesn't get to you first. Nod your head if you understand me."

He nodded and I swung again. This time, he lay flat on the ground and didn't move. I nudged him with my foot. He jerked his legs.

"Now, when you get up from here, you go in the house and tell Momma that you fell out of the hayloft onto the harrow. You got that?"

I saw his head move slightly. That was enough. Taking the two-by-four with me, I left the barn on the back side, away from the house.

I was shaking by that time, and I felt sick. Going the long way around, I went to the creek and set the board afloat in the moving water. I wanted all of this to disappear like that piece of wood, so I'd never have to think of it again. I'd done what needed to be done, but there was no satisfaction in it. Leaning my head over, I retched into the water, then watched as my vomit floated away, too. All the bad stuff floating away. Somehow that made me feel just a little better. Reaching down, I scooped up handful after handful of clean water and splashed it on my face. Then I sat on the bank awhile, leaning against the same log that Ned and I always leaned on, praying that things would get better now. For Flo, for Momma, for all of us.

I wrote Ned once a week, just like before, but I hadn't yet told him of my condition. I knew what the first thing to go through his mind would be, but I hoped he would choose to believe the best and accept the child as his. In the middle of March, I wrote and told him I was expecting. He didn't write back for a long time. In June, I received a brief letter from him, mostly asking about the girls, and never mentioning the pregnancy. I knew from the letter that he was angry.

When he left on New Year's Eve, things were not normal between us, which was to be expected, but it had seemed to me that the rift was mending. At that time, we'd not talked any further about my being with Gerald, not even the fact that I was sick and delirious when it happened. Looking back, maybe we should have. Maybe I should have made him listen to all of it. Now, on top of the torment of dealing with the damage to our relationship, we were separated by time and distance, which made it difficult, if not impossible, to put things together again.

I decided—actually, I had no other choice—I would stay calm and give him time. I continued to write him once a week, and prayed that my constancy would win over his heart and draw him back to me.

I didn't hear from him again until after my delivery.

CHAPTER 19

In June, after a brief visit home, Carl and Luther left again to work on the seasonal crew, while Pa hired an older fellow, Gus, to help him with the farm work. He really needed two workers, but he was too stingy to spring for it. The boys knew how he was, knew that if they stayed and worked hard all summer, they'd end up with nothing to show for their labor, so they chose to go with the crew again, where they could earn decent pay and save it for when they went out on their own.

Flora and I were both six months along by then, and we tried to do all of our gardening and field work in the cooler morning hours. Momma's arthritis had grown worse over the winter months. She found it difficult to carry out some of her usual chores and activities, so I tried to pick up the slack. Sally was old enough to help in many ways, especially watching over Susie, but I also taught her how to cook a few things, and how to keep the house clean. Flo still went to help Mrs. Jamison, but only twice a week now.

One day in late June, one of Flora's work days, Sally and Susie were helping me weed the garden. I came in to start dinner and found Momma on the floor in the kitchen, unable to get herself up. I tried to help her rise, but she couldn't put any weight at all on her left leg. I got a pillow and some quilts and made her as comfortable as I could on the floor, then sent Sally to get Pa and Gus.

The doctor's findings were not particularly hopeful. Momma's hip was broken. There was a chance it could heal properly on its own, but the more likely outcome was that she would be bedridden for the rest of her life. The option of going to the hospital for an expensive operation was offered, but Pa said he didn't have the money. There was no more talk of the hospital after that. The doctor left some pain medicine for Momma, and instructed me on its use and dosage.

Everything changed after Momma broke her hip. Schedules and arrangements had to be made and adjusted, and the household duties had to be reassigned. I took on most of the responsibility, though Flora did pitch in her share on the days she was home.

She wasn't tolerating pregnancy as well as I was, though. The months of July and August were hard on her. She retained water, and looked swollen all over by the end of the day, especially around her ankles. Many times, I had to order her off her feet, making her go lie down on her bed for hours, until the swelling went down some. Sometimes, it seemed like the needs of the whole house and everyone in it rested on my shoulders alone.

Momma progressed to the point that she could sit for an hour or two at a time, and she was grateful whenever I could give her something to keep her hands busy. Sally and Susie became her constant companions and helpers.

The most grueling chore of the summer, for me, was the canning. It had to be done, and it couldn't wait. Flo helped as much as she could when her legs weren't too swollen, and Momma was a big help with peeling and cutting, the things she could do from her chair.

Even Sally helped with washing the jars and laying out the supplies. But I wouldn't let her anywhere near me when the hot vegetables had to be poured up. It was too dangerous. Most of the hard work fell to me, but somehow, with everyone doing their little bit, we made it. The canning was done.

As the summer drew to a close, I was exhausted, tired deep in my bones, and I wished I could take just one day to rest. Still, I had to be thankful that Momma continued to improve, so much so that by the end of August, with the aid of two canes and the support of a family member, she could take a few steps at a time.

September arrived, bringing with it just the slightest relief from the summer heat. No one was more appreciative for even that small bit of respite than us two expectant mothers. Both of us were ready to be through with this miserable summer of too much heat, too much work, and too much weight to be carrying around. Flora's swelling was so severe now that she stayed in bed most of the day, getting out only in the late evening when it was cooler and she could sit out on the front porch in her nightgown and put her feet up on a crate. I took to sitting out there with her. It was quiet and peaceful, once the girls were in the bed.

On this particular night, the wind was blowing a storm in. It had been hot and muggy all day, but now the air was cool and damp and fresh, and it felt wonderful. Flo and I had just gotten settled with a nice glass of tea for each of us when I heard Momma call out. We had moved one of the twin beds into the front room since she'd been down with her hip. It made it easier to help her and keep watch over her.

"I'll go," I said, setting my tea down.

I could tell when I saw Momma's face that the pain was severe this time. "What do you need, Momma? Do you want some pain medicine?"

"Yes, please." Momma licked her lips. "Can I have a little more than usual, Birdie? It's more than I can stand tonight. Do you think that would be all right?" she asked, her voice shaking.

"Sure, Momma. I'll put a little extra in the spoon." I measured out the liquid with a generous hand, adding an extra drop or two for good measure. I lifted Momma's head for her to swallow. "I was afraid you were trying to do too much today. I guess it's time to pay the piper now, huh? Do you want me to rub your back for a minute?" Sometimes that helped to ease her distress a bit.

"Yes, please. Thank you, Birdie. You're a good daughter."

I could only imagine how difficult it was for my once strong and active mother to be dependent now on others for so many details of her life. Gently, I helped Momma turn on her side so I could massage her back. I felt the tense muscles relax after a few minutes, then eased my mother back down on the mattress. "Is that better now, Momma?"

"Flora, is that you?" Momma said.

"No, Momma, it's Birdie." That pain medicine played tricks with Momma's mind sometimes, especially if she had a little extra, like tonight.

"Flora, you were such a sweet little thing when you were born. My precious little baby, I thought you were the most beautiful baby in the world, you looked so much like your father."

I saw no need to keep correcting her about who I was. I just let her talk.

"You were perfect to me." Momma got quiet then, and I thought she had drifted off to sleep. I was just about to return to the front porch when she started back up again.

"Of course, Pa didn't think so. That was only natural, I guess. Just the sight of you reminded him of what I'd done." Momma smiled at something. "Jim. That was your real daddy's name. He was a traveling preacher, you know. Came by here one summer to preach a brush arbor revival. He was a handsome man, Jim was. I just couldn't stay away from him."

The smile vanished. "Then he was gone, and somehow Pa found out. He beat me within an inch of my life, that's what he did. He didn't want me to keep you. But I did keep you, Flora, my sweet flower. And I got the last laugh, too, because he had to claim you as his. He couldn't very well admit otherwise, could he? Oh, mercy, you were a beautiful child."

Momma's voice drifted off on the last few words, and after a minute, she began to snore softly.

What did my momma just say? Surely not. But she said it as if it were the gospel truth, didn't she? The door to the back porch was propped open to catch the night's cooling breeze, but now it made me shiver as it brushed along the hairs of my arm. In the air, I could smell the minerals from the well, bringing to mind the icy coldness of the water. I wrapped my arms around me and watched my momma sleep.

I sat there, wondering what I should do, whether I ought to say anything to Flo.

No. If it was true, Momma should be the one to tell her, not me. Even though it sounded like a true admission, Momma couldn't be considered of sound mind at the time because of the effects of the painkiller. I myself had heard her say strange things before when she was medicated.

No. I shouldn't say anything at all to Flo, especially not in her current condition. It could get her all upset, and then turn out not to be true.

Down in my gut, I had a feeling that in her delirium tonight Momma spoke the truth, and that this incident long ago was the catalyst for my pa's meanness to erupt, as well as providing him an excuse for treating Flora the way he did. It didn't make it right, mind you, but it did explain where it came from.

Still, I couldn't be the one to say it. First chance I got, I would bring it up with Momma and let her sort out what to do. The truth had been hidden for a long time. A day or two longer wouldn't make any difference. Or so I thought.

It turned out to be way longer than a day or two before the truth came out. The issue of Flo's lineage was put on the back burner because we ended up being very busy that night and for some time afterward.

CHAPTER 20

I couldn't sleep, so I lay there awake, thinking about my life. Soft puffs of breath came from Sally and Susie, who slumbered peacefully in the other single bed just a few feet away. We'd been here in this storage room much longer than we ever expected. I was grateful, truly I was, that we had a roof over our heads and food to eat. Things could be worse.

But this wasn't the life I had imagined for myself or my family. I wanted better for my girls and for this baby, who seemed to be poised to enter the world this night. Right now, what I wanted most was Ned. But he was far away, in the mountains of West Virginia, and truth be told, the distance was not the most crucial thing separating us at present. More than eight months now since I'd seen him, and three months since his last letter.

Another labor pain. I moaned quietly, so as not to wake the girls. I hoped to make it through several more before waking Sally to fetch her Aunt Flora to help with the delivery. Momma had been teaching both of us how to deliver the babies. Even though I'd experienced childbirth twice, I had almost as much to learn as Flora, particularly in knowing what to do if something went wrong.

Having a baby and delivering a baby were two different things, as Momma kept telling us.

I panted through another contraction—a little stronger, but still bearable. I should think of something pleasant to keep my mind occupied. Something that would make me feel happy. Like when Ned and I first met. Or when we first got married and had the little apartment in town. We were so in love. Or when we had the girls and Ned had a good job. I realized most of the happy times in my life centered around my husband and I wasn't surprised by that.

It was now two o'clock in the morning. I was so sleepy I was actually falling asleep between contractions. A strong one had just awakened me, though, and then my water broke. I knew it wouldn't be much longer now. It was time to wake Sally.

Before I could speak, I heard a faint call. "Bir-die! Bir-die!" It was Flora. In my tired state, all I could think was, What now? Can't I have a baby without having to tend to somebody else's needs first?

Even so, I rolled to the side of the bed and sat up slowly, holding my belly carefully. I remembered then that Flo had been awful sluggish the day before, and even more swollen than usual. Maybe I'd better go see about her before the next pain got hold of me.

As I went through the front room, Momma whispered from her bed, "Birdie?"

"Yes, Momma." I stood still in the dark and listened.

"I think your sister's been having pains since early yesterday," Momma whispered. "I've been hearing her ever since we all went to bed. They're right close together now. Do you want me to come help you?'

I wished my momma *could* come help me, but right now, she still required so much help herself that I was afraid I couldn't see about her and tend to Flora, too. "No, Momma. I think I can handle it. You just go on back to sleep. I'll call you if we run into any trouble." What was I saying? We were in trouble already, if both of us were in labor at the same time.

Flo called out again, but there were some things I needed to do first. Padding back into the kitchen, I stirred up the fire in the stove, then filled a kettle and a large pot with water and placed them on the burners. Then I went to the big bureau and took out a pair of scissors and all the towels and extra sheets I could find.

I hoped to make it to Flora's bedroom, but as I crossed through the front room, I felt another contraction coming. I managed to hold on to the linens and shuffle over to Flo's bedroom door before it reached its peak. I heard Momma call out to me, but I couldn't answer. I opened the door, dropped the linens, and grabbed hold of the bedpost.

When the pain eased off, I turned on the lamp by the bed and got my first look at Flo, who didn't seem aware that I was there. I tried to rouse her, but got only a moan or two in response. Checking under the covers, I could tell by the dampness that Flo's water had broken, too. I tried again to wake her. This time she opened her eyes and groped until she found my hand to clutch.

"Something's wrong, Birdie. My baby didn't move all day. I'm..." She tensed as a contraction came. I spoke soothing words to her and stroked the hand that was squeezing mine like a vise. When it passed, Flo was still alert and looking at me with fear in her eyes.

I tried to reassure her. "That happens sometimes, Flo. It's probably nothing to worry about. And maybe before daylight gets here, you'll be holding that baby in your arms." Somewhat reassured, Flora gave me a faint smile. Looking down at my sister, I prayed that my own baby would not be the cause of hurt for

Flora. For months, that had been my prayer—that my baby would not have Gerald's darker coloring of hair and complexion. Though Flo and I both had darker hair now, when we were younger it was almost blonde, and Ned's had always been light. If my baby was born with dark hair and swarthy skin, he would be an unwelcome and constant reminder that vows had been broken, and that the baby I bore was Gerald's and not my husband's.

I grabbed my stomach as another pain struck me. I saw Flo's eyes open wide as she realized what was happening. When it eased off, she asked, "Are you...?"

I nodded. "I'm afraid so. We might just have us two babies before the sun comes up."

Flo looked bewildered. "Well... how are we going to do that? I was going to help you, and you were going to help me, so..."

"So I'm going to help both my girls," said Momma, using her two canes to move slowly into the room. "Birdie, do you think you can fetch my rocking chair for me? It'll be easier if I can sit down in between."

I was so relieved, I kissed Momma on the top of the head as I went to get the chair. When I came back, she was examining Flora. I pulled over a small table for her to use, then together we covered the bed with extra linens in preparation for the birth. By the time everything was ready, I had two more birthing pains, and another one was coming on.

"Birdie, go on now and get up on that bed. You're going to have to deliver in here, too. It'll be all I can do to stand up just this little bit and get these two babies on out." Momma sounded almost like her old self tonight.

Leaning against the bed until the pain passed, I said, "Just one more thing. I'll go get the water for you first."

"You'll do no such thing. It won't hurt your pa to get up and do that one blasted thing. Now, Flora, you scoot over a little, and Birdie, jump in." Momma shuffled over to the door and yelled for Pa until he answered, then she sent him about her business and told him to stay awake in case we needed anything else.

Flora and I had taken hold of each other's hand. "This reminds me of when we were growing up and had to share a bed," chuckled Flora. Just then she shuddered, and her eyes rolled back in her head.

"Momma, something's happening," I warned, shaking Flo hard but getting no response. Momma hurried as best she could to Flo's side of the bed. She made sure Flo was still breathing, and held her fingers against her neck to feel the blood flow.

"What's wrong? Is she all right?" I asked.

Momma didn't answer, which scared me even more. She was busy feeling for the baby now and seeing about Flo.

Meantime, my contractions were coming hard and fast, one right after the other, and within a few minutes I could feel the baby's head crowning. "Momma," I gasped. "My baby's coming. Now."

She moved over to my side of the bed just in time to catch the infant's head, give it a turn, and with the next contraction, ease him out the rest of the way. Momma lifted the baby up, screaming and healthy, and laid him on my stomach. I was afraid to look, but I made myself do it. There he was, Gerald's son. Olive skin, thick black hair and eyes like coal.

Ned was lost to me now. I knew it.

Momma had no time to cut the cord or clean him up right then, for Flora, still unconscious, was having frequent, strong contractions. My mother was preparing to deliver her second grandchild of the night.

I lay there with the weight of the baby on me, crying silent tears. It felt like a rock had been tied around my heart and dropped down into the darkness of a deep well. My thoughts were jumbled and frantic. I didn't know how I could ever face Ned again. How could I ask him to do this? Look what had happened to my pa. Maybe he had started out as a decent kind of man, but when Momma strayed, it broke him and crushed him and made him mean and unhappy. Ned was a very good man, but could he accept a child who was obviously not his, and suffer through the barbs and unkind comments that were sure to follow us for the rest of our lives? This baby looked nothing like either one of us. Ned didn't deserve this. I was the one who deserved it. I was the weak one, the one who broke one of the commandments of God. After this, could Ned ever love me? Or would my sweet and gentle husband become bitter and hardened? That was something I couldn't bear to see.

"Come on, Flora, push," instructed Momma. On some level, Flora must have heard her, for she seemed to gather her energy for one big push, then another one. Then the baby was out. Another little screamer, this one. Another boy, too, but with the lighter colored hair and soft blue eyes of Momma's side of the family, the same blonde hair that Flo and I had been born with, which later turned to dark brown. Momma cut the cord and let him rest on Flo. She studied Flo's face.

"I think she's just sleeping now. Worn out," said Momma. "She's not bleeding too much and the baby wasn't in distress." She took hold of Flo's cheek and jiggled her face. "Flo? Can you hear me?"

"Leave me be," Flo replied, sounding irritated.

Momma chuckled. "She'll be fine." She walked around the bed again, so she could get to me. I cringed to think what pain this was costing her. "Let me clean up this little one, now," said Momma, tiredness creeping into her voice as she cut my baby's cord. Picking him up off me, she carried him to her rocker and began to gently wash him.

I couldn't take my eyes off the baby whimpering on Flo's stomach. My baby should have looked like this one. I wished he could have been mine. Ned could believe this baby was his, and Flora would be thrilled to have a baby who would remind her always of Gerald. God seemed to have made a big mistake this night, and that was the truth of the matter, as I saw it.

Momma brought my baby back, all cleaned up and wrapped in a receiving blanket. Then, she lifted up Flora's boy and took him to the rocker. Flo still hadn't stirred.

I touched my baby softly. I looked down at his little face and pulled one tiny hand out from under the blanket. I considered what I was about to do, then I put my hands around the little bundle and transferred it to Flora's arms.

When Momma came back with the light-haired infant, she stood stock still, then jerked her head to stare at me with an unspoken question in her eyes.

I simply said, "Please, Momma. It'll be better this way."

Momma didn't move for a long time. I knew she was traveling back many years in her mind, to a mistake she'd made, consequences she had to pay, and the costs that others suffered because of her.

She laid the baby in my arms.

There isn't time -- so brief is life -- for bickerings, apologies, heartburnings, callings to account. there is only time for loving -- & but an instant, so to speak, for that.

-- Mark Twain

Letter to Clara Spaulding
20 August 1886

CHAPTER 21

The mountains were beautiful, stretching far away to the horizon, in every shade of smoky blue. We were in a world of our own, travelling by train to our new home in West Virginia—the girls, myself, and baby Tommy. I'd never been on a train before and found it exciting, to say the least. I hated to spend so much of my money to buy the tickets, but Ned insisted. All things considered, he was right. With all our bags, the two girls, an infant and all the necessary paraphernalia, any other mode of travel would have been difficult to negotiate.

Momma gave me a traveling suit to wear. She insisted that I couldn't be riding all day in a simple everyday dress. I only had two Sunday dresses, and she said I needed to keep them nice for church, because who knew when I would be able to buy more. I told her I could make my own clothes, to which she replied that I might not be able to buy enough fabric for myself, since I'd also be needing to buy fabric to make clothes for the children. Flour sacks would only go so far. I stopped arguing and thanked her for the traveling suit. It was a bit old-fashioned, but I redid the collar and put some trim on it, and it wasn't so bad after that.

Ned hadn't seen the baby yet. I wrote him the day Tommy was born, and told him all about our son, what he looked like, and how big he was. I named him Thomas, after Ned's father, who had passed away some twenty years before, and Arlo, after Ned's uncle who had moved to Texas. Thomas Arlo Parker. I thought that had a nice rhythm to it.

When Ned wrote back, his letter sounded as if he had gotten over being so angry with me. He said he had his name on the list to get one of the company houses, and now his name was at the top of the list. He had a house for us, and we could come to West Virginia just as soon as I could travel with the baby. He was anxious to see his girls, as it had now been ten months since he'd been home.

I was never so nervous about anything in my life as I was about seeing Ned. Whether he was ready to forgive me completely remained to be seen, but I was going to put everything I had into building a new life for our family in this new place.

We passed over the state line into West Virginia. I was going to miss the gently rolling hills around Deckler Springs, but maybe I could come to love this place, too. There was a certain mystery that came from not being able to see beyond the mountains that encircled me. Who knew what might be hidden in the next valley, or around the next hairpin curve?

When the conductor said we would arrive in a quarter hour, I marshalled my forces and gave the children a little spit-shine. I brushed the girls' hair and twisted it into ringlets. Then I changed Tommy's diaper and his bib, so he was sweet and clean. Finally, I took out my compact. Pursing my lips, I applied the new lip color Flora had given me. I wasn't used to it, so it looked fake and cakey to me, but Flo said it was the cat's meow, whatever that meant, so I put it on and hoped Ned would like it.

"Sally, hold Susie's hand and don't let go." I wiped some spit-up from Tommy's mouth and packed away the last of the baby blankets and toys. "Do you think you could carry these satchels, girls?" Good girls that they were, they both tried to grab the biggest ones. "Here. Susie, this one's just right for you. Sally, you can carry this with one arm and hold on to your sister with the other." I was thankful again to have them with me; they'd been such a help with the baby, Sally especially.

"Momma, will Daddy be there when we get off the train?" asked Sally.

I probably sounded like an excited schoolgirl myself. "He said he'd be right there waiting for us."

Susie had to get her share of the moment. "Momma. Will he know who I am?"

"Oh, yes, darling," I answered quickly. "Daddy knows exactly what we all look like."

"Except for Tommy," Sally corrected me.

Just then the whistle blew, indicating we were drawing near the station.

"Look for your daddy, girls." My eyes scanned the platform. "Do you see him?"

"I don't see him anywhere," said Sally. She sounded disappointed.

Wanting to cheer her, I said, "He's probably inside the station house. Everybody get their bag now, and hold on to it. And I'll just get my bags. And the baby." We stood in the aisle and I looked around one last time, not wanting to leave anything behind. "All right, then, I think we're ready. March, girls."

We stepped off the train and into another world. Though we had come out the other side of the tallest peaks, we were still high up. The small town of Lily's View was surrounded by mountains on every side. We were so isolated. Beautiful, but isolated. I felt a little chill run through me—call it a premonition, if you like. I ignored it, and let my eyes search for my husband, while the children and I huddled together on the platform.

A young woman with pale blonde hair came toward me, smiling. She had the sweetest expression on her face, and I knew immediately that we would be friends. "Birdie?" she said, in a soft, lilting voice.

I nodded, "Yes, I'm Birdie."

"Oh, of course you are, and didn't Ned tell me how lovely you'd be." Looking down at the girls, she continued, "You're the older sister. You must be Sally. And you must be Susie. Your dad told me you were pretty as two pink rosebuds." Then she held out her hands for Tommy, and I gave him to her. "And who is this handsome young feller?" She looked to me for an answer.

I realized Ned must not have mentioned the baby. That hurt my feelings and scared me, too, but I stuffed it down, to deal with it later. "That's our sweet boy, Tommy."

"Oh. Tommy," she cooed. "That's my brother's name, Tommy, so you must be special, little one."

I wanted to know where my husband was. I was tired and ready to settle in somewhere. "I thought Ned was going to meet us here."

My new friend's head popped up. "He was. But they had a side wall cave-in, so they're all working an extra shift. He got word to me, so I could come instead."

"Oh. Well, we'll see him soon enough, I guess. I guess he told you all of our names, but I don't know yours yet."

"Goodness, where are my manners? I'm Fairy. Fairy Truelove." With her free hand, she motioned for us to follow her. "Come on. I'll show you to your house." Still holding the baby, she took one of my bags from me. We walked down the main street of Lily's View, past a few stores and other businesses, then took a right onto a narrow residential lane that seemed to lead right up to the sky.

I stopped at the bottom of the hill. Surely we didn't live at the top of this thing.

Fairy turned around and came back to me. Smiling sympathetically, she said, "You'll get used to it, I promise. It's really not as bad as it looks."

Hmph. I can tell you now, it *was* as bad as it looked.

The house was so, so tiny. Two rooms. We did have running water, but no bathroom, just an outhouse. Fairy said they were working on building bathrooms onto every company house, but it would be a while before they got to ours. But—good news— probably before the year was out, we'd be in line to move into one of the bigger, better houses. One with four rooms and a bathroom.

Fairy had most kindly fixed supper for us, and kept it warm in the oven. Beans, cornbread and some ham. That sounded wonderful to me. She stayed a little while, and told us all the little things a woman knows to tell another woman, things a man would never think to mention. As she was leaving, she told me she and her husband and their four children lived the next road over, halfway down the hill. "But you can go through your backyard and the neighbors' back yards, and we're only three houses down." She gave me a hug and said, "Come and see me soon." Then she was gone.

Ned got home at midnight. He was black with coal dust, and he had grown a beard. If I met him on a dark road somewhere, I'd be terrified. Even in our own house, knowing he was my husband, I was a little intimidated, he looked so different.

"Ned? Hey, honey." I went to him as soon as he opened the door. He smiled hesitantly, but held his hands up.

"I'm dirty. Don't touch me yet." But he leaned over and kissed me. He looked happy to see me, but wore out.

I'd kept some water warm for him, so he got some towels and washed himself. And washed, and washed, and washed. When he was finished, I could still see the shadow of coal dust on him here and there. He took his clothes off and left them right by the door, leaving just his long johns on.

He came over and hugged me then, and kissed me good. I admit, I was thankful the baby was asleep. I wanted Ned to meet our son, but even more, I wanted time to be with my husband again, to get a feel for how things stood between us.

Still holding me, he asked, "How was your trip?"

"It was good. And you were right about paying for the train tickets. The girls tried to stay awake to see you tonight; they've missed you so much. But all that excitement from the trip tuckered them out and they had to succumb, finally."

He nodded. "Sorry I couldn't meet you at the station."

"It's all right. Fairy explained everything."

He hugged me again, hard. "I'm so glad you're here. I missed you."

"I missed you, too." I felt him sway on his feet. "Here, now." I guided him over to the rocker. "You sit down and I'll bring you your supper. Fairy was kind enough to have it ready for us tonight."

We didn't say much else that night. I could tell he was bone-weary and hungry and sleepy, so I had mercy on him and didn't expect any more attention. After he ate, he walked into the back room, where the girls' bed shared the space with the kitchen area. He kissed them both and tucked their covers closer.

As there wasn't a cradle or a crib in the house, I'd laid the baby in the middle of our bed. Much to my sorrow, Ned did no more than glance at Tommy before climbing into the bed on the outside, leaving me to crawl to the inside, against the wall.

"Sorry, Birdie. I'm real tired," he muttered. "We'll talk some more tomorrow…" He had already drifted off.

I told him he should wake me the next morning whenever he got up, so I could cook him some breakfast, but I don't think he heard me. I didn't sleep very well, being in a new place and all, and I had to get up with Tommy a couple of times during the night. I guess that kept me from waking up early, as I'd intended. Anyway, by the time I woke up on my own the next morning, he was gone.

Later that morning, when I got myself and all the children ready, we walked to town to find the schoolhouse. It was a nice-sized building with four large classrooms, three grades in each room, with the first through third grade students in the same room. I hadn't intended to leave Susie, but she begged and so did Sally. The teacher said Susie was old enough if I wanted to leave her, and the two of them were clinging to each other. I found I couldn't deny them. They were in a new place and they didn't want to be separated. I couldn't say no. I told them I'd be back for them when school let out at three o'clock. After a day or two, they'd be fine to walk back and forth on their own.

When I left the school, it was only mid-morning, so I decided to visit my new friend, Fairy.

CHAPTER 22

I've never met anyone else quite like Fairy, neither before nor since. When I showed up at her door, she giggled and clapped her hands. "Oh, I knew you'd come straight away, Birdie. We're going to become the best of friends, aren't we?"

"I believe we are," I replied. And it turns out, we did.

I don't know what I would have done if there'd been no Fairy in Lily's View. She was part brilliant and wise and part whimsical fairy, just like her name. You never knew which side was going to pop out.

I wasn't accustomed to being alone, and Ned worked six days a week, usually ten hours a day. I know he had the harder lot of the two of us. I'd never say different. But I was in a new place, pretty much on my own, lonesome and bored. I took to spending at least an hour or two with Fairy almost every day. Simply to walk into her house was soothing, for the smell of lavender permeated everything.

That first day, she explained the company store to me.

"It's *wonderful*, but it's *awful*," she moaned, quite theatrically.

"Huh?"

"Well, it's *wonderful* because the company makes sure there's a place for us to buy the things we need. They provide the store for the miners' families, and they arrange to have the goods delivered way up here in Lily's View. We don't have to worry about that. But it's *awful* because their prices are high, and they discourage anybody else from opening up their own store to compete with them. Or maybe nobody else wants to. I don't know about that." She handed me a glass of tea and continued.

"And then the store is *wonderful* because when work is slow, and the men don't make enough to feed their families, the store lets us charge whatever we need. Or maybe it's not slow, but a man just wants to spend more than he makes, and the store lets him do it. Well, you see, that's the same reason the store is *awful*. The men go into debt with the store, and then they can't ever get it paid off. They can't ever get ahead because they're always having to pay off what they owe, and they can't leave the mine, because they owe too much to the store."

"Oh, golly." I didn't like the sound of this. "Does everybody owe the store?"

"Almost everyone. But for the past few months the men have worked a lot of hours, so most people don't owe so much right now."

It sure seemed to me that we gave up a lot by leaving the open spaces and the good clean dirt and the home-grown food on the farm. All we got in return was a tiny house, no bathroom, canned food, coal dust covering everything, and a dangerous place to work sixty hours a week. "Is there anything good about working in the mines?" I asked her, hoping she could share some redeeming qualities of the coal miner's life. I suppose she could see the distress on my face.

"Oh, I'm sorry I was all lopsided in my telling." Fairy put down the potato she was peeling and came to sit beside me. "This company is one of the good ones, with a fine owner, Mr. Higgins. He looks after his people and he does as much as he can to keep the mine safe. Some companies don't do that. They work their men like dogs and pay them next to nothing, and they don't even try to keep the mines safe. So all things considered, we have it good here in Lily's View."

"Well…what do the women do while the men are working six days a week?"

"Oh, we find things to do. There's a quilting circle meets twice a month."

"I do like to sew," I said.

"And the county has a library bus that comes through every two weeks. Do you like to read?"

"I enjoy it sometimes. Just haven't had a lot of time for it before."

"You will. During the winter here, especially when the snow's on the ground and nobody can get out much, you'll have a lot of time on your hands."

"What do you like to do, Fairy?"

She looked a little embarrassed, like she didn't want to say.

"Come on, you can tell me," I urged her.

She looked around, as if afraid someone might be listening. "I like to paint."

"Really? What do you paint?"

"Most anything, but mostly people and nature, I guess."

"May I see some?"

She shook her head no. "Not today. Maybe next time."

After that first visit with Fairy, I went back to our tiny house. That's what I began to call it, in my mind. The Tiny House. I went through all the cabinets and drawers and the one chifforobe, making mental note of our supplies and belongings. There wasn't much in the way of food to cook for supper. Maybe I'd go by the store and pick up a few things after I got the girls from school.

Sally and Susie bubbled over with tales from the first day at their new school. They adored their teacher, Miss Cuddy, and I could understand why. She was young and sweet, and treated them with kindness. They would do well with someone like her. At least one aspect of our life here seemed to be on the right path.

To make it easier to walk and carry bags, I tied a long scarf around me to snuggle the baby in, but even with that, I was tired by the time we reached the general store. Maybe this wasn't such a good idea. I started to not go in. But then I thought about it being our first real evening together, Ned and I. And I couldn't bear to serve him only rice and gravy, with maybe a few canned peaches thrown in for dessert. No, I had to buy at least a few groceries. A small piece of beef, perhaps, to have with the rice? And some carrots and potatoes would be good, too.

Keeping the girls close, I roamed the aisles of the store. Fairy had said the prices were a bit high, but she didn't mention they were double the prices elsewhere. My, oh, my. I was going to have to economize. In the future, rice and beans and potatoes would be served frequently at The Tiny House.

But not tonight. I bought the beef and the carrots and the potatoes, and a can of cherries and some butter. Tonight, we would have cherry cobbler for dessert. I wanted Ned to feel that bringing me here was exactly what he needed and wanted. And I wanted him to be in such a satisfied, happy mood that he would feel not just tolerant but welcoming toward Tommy.

Since today was a normal workday, only ten hours, I expected Ned home around six-thirty. I fed the children and got them ready for bed, and had just enough time to bathe myself and put on my blue dress that I knew Ned liked. I fixed my hair and brushed my teeth, and then he was there.

Knowing the girls would want to climb all over him, I'd warned them ahead of time that they could give him one kiss and talk to him for just a minute, but then they had to let him wash and change clothes. After that, they could sit in his lap as long as he would allow it, even if it was past their normal bedtime.

When he finally sat down in the rocker, a girl on each knee, he was overcome by the joy of it. Trying hard not to cry, he hugged them over and over. He let them talk, nodding to show he was listening, and wiping a stray tear away once in a while. They'd drawn him a picture and colored it, of the cherry tree back at the farm, with a large, ferocious-looking cat standing guard over it.

"That was the mean cat, Daddy," said Susie.

"He kept stealing the eggs from the hen house," clarified Sally.

"But Grandma said he was a mouser, so he got to stay anyway," finished Susie.

"Is that so? Must be quite a special cat." He looked at me then, with his same old smile. "We'll have to hang this picture on the wall somewhere." There was certainly no doubt about the love he had for his daughters.

I had Tommy asleep in my arms, still no more than an infant at less than two months. This seemed as good a time as any to introduce them properly. I drew closer. "Here's your son, Ned." I leaned over and pushed the receiving blanket aside so he'd have an unobstructed view. "He's such a good baby. Isn't he beautiful?"

Obediently, Ned took a good long look at the baby.

I pushed on. "I think he's got your nose. Looks just like Arlo's, don't you think?"

He looked some more. "I don't see it." Then he turned his attention back to Sally and Susie. I sat down in the other chair. So. This was how it was going to be. He wasn't going to make it easy for me. But I knew my husband. There was no way in heaven that my kindhearted, selfless man could keep from falling in love with this precious child. Eventually. I would be patient, and give him time. I was certain he would grow to love Tommy, as I did.

A few minutes later, I shooed the girls away, and sent them to the other room to play and watch Tommy while Ned and I ate our supper and talked.

I'd written him every week, so he knew of most of the goings-on back home. I, however, knew very little about the mine, the town, his friends, and what he'd been doing for the last ten months.

I wanted to know all of these things. "How is the work, Ned? Is it real hard? Is it too dangerous?"

He seemed to relax, now that it was just the two of us. "It's hard, but it's not a bad life. The pay is decent, and it's fairly steady."

"What about the wall that fell in yesterday?"

He shrugged. "Happens all the time. You get used to it. Nobody got hurt. It just took some work to repair the wall."

"And you're the crew leader?"

He nodded. "We work in five-man teams. I'm the team leader now." He grinned. "But you know me. I'm not one to boss anybody around. The five of us just figure out what we need to do and we get it done. That's really all there is to that."

Ever the modest one, my Ned. "Have you made some good friends?'

"Oh, yeah. Fairy's husband, Sam. I've spent more time with him than anyone else. But most all the guys are fine fellows. Only a few bad apples, just like anywhere else."

"I went to see Fairy today. I like her."

"Different, huh?"

I laughed. "Yes, but in a good way."

We talked a bit more, then I took care of the supper dishes. Sally and Susie were already asleep, Tommy tucked safely between them for the time being. I'd be back to get him in a bit.

Ned was already in the bed by the time I finished everything. He watched me as I undressed. I didn't mind. I'd dreamed of this night for over a year. I was finally with my darling again. There were many things not right yet, but I had faith that someday they could be set right once more.

But tonight... tonight I would put them from my mind for a little while. Tonight was just for Ned and me.

CHAPTER 23

I promised Momma I would write her every week. Having arrived on Wednesday, it was Friday before I had time to compose a letter. Of course, there were some things that had to remain unsaid, namely Ned's indifference to the baby. Not wanting to worry them and not sure myself of whether this life was going to be tolerable, I stuck to the safer topics, and I wondered when I would get my first letter from Momma. I sure did miss her. Fancy that. Here I was, a woman of twenty-six years, with three children of my own, and after only two days, I missed my momma.

Friday was also the day I washed my first pile of diapers at The Tiny House. I was thankful I had enough to last a few days between washings, for it wasn't one of my favorite chores. Hanging them out on the clotheslines in the backyard, I was surprised at the icy fierceness of the wind coming down from the top of the ridge. Add to that the slope of the yard, and there were several times it nearly blew me over. It being only November, I feared full winter here in Lily's View might be hard for us less seasoned folks to manage.

After a light dinner and Tommy's nap, I bundled him up good, and myself as well, in my heavy coat which didn't seem heavy enough anymore, and skittered down the hill through the backyards to Fairy's house. I definitely liked entering her home, for her spirit seemed to lighten the whole place. I hoped she might show me her painting today.

"Quick. Come in from the cold," she said, as she pulled me through the doorway and took the baby from my arms. "Get over here next to the stove and warm yourself." She unwrapped Tommy like she was unrolling a mummy's wrap, for I'd wound several blankets and quilts around him to keep the wind out. "Oh, he's such a beauteous fellow," she said as she handed him back to me. "Now, you sit right there, and I'll get us something warm to drink." I wasn't used to being waited on, and so kindly, too.

Fairy came back with two steaming cups of tea. "Are you getting settled in? Can I help you with anything?"

"I think it's a matter of getting used to things. I stopped in at the general store yesterday."

"And? What did you think?"

I hesitated. "Well, I can see why it's so easy to go into debt to the store. The prices..."

"Oh, but you're a wise girl with a good head on your shoulders. You'll manage fine."

"What do you do all day, Fairy? Besides your painting." I remembered how I felt when Ned and I lived in the apartment, right after we were married, and I had nothing to do while he was at work. I knew I would go a bit crazy again, alone in The Tiny House most of every day, if I couldn't find something to occupy my mind and my hands.

She gave me a wry sort of smile. "Well, you know, I have four children. The oldest boy, Sean, works with his pa in the mine. The other three are still in school, so there's a lot of cooking and washing and cleaning to be done in this house. When I do have time, my favorite thing to do is paint. But I go to the quilting circle for the socializing." She lowered her voice and leaned forward, saying, "It's better to go than not go. They can't talk about you if you're sitting there." Then she laughed, a soft flutter. "I'm teasing you, but there's some truth there, too."

I laughed. "I'll be sure and go with you, then."

"I like to know what's going on in the world, too, so almost every day I listen to the news on the radio at noon."

"Oh. You do?" That seemed strange to me. Even when we had our own radio in Deckler Springs, before we had to sell it, we never listened during the day, only at night, and then mostly to music. We got our news from the newspaper. The radio at the farm was under Pa's strict control, and he never turned it on except to listen to the Opry or some such. I didn't even know if Ned had a radio here.

"Yes, I do. I think it's important, now that women have the right to vote, to school ourselves on the affairs of our country. That means we have to watch out for what's going on in the rest of the world, too."

I'd never really thought much about that, nor had I ever been around a woman who expressed such ideas. It had been twenty years since the amendment passed that gave us our voting rights, and I had voted several times, but I always cast my vote according to whatever Ned advised. It was a new thought, but maybe I should be informed enough to form an opinion on my own.

"Will you show me your painting today?" I asked.

"Yes. But you mustn't expect too much," she cautioned. Rising, she walked across the room to a large cabinet. Opening both doors wide, I noted the jars of paint and other supplies on a top shelf, and below perhaps twenty canvasses of varied sizes, standing up, leaning against each other. I recognized a homemade easel folded up beside the cabinet.

"I'll just show you a few," she said, taking out a small square from near the front. "I like this one. It's one of my favorites." She turned it around so I could see.

My lips parted in delight. The painting was of a very young girl, her eyes wide with wonder, surrounded by a field of wildflowers. The girl's face was so true it looked like a photograph, and the colors were all soft and ethereal.

"It's my daughter, Iris, the baby of the family. She was three when I painted this. She's eight now." Fairy smiled at her daughter's likeness.

"Fairy, I don't know what to say, it's so lovely. And so much more than I expected. Show me more?"

She nodded, and laid the first painting aside. Then she drew out one of the largest canvasses from the back of the cabinet. It was a painting of a dogwood tree growing near the edge of a lookout point, with the mountains laid out like waves in the distance, and all of it glowing in the colors of a sunset that had almost slipped behind the last mountain. It was magnificent, and made me want to thank God for all the beautiful sunsets I'd seen.

I couldn't speak. I looked at her, wondering how this little sprite of a woman could contain so much talent and vision. With no other words sufficient, I hugged her and simply said, "Thank you. Thank you for showing me."

Sunday finally rolled around, along with our first attendance as a family at Lily's View Baptist. I found it very much the same as our church back home, except that the preacher here was way up in years. Ninety-two, I heard someone say, adding that Reverend Hoke had fought in the Civil War, then started preaching right after the war ended. Maybe he'd been delivering the gospel so long he knew how to winnow out the chaff, or maybe he was so old he could only hold out for so long, but that reverend could deliver a speedy sermon and yet leave you knowing that the Word of God had been spoken that day.

You'd think, having been raised up in the church, that these things would not be new to me. Maybe I had only now reached an age to begin to understand. Whatever the reason, I soaked up the words of the old pastor. Sometimes the message gave me hope and sometime I felt convicted. I guess that's what it was supposed to do. For the time being, I just let it sit in my heart and didn't try too hard to unravel those mysteries.

Once we'd finished with church and dinner, I wondered what Ned and I would do with a whole afternoon together. I needn't have worried. He spent an hour reading the newspaper, which we'd picked up at the train station that morning, fresh in from Charlottesville. Then he fell asleep for a couple of hours while I tried to keep the children quiet, playing on the girls' bed in the other room. When he woke up, he took the girls on his lap and told stories and taught them some silly songs.

I watched from our bed, where I was lying down with Tommy. Whenever I looked down at the baby, he was staring at me. I smiled at him and tickled his neck or tummy. Every time I did it, his eyes would grow big with pleasure. I turned away for a few minutes, listening to the girls singing with their daddy. When I smiled at Tommy the next time, he smiled back at me, perfect as you please. "He smiled," I told them, interrupting their singing. "Ned, he smiled at me. Girls, your brother can smile now."

Right away, Sally and Susie jumped off his lap and onto the bed. "Do it again, Momma," they urged. So I repeated the process, and Tommy obliged by showing off his gummy smile. The girls were wild with delight, giggling every time he performed.

"Daddy, come see," said Sally.

"I'll look later," he replied, picking up the newspaper again.

I sighed, reminding myself to be patient. It had only been four days. It might be months before Ned would do more than acknowledge the existence of this child. I loved my husband and my baby, both. I would wait.

On the following Wednesday morning, Fairy introduced me round at the Pauline Beatrice Carswell Quilting Circle meeting. We were two of about twenty ladies, circled around two large quilting frames which were let down from the ceiling in the community building provided by the mining company. Most of the women were in their twenties and thirties, with just a smattering of older ladies.

As to the virtues and the pitfalls of the quilting group, Fairy's astute observations were correct. Gossip was zealously pursued, and those not in attendance were thoroughly picked apart, and usually found wanting in some way. On my right sat Fairy, and on the left was a sweet woman about my age named Martha Brennan. She had four children, all under six years old, and had bravely brought all four of them with her. So much for patting myself on the back for bringing one infant with me. All the children were corralled in one corner, with baby dolls, toy trucks, blocks, and bottles of milk. When needed, the mothers would excuse themselves from the circle, take care of their child's needs, and return to the circle. Somehow, it all worked out.

In her timid way, Martha was quite friendly. "Birdie, where are you from?" she asked me.

"North Carolina. Close to a little place called Deckler Springs."

"My husband Harold is on Ned's team," she said shyly. "Ned's told them all about you and the girls."

I noticed that she didn't mention our son, but I smiled at her, sensing that she was a sweet soul. "I hope it was mostly good."

"Why, of course, it was all good. Ned couldn't wait for you to get here."

"Do you have family close by, Martha?"

She shook her head. "No. There's nobody. I grew up in an orphanage in Richmond. Harold's daddy delivered milk to us, and sometimes Harold came with him."

"Well, I'm looking forward to meeting Harold sometime."

"I guess you can meet him at the company Christmas dance. It's only three weeks from now. Did Ned tell you about it?"

"No. What kind of dance?"

"They've got musicians coming from Fayetteville to play for us. Square dancing, the Virginia Reel, maybe even the Charleston. Do you know how to do the Charleston?"

"A little. Not much, really. But Ned's a great dancer. He'll be able to follow along, no matter what they play, and I'll follow him."

"Harold and I don't dance much, but we like the music. The company pays the older teenage girls to watch our children during the dance. Isn't that wonderful?"

I agreed with her. But just now a conversation was heating up on my right, centered around Fairy, and I began listening in.

"Well, I don't care what's happening over there. We got drawn into their fight in The Great War, and look where it got us.

We lost a host of our best young men. This time we need to mind our own business and stay out of it." This was from one of the older ladies who, Fairy later told me, lost two sons in that war.

"With all due respect, Maggie, we can't close our eyes to what happens in the rest of the world. Even if we wanted to insulate ourselves, evil will eventually come and find us," Fairy said. "Have any of you been paying attention to what Germany has done this year? The Netherlands and Belgium have fallen. The Allies were forced to abandon France and Norway, both of which are now occupied by the Germans. Great Britain is being attacked by air, and German U-Boats are instructed to sink any and all vessels, including ours. And there are rumors of much worse things than that."

The table had grown silent as all of us listened. I imagined the other ladies, like me, had no knowledge of those world events, and many of us probably wished to know nothing. I was ashamed to be a member of the first group, and even more ashamed to realize I was an unthinking member of the second group.

CHAPTER 24

The company chose to honor President Roosevelt's designation of the next-to-last Thursday in November as Thanksgiving Day. Almost all of the men were on holiday, with only a few required to work a half a day each. Ned volunteered to work the morning shift so all of his crew could have the whole day off.

Since there were only four of us to share the meal, I bought a large hen instead of a turkey, but with plenty of dressing and sweet potatoes, and a couple of pies, we didn't miss ole Tom Turkey. The girls had brought home paper pilgrim hats and collars from school on Wednesday, so I helped them practice a little show to put on for their daddy, complete with songs and very brief recitations.

Once he got home, a little after one, Sally escorted him to his rocker, and scooted back into her bedroom to don her costume. "What's all this?" he whispered to me.

"They want to perform for you. It won't take long," I promised.

The Tiny House was full of good smells that day. The children were excited and happy. Ned seemed rested and in a good mood.

Tommy was happy in the crib we had borrowed from one of Ned's crew members, and I was feeding off of the peace that had settled on us.

Marching proudly in, with their paper hats askew, Sally and Susie performed with confidence, with only a few stumbles over forgotten words. Ned was properly impressed by their stage talents and congratulated them heartily.

It was a very good day. I even handed Tommy to Ned at one point, and he took him without a word, held him while my hands were busy, then gave him back to me. It felt natural, and it resurrected new hope in me that our family could be complete and whole again, perhaps sooner than I'd dreamed.

The month of December turned even colder, the days grew short, and going abroad happened less frequently. I had to buy warmer clothing for the girls, mufflers and mittens and boots, and even then, I sometimes had misgivings about sending them off to school in the morning alone. My visits to Fairy were reserved for only the fairest of days, but usually once a week she would hike up the mountain to see me. I was grateful for her visits. Our nearest neighbors were good, decent people, and I didn't hesitate to ask for help if I needed it, but I didn't seem to have as much in common with them as I did with Fairy.

Ned seemed to withdraw inside himself during those cold months. Fairy told me it happened to some men that way. They were deep underground during the day, hidden from the sunlight, and because of the short days, they were deprived of the sunlight both before and after their workday. She said he would probably come out of it when spring came around, but it still worried me, as I remembered other times, back home, when he would fall into those dark spells.

I hoped the Christmas dance would bring him a little cheer. I wore one of my Sunday dresses, the dark green one, and I pulled my hair up on my head and made little pin curls all over the crown. Topping it off was a green velvet bow Fairy loaned me.

Ned sat on the girls' bed, watching them play with Tommy, waiting on me to come out of the front room so we could go. At the doorway, I stopped and took in the picture.

Ned looked so handsome, with his white shirt and string bowtie, and his hair combed over to the side with a little Brylcreem on it. It reminded me of the times we'd gone out dancing when we were first married. That seemed a very long time ago, and the difference was, where once Ned's face was smiling and always laughing, now his eyes were sad and he rarely smiled.

Sally and Susie caught sight of me then. While they oohed and aahed about their dressed-up momma, I watched Ned. I wanted him to notice me, say something, but he didn't. He scooped Tommy from the bed and brought him to me to wrap up.

Bundled up and loaded with all of the baby supplies, we walked down the hill on our way to the community house, but before we were halfway down our road, a neighbor from further up stopped in his wagon and gave us a ride the rest of the way.

We sat in the back, leaning against the buckboard, Ned and I on the outside with the girls between us, while I held Tommy. We hadn't gone far when I felt a touch on my shoulder. I turned to Ned to see what he wanted. He smiled at me. I smiled back, wondering why the change in him. Then he said, "You look pretty, honey." My heart soared.

That was all I wanted. The evening was off to a splendid start, and with the wagon ride, now my good shoes would not be wet and dirty when we arrived at the dance. Hallelujah.

The musicians were quite accomplished, and they managed to perform adequately in a wide variety of styles. They even managed a few big band tunes, by letting the fiddle carry what would normally be the horn melody. Not to sound arrogant, but Ned and I did ourselves proud that night. There was no one who could rival us on the dance floor, and it did us good to be a couple, doing something together.

The only uncomfortable moment of the evening was when one of the men, Lester Desmond, who'd imbibed more than he should have, kept pestering me to dance with him. Though no alcohol was served at the party, a number of the men were going outside and taking their swigs.

Coming up to me for the third time, he said, "Come on. Dance with me, just a li'l bit." The alcohol was strong on his breath. From the other side of the room, Ned caught my eye and frowned. I was afraid if Ned came over, they would get into a fight, right there in the middle of the dance.

Thinking it the most peaceable scheme, I decided to maneuver Lester to the door, so Ned could then get him outside. "All right. Let's dance. But it's too crowded. Let's go over there, closer to the door."

Grinning like a cross-eyed idiot, he put his arm around my waist, and we started moving in the right direction. I tried to lean away from him, but his grip was tight. Then, when we were almost to the door, his hand slipped lower and he grabbed me where he shouldn't have. I pulled away from him and whispered, "Get your filthy hands off of me." I slapped Lester's hands away, but he wouldn't stop trying to get hold of me. Finally, I put my hands on his chest and pushed, but he hardly budged. Instead, he reared back his fist and swung at me.

Seeing the punch, Ned flew through the air the last couple of feet and knocked Lester to the ground. Then he grabbed the drunk by the collar and flung him out the door, following behind him.

Being pretty sure Ned wouldn't want me out there, I waited. It wasn't long before he came back in, straightening his tie and his hair. "Some of his friends are taking him home," he said. Pulling me to the side, he asked me, "Are you all right? He didn't hurt you, did he?"

"I'm fine. No harm done."

"I don't like Lester very much, but to be fair, he lost his wife two months ago, and he has a four-year-old and a three-year-old to care for."

"I'm sure that's hard."

"Yeah, but no excuse for bad behavior toward a lady." Ned scanned the room, then his eyes lingered on me. "Are you ready to go?" I read the look in his eyes and answered it with my own. A night of love with my husband would always win out over a few dances.

"Yes. Let's go home." I put my arm through his, and we went to get our children.

For Christmas, I suggested to Ned that we buy a radio instead of gifts for each other. He agreed, and let me go to the general store and order what I wanted. Afterward, I couldn't figure how we'd gotten along without it for so long. Though the reception wasn't perfect all the time, it was as if I had company, or least an alternate form of company, when I needed it. And for once, I was grateful we lived at the top of the hill, because our reception was much better than those who lived at the bottom of the hill. Life can be fair occasionally, I guess.

Letters from home usually arrived on Thursday, so I always looked forward to that day of the week. In her letters, Flo was good about sharing all the news of little Gerry, and I admit I was hungry to know.

Most folks would probably find it peculiar that, after the night the boys were born, I wasn't constantly fearful that the truth would come out. For the first week or so, I was. I was afraid Flo would somehow discover my deception, or that my momma would find the secret impossible to keep. But as time passed, my anxiety lessened and it came to my mind less frequently. Tommy became mine and Gerry was Flo's child. This became the truth to me, at least the only truth I would allow.

Of course, it wasn't the truth, and I knew it. I had two secrets hiding inside of me, and they were burning a hole in my soul. The first wasn't really a secret, it was simply a matter of not admitting the truth. I pretended that Ned was the father of the baby I bore. Flo was more than happy to go along with that lie, even though she knew better, for it allowed her to ignore her husband's adultery, but my husband refused to play the game with me, though I used every tactic I knew to induce him to join in.

The other secret was the most treacherous. I rarely allowed it to surface in my mind, for it had the power to destroy me, my husband, my sister, everyone I held dear.

I committed a sin when I switched the babies, and that's the truth.

I told myself at the time that I had simply corrected God's blunder. If I'd left it in God's hands, my sister would be constantly reminded of her husband's infidelity, and Ned would have to live with a constant reminder of mine. For myself, I accepted the burden of carrying the secret to my grave, believing that this choice would cause the least pain to all of us. As I looked back later in my life, I didn't see things precisely in that way, but at the time, it seemed necessary and the right thing to do.

When signs of spring appeared in the mountains, shedding the darkness of winter was a relief to all of us, but most particularly to Ned. One Sunday in April, it was a soft, warm day and we were all out in our sloping front yard, soaking up the sunshine. The girls were giggling. They made a game of chasing the ball as it rolled down the hill, which it did, of course, every time they set it down, leading to even more giggles. Lying on his blanket between me and Ned, Tommy was thoroughly occupied watching the newly budded leaves dance in the treetops above him. Ned seemed almost happy, and I wondered if he really was.

"Honey?" I said, and he turned to look at me. "Are you happy here? Say, if times got better back home, would you want to stay here anyway?"

He lay back on the soft, thick grass, hands behind his head. "Right now, I'm grateful to have a job. Thankful I can support us. But if times were better, and I could pick and choose... I'd prefer to work in the light of day. I'd like to use my mind and my hands in a way that gave me more pleasure."

I reached over and squeezed his leg above the knee. "I'm sorry you've had to do this, baby."

He waved my concern aside. "It hasn't been that bad. I'd do it again if need be."

I twisted around and lay back in the grass beside my husband, with only the baby separating us. Ned seemed in a receptive mood. Perhaps I could persuade him...

I had to try. "Honey, I've been here six months. Tommy's seven months old. I was hoping by now you'd warm up to your son." *Please go along with it, Ned, and let's just be a happy family,*

*like we were before. Can't you please just love the boy? He's so
loveable...*

Ned pushed up from the ground, and checked to see where the
girls were. He spoke softly so they wouldn't hear. "Birdie, I love
you. I always have and I always will. Our home can be Tommy's
home, because he's yours. And I won't treat him bad, I promise
you. But he's not my son. And he won't ever be my son." With
that, he walked off down the road, and didn't come back until after
dark.

After that, as far as Ned was concerned, the first secret, the
pretending, was over. From then on, I didn't try to finagle around
and trick him into holding Tommy or such as that, for there was no
longer any need to sustain the lie. As long as I left Tommy out of
it, Ned and I got along fine most of the time, but it was festering
inside of me. I could feel the prickle of it. I reckon it was festering
inside of him, too. And then, of course, there was the second
secret, waiting in the wings.

By that spring, Tommy was sitting up on his own, jabbering
and smiling. He had a dimple in his left cheek that was just like
Flo's, and whenever he smiled, I felt a twinge in the area of my
heart, a twinge of something I didn't want to examine too closely.
Maybe it was guilt, stirring around from time to time, reminding
me of the fact that, because of me, Flo would never know he was
her flesh and blood.

On the other side of that coin was Gerry. Maybe, underneath
all of his father's looks, there might be a little bit of me in him. I
couldn't think about it, though. It was too much to bear, so I buried
it and did my best to leave it buried, even if it meant lying to

myself. I had chosen this path. The only thing I could do now was to be a good mother to Tommy, my chosen son.

I did adore him, and he seemed to adore me, too, for he lit up whenever I was around. Even Sally and Susie, who were devoted to him and played with him as if he were their own little "live" dolly, didn't elicit the same level of response from him. There was a bond between him and me, born of hours in each other's company, with no one else around. In a time when we both needed someone, he rescued me just as much as I rescued him.

CHAPTER 25

The distance grew between Ned and me. It wasn't what either of us wanted, but it couldn't be stopped. As our hearts grew harder, it became difficult to be pleasant and reasonable with each other, as we'd always been before. As unfathomable as it was to me to even conceive of such a thing, I worried that he might up and leave us.

But then, every time it seemed we reached a point where it was useless to try anymore, there'd be a kind gesture, an apology, a look passing between us that no one else could ever understand, and then we'd reach for each other again, laugh together at something silly, and spend the night in each other's arms. Things would be almost the same as they used to be between us. Almost, but never quite.

Spring passed, as did summer. The mountains were so lovely that time of year. Fairy and I hiked with our children several times to nearby points of interest. We trekked to Cater's Artesian Spring, to Lily's view (the actual lookout point), and to the Wenslow River, where the children spent all afternoon sliding down the rocks. Even though it wasn't Deckler Springs, it would have been a near perfect summer, if only there was no barrier between my husband and me. I missed the old "us," and that's a fact.

It was the end of August when our world turned upside down. In the cool of the morning, the children and I went with Fairy and her children to pick blueberries. We'd been picking for about thirty minutes when we heard a huge boom that shook the hills. I looked to Fairy, wondering what it could have been. "What...?"

Her face was deathly white. "The mine. There's been a cave-in." Looking anxiously around her, she said, "Children, get your buckets and all your things. Quickly!" I'd never seen Fairy when she was not at peace with herself and the world, but at that moment, her world was being shattered by fear of the unknown. I hurried to move the children along.

When we trudged back to Lily's View, the whole town was in turmoil, with people running here and there on important business of one sort or another. "What do we do, Fairy?" I asked her. "Should we go to the mine and wait?"

More her usual self now, she instructed her oldest daughter, "Posey, you take all of the children to our house. You're in charge. Do whatever is needed to take care of Birdie's three until we get back from the mine." We hugged our children, and I handed Tommy to Posey.

I was scared. What if something happened to Ned and I never had the chance to make everything good and right between us?

Almost everyone from the town was gathered at the mine, waiting for news. As soon as we arrived, we were told that the cave-in of a side tunnel had trapped only one team, Ned's. All the other teams and men had been accounted for. Still, no one left the vigil. All stood together, showing their support for the families of those trapped inside, knowing full well that it could have been one of theirs who was still in danger.

Coffee and food was brought to the waiting wives, but few were partaking. The initial bustle gradually quieted, so that now there was only the occasional figure entering or exiting the mine. After an hour or so, someone brought us chairs, and found a place for us to wait where there was a bit of shade. It didn't matter to me or to the other four women who waited for news of their men. Nothing could comfort us but the sight of our men returning safely. I was grateful that Fairy stayed by my side that whole time, bolstering my spirits, keeping me calm, talking to me.

We were told that the other miners were taking turns digging through the debris, moving as fast as they could to get their fellow workers out as soon as possible. They hoped to break through by sundown.

At twilight, we heard shouts coming from the mine. Men poured out, pickaxes on their shoulders and shovels in their hands. Finally, at the end of the line, Ned's team members were being helped out. Three of them were on stretchers, and someone had covered the face of one of them. The other two came behind the stretchers, walking on their own, supporting each other. One of the two was Ned.

Out of the corner of my eye, I saw Martha Brennan slump, her knees buckling, held upright only by the friends supporting her on each side. I recognized the faces of the four men who'd made it out alive, including Ned's. Harold was not one of them. My heart went out to her. Later, I would go to Martha and do what I could, but right then, I had to see to my husband. Giving Fairy a quick hug, I left her and ran to Ned.

Someone had a wagon waiting, and took us straight home. Once I got him inside, I sat him down in the rocker, coal dust and all. As soon as I had the water heating, I came and knelt in front of him. I untied his boots and began to remove them.

"Honey, are you all right? Are you hurt anywhere?" I could see a rip in the arm of his coat, as well as a few tears in his pants.

He shook his head.

"Let's get your coat off before you get too hot." I made him lean up, and got the coat off of him.

The kettle whistled. I turned to go see about the water, and he grabbed my wrist. "Harold's dead," he said. There was agony in his eyes, and I knew what he was saying to himself. He was telling himself he was responsible, he was the team leader, he should have kept this from happening.

"I know." Standing by the rocker, I pulled his head against me and stroked his hair. "It's not your fault, Ned." He grabbed me then, and pulled me closer, burying his face in my stomach, while sobs erupted from deep in his gut.

"Shhh, shhh, shhh."

The kettle was whistling, but it would have to wait. My husband needed me near right now.

Harold Brennan's funeral was the next day, and Martha asked Ned to be a pallbearer. I was glad she didn't ask him to sing; for once, I don't think he could have borne it. The mine was closed for the afternoon so all could attend. It was a sorrowful sight—Martha and her four young children, lined up on the front pew of the church. What would they do now?

Two weeks later, I was in the general store and I saw Martha speaking with the store manager. I wasn't trying to eavesdrop, but it wasn't hard to figure out what was taking place, whether I heard them or not. She was begging to charge some things, and the manager wouldn't extend any more credit. I couldn't imagine how she felt, and I knew it could have been me who lost my husband, instead of her.

In my purse, I had a little bit of money. Martha had her few meager purchases sitting on the counter, so I walked over and asked the manager, "How much for these items?"

He looked it over and answered, "Three dollars and eighty-seven cents."

I counted out the money, and turned to give Martha a hug. "Thank you," she whispered.

A week later, the children were back in school, and Tommy and I visited Fairy one morning. After blocking off the room to corral Tommy, who was walking now, my friend handed me a cup of tea and said, "I heard some news this morning. I don't know if it's good or bad."

Wondering what that could mean, I said, "Then do tell."

"Martha Brennan has up and married Lester Desmond."

I was stunned. "Martha and Lester? Oh, that can't be right."

"Well, it is."

"Poor Martha. But why would she do such a thing?"

"Think about it. She has four little mouths to feed and no money. She doesn't have any family, and I think all of Harold's family are dead. What choice did she have?"

"But Lester? He's mean and he's a drunk."

"I know. Let's just hope and pray he'll do better, now that he's got a wife."

My worries seemed small indeed when compared to the heavy burden Martha would now be carrying.

Ned was in a somber mood after the mine accident, which made me worry about the dark winter months to come. All the time now, he seemed to be bothered by the coal dust. He said he could feel it in his throat and down into his lungs. He wasn't playful with the girls and he never sang. Trying to assure me that this was normal, Fairy told me that it took most miners who'd lived through a cave-in at least a few months to work through the shock of it all. I tried to follow her advice, which was to stay close by and let the little things go for a while, let him spend time with his family and be ready to talk about it, if he decided to open up.

It came home to me then, as never before, just how much I loved my husband. In the disaster at the mine, in the bowels of the earth, I could have lost him forever, and I never again wanted to feel as I had that day—that we had things to settle, things to finish, things left unsaid. We had been so close in the early years, as if we were one person instead of two. No secrets, no hiding things, no lies. Not always of the same mind, but always seeking what was best for the other. I wanted that back, and not just on the surface, as it had been since before Tommy was born.

But I was torn. If I was totally honest, our relationship might completely disintegrate. And if I was honest with him, should I be honest with Flora, too? Would it serve a purpose to hurt these two people I loved? Or would I be seeking only my own selfish needs? Would it be kinder overall to keep my secret and play it out until the day I died?

CHAPTER 26

S ometimes I longed for the sight of our open fields back on
the farm and the blue morning glories climbing up the
columns on the back porch and the taste of our well water. But I
knew I had what was most important right here with me in Lily's
View, and we could live the rest of our lives here if need be. The
thing is, it was sapping the joy right out of my husband, and we
needed his strength to keep us going.

Ned was not happy in the coal mines, but as he said, it was a
decent, steady job that allowed him to feed his family. I wished for
something better for him, something that would make him happy
to get up and go to work, something that would put a song in his
heart again. But until there were jobs available back home, here is
where we would stay.

Now that we had a radio, I tried to become a better informed
citizen. The newsmen said things were getting a little better all
across the country, but the reports from Momma and Flora were
that the mills and factories around home were still not running at
full capacity. I wrote and asked Flo to get in touch with the
manager at the furniture factory and tell him that when a job came

open, Ned would be available. I didn't want to get Ned's hopes up, so I didn't tell him about that.

About the middle of October, my spirits were low. We were soon to begin another hard winter, and I dreaded it. The girls were in school, Ned at work, and I didn't even feel like visiting Fairy as much as before. For the most part, I spent my days alone, the only bright moments existing solely because of my baby boy. He had become such a charmer. Loving, smart, almost always happy. Several times a day, he would come up to me, put his chubby little hands on my cheeks, and carefully place his puckered lips on mine. Then he would pat my cheeks twice and hop down, ready to go play again.

Weekly letters to and from the farm continued. Flo said Gerry was rambunctious, and now that he was walking, always into things. She clearly enjoyed being a mother, and I was happy for my sister.

November arrived, and with it, the first bitterly cold day of the season. Sally and Susie both came home with the sniffles that day, and by midnight their colds had grown into something more sinister. Their fevers raged all night long. Several times I considered sending Ned for the company's doctor. In the early morning hours, though, Susie's fever broke, then Sally's, and by dinnertime, both of the girls were able to sit up in bed to eat some soup. Tuckered out, and now with their tummies full, they went right back to sleep.

Having had no sleep at all during the night, I settled into my rocker by the coal stove, after blocking off the bedroom so Tommy couldn't go in there and disturb the girls. I tried to stay awake until Ned got home from work, but several times I fell asleep, a few minutes at a time, only to wake with a jerk, when Tommy would push against me or holler at me. With a set of his jaw that said he intended to have his way, he was having one of his cranky spells. I wondered if he was getting sick, too. I pulled him into my lap to feel his forehead. Just a little warm. I snuggled him close and he quieted. We both fell asleep.

Finally, exhaustion won out. A hard, deep sleep came upon me and I didn't rouse for an hour or more. By that time, the sun had gone behind the ridge, and with the absence of its warmth, the temperature fell rapidly. At quitting time, when Ned came stomping in, I woke and immediately scanned the room for Tommy. He wasn't there.

"Where's Tommy?" I asked Ned. Not waiting for an answer, I began looking.

The suitcase I'd used as a barricade into the girls' room had been shifted to the side. He must be in there. Moving the luggage out of the way, I stepped into their room and looked everywhere, under and over the beds, and anywhere else a one-year-old could hide. Ned followed me.

My voice went up a notch. "Did you let him out the door when you came in? Did you see him outside?"

"No. No. I haven't seen him. I just got home." He followed me back into the front room. "Why isn't he here with you?"

"I fell asleep. I was up all night with the girls," I said defensively. "He was supposed to be in the front room with me, so I could watch him." I went in the back room again. The back door was shut. "Girls, have either of you been to the outhouse this afternoon?"

They looked at each other, then back at me, nodding their heads, their eyes huge with fear that they'd done something wrong. *The door didn't catch and he followed them out the door. That's probably what happened.* I couldn't put that guilt on them, though. It was my fault and no one else's.

I looked once more in the front room and then headed out the door. Turning back, I yelled at Ned, "Help me! We've got to find him *now*."

The girls stood at the door, watching us, crying, scared. We both yelled, up and down the hill, stopping from time to time to listen. Neighbors poured out of their houses to ask what was wrong, then joined the search, some already armed with flashlights. One older man went to get the sheriff. Within the hour, the search was organized and all of the day shift men from the mines were out scouring the mountainside for my baby.

Just after midnight, a neighbor found him, ice cold but still alive, in a narrow ditch in the open woods across the road. The doctor was out delivering a baby, but sent word he'd be there as soon as he could. Ned stoked up the fire with extra coal and I sat close with Tommy in my lap, rubbing his little arms and legs, trying to get the circulation going to warm him up, frantic to get some kind of response from him. At last, his eyes opened and he reached for my cheeks, puckering his lips for a kiss. I was so relieved, certain that he was going to be all right now.

But as he revived further, he became more agitated, often coughing to the point of choking, spitting up the water and milk I'd given him. Then his temperature rose, fast. Ned went and got the thermometer, but I knew even before we read it that his temperature was getting dangerously high, higher than the girls' fevers the night before. It was 104 degrees and climbing. I laid him on my lap and rubbed his arms and legs with rubbing alcohol. I couldn't tell if it helped at all.

The doctor arrived just before daybreak and examined Tommy. His thermometer read 105 degrees.

I was becoming hysterical. "What can we do? Can you give him something?" I was about to fall to the floor, when Ned caught me and pulled me up against his side.

"Not much that can be done, except to try to keep the fever down," said the doctor, an older whiskered fellow, obviously tired out, here in the early morning hours. "Give him the aspirin every couple of hours. Put you some wet rags out on the porch rail. When they're good and cold, rub him down with them. You've got to keep that fever from going any higher."

Then he told us there was nothing more he could do, and that he was going home to get some sleep.

Not long after, Ned got ready to leave for work. He kissed me goodbye, but I wasn't paying much attention to him. So, he took my chin and forced me to look at him. "Don't worry about anything but the baby today." He paused and swallowed. "And I'll say a prayer for him." Then he left.

The girls woke, feeling better and very hungry. I let them fix their own oatmeal, then told them to go play quietly in the other room. My only concern at that moment was my baby boy. He was pale and still burning up. I could tell he was probably having fever dreams. because he was jerking and moaning in his sleep.

When the seizure began, I didn't understand what was happening. All I knew to do was to hold him and talk to him, hoping he could hear me and be comforted somehow. The seizure ended and I lowered him to my lap so I could look at him. He was still and calm, now. Relaxed. I thought at first he was better. Then I saw that he wasn't breathing.

The small church was filled with all the miners and their families, and I was thinking it was much too soon to be here for another funeral service. Ned held me up, and the girls clung to his other side. I should have felt the love and comfort coming from all the friends around us, but all I could feel was my own pain. God had made a mistake again, just when I had begun to entertain the thought of giving Him another chance. Last time, I'd taken upon myself the task of correcting His mistake, but there was no way to correct this one. There was nothing I could do to fix things, nothing I could do to bring Tommy back.

Ned was given two days off to spend with us, but we didn't have much to say to each other, Ned and I. He'd always known that Tommy was not his son. In spite of my attempts to make him believe Tommy was from his seed, he'd known. So deeply had I embraced my false reality of being Tommy's mother, I never fully acknowledged the fact that he wasn't even a child of my womb, but of my sister's. But he was mine, in every way save that, and I loved him as my own. That was my truth, and nothing else mattered at the moment.

I had hoped that Ned's goodness would win out over his pride, or at least that his love for me would enable him to love Tommy simply because I loved Tommy. Maybe that much love isn't possible. I could tell Ned was feeling regret and shame, but at the moment I had no mercy to give him.

I was alone at the bottom of a deep, dark pit, grieving that my own little sun wasn't going to shine and warm up my life anymore. Everything inside me was frozen and cold. I hadn't a thought for Ned at that point, and little enough for the girls.

On the third day, with Ned at work and the girls at school, I stayed in my rocking chair by the coal fire and cried all day long until, finally, I was spent. When the girls and Ned came home, there was no supper, for I hadn't fixed any, so Ned heated two cans of beans for their evening meal. I refused to eat, or later, to come to bed. All through the night, while my family slept, I sat by the fire.

The rocker creaked softly, breaking the absolute silence of the night, and the coal fire lit the room with a subdued glow. I pondered for a long time on how I had tried to outsmart everyone, even God. And now look at me. My baby was gone. And the child that was from my own womb was alive and happy with my sister. You reap what you sow, wasn't that what I'd always heard? Now, in spite of my best efforts to avoid it, I would have to live with the consequences, just as my momma did.

Maybe paying the consequences was like paying on a debt. Maybe someday my debt would be paid and life would be good, as it used to be a very long time ago, before Ned lost his job and before Gerald. But then again, maybe it was like the company store and there was no way to ever be free of it. Maybe this burden of sadness and regret would always be with me, for the rest of my life. If that was the case, I'd better start learning to live with the weight of it.

I hadn't written Momma and Flora in more than a week, and they would be wondering what was wrong. I was going to have to tell them. I got out my pencil and paper and began to write.

CHAPTER 27

Ned tried to comfort me. He was good to me in every way, but all I could think of when I looked at him was how he had rejected an innocent baby. Though I knew I should, I couldn't forgive him. Maybe I would at some point, but right now, I was angry with him.

Before a week passed, I shouldered my responsibilities again, but they seemed too light without Tommy there, needing diapers, needing to be carried, needing to be fed. I visited Fairy almost every day, in spite of the cold. That helped, for she always had something to show me, or feed me, or discuss with me. The current subject of discussion was our imminent entry into the war. Fairy felt it was coming, and soon.

The first Saturday in December, Fairy and Samuel invited us and two other couples to eat supper with them, while Posey watched the girls at our house. It had only been a month since I lost Tommy, and I didn't have any desire to be around so many folks, but Fairy promised me it would be a quiet gathering, so I agreed to go. After the meal, the men gathered around the stove, questioning the possibility of the United States jumping into the fray.

"Well, I personally don't believe that will ever happen," said Johnny, a member of Samuel's crew. "Washington won't stand for it."

"That's right. We learned a hard lesson just twenty-something years ago. Mind our own business, that's what we've got to do." This came from Bob, also on Samuel's crew.

"I don't know, boys. Look what Germany's been doing the last five years. Look at how many countries have caved in. They're getting brave. Just a little longer, and they might get brave enough to come over here, on our own soil," said Samuel.

Ned spoke up. "I'd like to see 'em try it. Our boys are the best and we'd blow 'em right back across the ocean."

"You got that right," said Johnny.

Bob agreed. "Probably wouldn't take us a week to send them packing."

In the kitchen, Fairy and I stopped our work and listened by the door as the men talked.

"You know what that reminds me of?" I whispered to Fairy.

"What?"

"You remember in Gone With The Wind, at the start of the book, when the southern boys are talking about how they'd whup the northerners in no time flat?"

Fairy giggled. "Does kinda sound like that, doesn't it?"

I sobered. "I hope we don't go to war. It's not a grand thing. It's devastation and destruction and death."

Fairy sighed. "Yes, my friend, you're right. But evil can't be allowed to win, so sometimes good people are left with no choice but to fight."

We were to remember that conversation later.

The next day we went to church as usual, and on our way home, light snow fell. The clouds were low and gray, making it seem almost like dusk instead of the middle of the day. We had chicken and dumplings for dinner that day, and after that, we all settled down for a quiet, lazy Sunday afternoon. The girls played checkers at the table, I read a book, and Ned took his shoes off and laid down on the bed for a Sunday afternoon nap.

Our peace was interrupted just before three o'clock, when we heard people shouting outside, up and down the lane. While Ned put his shoes on to go see what all the fuss was about, someone knocked on our door. I was the closest, so I answered it. Our neighbor, Fred, was on the door stoop, shivering, but with no coat.

He could hardly get the words out, he was so upset. "On the radio. Did you hear it? We've been attacked. Pearl Harbor, out in Hawaii. The Japanese bombed us. Turn your radio on."

As Fred started toward the next house, I turned to Ned. He had heard all of it. "Turn the radio on," I told him.

All the rest of the day, until bedtime, we listened. There weren't many details to begin with, but gradually, the picture grew clearer. Thousands killed in a surprise attack. All day long, people in our small community dropped by, wanting to see what we'd heard, whether we knew something more than they did. When we finally turned the radio off, much later than our normal bedtime, neither of us could sleep. We weren't children any longer and we understood what this meant. It meant the end of innocence for another generation. Our generation.

The President's address to Congress the next day was broadcast on the radio, and it was stirring. A call to patriotism and honor and freedom. Where before the prevailing sentiment was isolation and self-preservation, now it was good versus evil and protection of the innocent. Even Charles Lindbergh, a known isolationist, reversed his stance and firmly supported an armed response.

There was no going back to the calm of before. Everything had changed. Our country was at war. By the time Christmas came, a number of the younger miners with no children had already enlisted in the military. Fairy's son Sean was one of the first. Fairy put on a brave, proud front, but I knew she was afraid of losing her son.

Between Christmas and New Year, Ned was preoccupied. I thought it was because one of his crew had enlisted, cutting their number down to three, making more work for him. I never dreamed he was thinking of enlisting. The second Saturday in January, when he got home from work and we finished eating our supper, he shared his plans.

"Sit down, Birdie. We need to talk."

I sat down and waited.

He continued, "A lot of the fellows have enlisted in the service."

"Yes, I know." A niggly little fear began to take hold of me.

"Well." He took a deep breath. "I'm going Monday to enlist in the army."

I was not over being angry with him for rejecting Tommy. Now I was boiling. "Are you serious? You can't leave us high and dry."

"I'm not..."

"You're not going to do it. I refuse to let you."

"It's my decision, Birdie. And I *am* going to do it." I could see in his eyes that he'd made up his mind. I tried another tack.

"It's not just your decision. You have a family to consider, and what you do affects us."

"Nevertheless, I'm going, because it's the right thing to do."

I shook my head. "That's not it. That's not all of it, anyway. You're not happy being a coal miner. And you haven't been happy with me for a long while. You just want to get away from all these things. Don't you?" I dared him with the truth, but I didn't want to hear his answer

"Maybe that's a small part of it."

I jumped up and put my hands on the back of my neck. "Oh, God. Ned, you can't leave me. You could be gone for years. The girls could be almost grown by the time you get back." I began to quiver inside.

"It won't be years," he reassured me. "A year. One year. Two at the most. I'll be back before you know it."

I couldn't be still. "I seriously doubt that." I walked around the tiny room in circles. "What are we supposed to do while you're gone? How are we supposed to live?" I had my hands in my hair, gripping it tightly.

"You can go back to the farm. You miss them all the time, anyway." His voice was too smooth, too conciliatory. He was playing me for a fool. He just wanted to get away from me. He was tired of living with a woman who was grieving for a baby that wasn't his.

I rolled my eyes, then put my face in my hands. I was paying my debt now, wasn't I? I could see there was no use arguing with him. He had his mind fixed already, and he was going to do this thing, stubborn man that he was. "Go ahead, then. Go play war with all the other boys." I lifted my head up and looked at him. "But remember this, take this with you when you go. Right this very minute, I hate you, Ned Parker." I got my coat and went out the door.

Ned quit his job, packed his bags and left. I barely spoke to him, I was so mad at him. I wouldn't have kissed him goodbye, were it not for the girls standing there watching us. Poor little things. They didn't know what was going on, and they cried almost as much as I did, asking me, "Why are we moving back to the farm again? Why is Daddy leaving?" I had no answers to give them.

I sold everything I could the next week. The only things I packed up were our clothes and personal belongings, and my radio. It was actually Ned's radio, too, but I figured I deserved to keep it, and he certainly couldn't use it where he was going. We kept a few bags to carry on the train, but two other large boxes I shipped ahead of us. I had written Momma the day Ned enlisted, to tell her we would be coming the following Saturday. Hopefully, she received the letter in time. I would be glad to see my Momma and my sister, the creek and the fields, and the morning glories.

But I would miss the beauty of the mountains, and I would very much miss my dear friend Fairy.

Grief and tragedy and hatred are only for a time.
Goodness, remembrance and love have no end.

-- George W. Bush
Courtesy: National Archives
and Records Administration

CHAPTER 28

It took some getting used to, being back on the farm. While we were in West Virginia, I had remembered only the things I loved about the farm, and had conveniently forgotten all the things I didn't like. Things like Pa's mean nature, Flo's tendency toward selfishness, the hard work of running a farm. I know it's plain silly, but I think the thing I was most happy to see, aside from my family, was the bathtub.

And, of course, what brought me the most pain was seeing little Gerry, the same age that Tommy would be now, knowing that if things had been different, if Tommy had lived, he and Gerry would be playing and having the best time ever, growing up together as cousins.

Once, and once only, the thought crossed my mind that if Tommy had been here with Flo, and Gerry had been in West Virginia with me, maybe both boys would be alive today. But it was too hard a thought in the midst of my grief, and I shut it out. Someday, if I had to, I would examine that thought, but not now.

From time to time I thought I saw a glimpse of myself in Gerry, but he was so much the spitting image of Gerald, it was hard to see if he favored anyone else. His feet looked just like Sally's, though, and his eyebrows had the same funny twist on the end that Susie's did. If Flo ever noticed anything, she never commented on it.

You might think I'd be wanting to steal back the child of my own womb, but that wasn't the case. My grief for Tommy was so strong, that to turn around and covet the living, just because Gerry was alive and Tommy wasn't, would have been the greatest disloyalty to the son of my heart. Tommy would be forever my son. Gerry belonged to Flora. I would be Gerry's Aunt Birdie, and nothing beyond that. I wouldn't allow myself to think any differently. If there were any heartaches or regrets inside the tangled mess I'd created, they were mine to bear, and mine alone.

Most of the time, I kept this attitude, for it was the right thing to do. The only times that resolve weakened was when Flora was harsh with the boy. She was truly a loving mother, but she could be heavy-handed with the paddle and scathing with the tongue. One day, he scattered his toys on the floor, and took too long to pick them up as she told him to do. She'd already taken a switch to him, and then proceeded to pick at him, saying things like, "You are a *bad boy.* You're never going to be worth anything, young'un, if you don't do like your momma says. But you don't even love your momma, do you, Gerry?" And she whistled the switch by his legs some more. Little fella, he was sobbing so hard, he couldn't catch his breath. Fat tears poured down his chubby little cheeks. He tried to pick up the toys, but he couldn't, because he was crying so hard.

I went over and pulled him into my lap, and hugged him. "Let's you and me get these toys picked up. All right?" He nodded slowly and I hugged him again. Flora tore into me then.

"Just what do you think you're doing? Get your hands off of him and quit your interfering. That is my son, and I'll raise him as I see fit."

I couldn't argue with her. I put him down, but not before hugging him again and stroking his hair another time or two, hoping to give him a few more seconds to calm down. I left the house and ran out to the orchard, biting my lip until it bled, praying for my sister and the child who belonged to her.

It was hard sometimes to keep my distance, but I had to. I'd had my chance to raise a baby boy, and through my neglect, he was dead. Could Flora do any worse?

In all fairness, my sister could be loving and kind when she wanted to be. She and Momma both, without a lot of words, let me know how sorry they were for our loss. They were tender toward me, at least for a few months, and gave me time to grieve, which I sorely needed. In a sense, I think I was grieving for the loss of Ned, too, and the disruption of our marriage. There was much to grieve right then.

Ned hadn't always been a consistent correspondent when he lived alone in West Virginia, so I didn't expect much better, now that he was in the military, especially after parting poorly. After he enlisted, he was sent to basic training for thirteen weeks at Camp Wheeler in Georgia. At the end of basic training, around the end of April, he would have five days off to come and visit us, and then he'd be sent to who knows where. Maybe by that time I'd feel a little more kindly toward him. Still, I wrote him every week, just as I'd done before, and Sally and Susie usually sent a picture or a little note, too.

When Carl and Luther signed on with the Navy, I had a hard time imagining my little brothers on a ship in the middle of the ocean. Pa didn't have much to say about that, except to grumble that there was no one to help him with the work on the farm. Later on, though, I noticed that, when asked about the boys, he seemed to answer with pride that they were serving here or there, in some faraway place.

I registered the girls at school and that first morning they went happily off, excited at the prospect of riding the bus to school. The house was now quiet, so Momma and Flo and I sat around the table after breakfast, having another cup of chicory coffee.

"Momma, you seem to be having more trouble getting around. Is your hip worse?" I asked.

She nodded. "Yes. It is. But I make myself get up every day just the same. I don't want to give up yet."

"I can understand that." I took another sip of chicory coffee. "Pa seems to be moving a little slower, too."

"He complains of his back sometimes," said Flora. "You know old Gus is getting up in years, too, just like Pa. It's more than those two old coots can handle sometimes. He's talking about hiring another man, younger, just for the spring and summer." She huffed a little. "You and I sure can't do all that plowing and planting the big fields. I guess we can handle the garden, though, like we always do."

"Of course we can. How about the Jamisons? Do you still work for them?"

"No, I had to give it up so I could take care of Gerry." She smiled. "I didn't mind. I do miss the pocket money, though."

"Well, what can I do around here?" I looked around the kitchen. "You know I won't be able to sit still for very long. Reading and sewing and resting only amuse me for so long."

Momma laughed. "Birdie, you just won't do. Something will come along. Maybe you should try to make it at least until Ned gets his five-day leave. Until then, you can get the garden ready to plant, and I believe the orchard needs pruning. It's time to do that, and I don't think your pa has gotten to it yet."

"And I could use a day in town, Birdie. You could watch Gerry for me. Momma can't keep up with him anymore since he can take off, running away from her. Can you, Momma?"

Momma shook her head.

"Okay," I replied, holding my hands up in surrender. "Maybe I can manage that long, until Ned's visit. Momma, has Pa ever thought about getting an automobile?"

A few days later, Momma and I were alone in the house, working on a flour-sack quilt. "Birdie, you haven't talked much about Tommy. Tell me what my grandson was like." She didn't look up, just kept on with her sewing.

I didn't know if I could talk about him. I didn't want to break down and cry, but I wanted my momma to know about Tommy, so I began.

"He was beautiful, with his blond hair and blue eyes. He was a good baby, too. Slept through the night after only a few months. He smiled all the time, and the girls could make him laugh until he'd lose his breath, he'd be so tickled. He started walking toward the end of the summer. Never crawled much, just took straight to the walking. We spent a lot of time alone, just him and me, so when he was gone, it was hard because I missed him being there with me every minute of the day."

"What did Ned think of him?"

Oh, there it was. There was the crux of the situation. How was I to answer that question? "He... uh... he was kind to him."

"Well, I'd never expect anything different from Ned. He's a good-hearted man."

For some reason, I wanted to tell her more. I wanted her to take my side, to tell me that my stance was justified. "He never accepted him as his son. He never tried to play with him, or take up time with him."

She looked at me then. "Well, he wasn't his son, was he?"

I felt like I'd been slapped in the face. I couldn't believe she wasn't going to criticize Ned. Instead, it seemed that she was laying the blame on me. I gritted out, "You know he wasn't."

I was too angry with her to say more. But it did start me thinking. Maybe I hadn't tried to see Ned's side in all this.

Springtime was upon us. The days were sweet with budding trees and the smell of dirt from the plowed fields, ready to receive their seed. The big day arrived when we were to meet Ned at the train station at four o'clock, so I drove the wagon to town and picked up the girls from school. They were so excited about seeing their daddy, I didn't want them to have to wait a minute more than they had to. I wanted them to see him as soon as he got off that train.

I was rather excited myself. Time and a new perspective had softened my anger, until it was now just a small ache from the past. But it bothered me that Ned and I had not parted well. I'd never apologized or taken it back when I said, "I hate you, Ned Parker." Still, I'd been writing him in a friendly, cordial way. Maybe he'd forgiven my words as those spoken from someone suffering in the throes of grief. Soon enough, I'd find out how things stood between us.

It seemed every time we were apart, my husband changed his looks. When we moved to West Virginia, he grew a beard and his hair was longer. This time, when he got off the train, he was clean shaven and his hair was in a military cut. The olive-green uniform suited his figure and showed off his leaner physique. He looked good.

He barely had time to descend the metal stairs from the train car before the girls were streaking toward him, calling "Daddy, Daddy!" Tossing his duffle bag down, he grabbed one in each arm, hugging them to him. I stood back and waited my turn.

When he put the girls down, he retrieved his bag and came over to me. I tried to show him in my face and eyes that I felt differently toward him now. He didn't seem to catch the message, or maybe he didn't want to. I gave him my best smile and said his name. "Ned…?" Then I hugged him and turned my face up to him. He gave me a quick kiss and said, "Birdie, it's good to see you."

I couldn't help but be dismayed by his lack of warmth. Hoping for more, I was frustrated. Were we never again to have our minds set in the same direction at the same time? Was it now to be always one of us hot and the other cold? I knew we were worth saving, but whether it could be done, I didn't know for sure anymore. Regardless of whether we could or not, Ned deserved an apology from me. I intended to make sure he heard one, and soon.

There was no time for talking until later that night, when supper was over and the girls had finally been ordered to bed. After tucking them in, Ned came out to the back porch and sat down. For April, it had been an unusually warm day, and warm enough still to sit out there without a jacket.

Pa was sitting on the porch, too, and I didn't want to share the night with anyone other than my husband. I walked over and held out my hand to Ned. "Come on. Let's take a walk. It's such a nice night," I coaxed.

He took my hand and we stepped off the porch into the night. It was a waning moon, but the night was clear, so we could see well enough. Without speaking, we both turned in the direction of the creek. The familiar path was spattered with splotches of moonlight, and the crickets and the frogs were in full voice. We'd gone down this path many times, but always before we'd been in perfect harmony with each other. I prayed that we could get that back.

At the creek, we found our favorite rock to sit on. Before, we'd always sat close together, our bodies touching so that you couldn't tell where one ended and the other began. Tonight, we were a foot apart. I reached for his hand and held it in mine. "Ned, I said some harsh things to you before you left Lily's View. I want you to know I didn't mean them, and I'm sorry for saying them."

"I know you didn't mean them. You were hurting, that's all. Don't worry again about it."

"You forgive me?"

"Yes. Yes, I do." He took his hand away, found a rock and skipped it across the water. Somehow, I didn't sense that anything had changed. What was I expecting? The wall was still there. Evidently, it was going to take more than an apology to tear it down. Maybe it was going to take time, but that was something we didn't have much of. Three more days here, and then he had to travel back on the fourth day. Not enough time to heal so much hurt and disappointment and lost trust.

Oddly enough, or maybe not so odd, the desire we'd always felt for each other was undiminished. While he was there, the nights were the only time we achieved the closeness of the past. Maybe the intensity of it was from realizing the possibility that we might never be in each other's arms again.

On the last night, after we made love, we lay entwined, clinging to one another for a long time, not letting go. Finally, I said, "Ned. Please be careful, come back to me as soon as you can." He didn't answer, and I realized he was already asleep. I didn't wake him.

Through the years ahead, when I missed him most, I remembered those last nights, when we reached back into the past and found our love, unmarked by time, pure and unblemished, strong and true. It was still there. I held on to that.

CHAPTER 29

The new man Pa hired to work on the farm was called Lumpy. His real name was Akin Lumpkin. Poor fellow had a limp, too. I could only imagine the nicknames he had to endure as a child. In spite of the limp, he had a strong back and turned out to be a hard worker. With the new infusion of help, Pa planted not only our own fields, but also fifteen acres on the Jamison's spread. I could tell by things he said that he was hoping for a standout year.

That summer, I put Sally in charge of herself and the other two young ones, since Momma couldn't be chasing babies anymore. Between Sally and Susie, poor little Gerry couldn't get by with much. I could tell they were still missing Tommy by the way they poured out all that love on Gerry. In fact, they did so much mothering and cuddling him, he was probably relieved to see his momma when she came in from the garden. When the beans and the peas started coming in, we blocked off the steps, and they watched him out there on the back porch while they helped Momma snap beans or hull peas.

The summer months were as busy as always, with canning and preserving. When apples and pears came in, we did our duty there, too, drying apples for pies and putting up applesauce and apple cider. Susie asked me, "Momma, why don't the flies or the ants eat up the apples?" She was asking about the apple slices we set out in pie plates on top of shoulder high poles, to let them dry in the sun.

"You know something, Susie?" I answered. "I don't have the foggiest notion. In fact, I think I'll add that to my list."

"What list?"

"The list of questions I want to ask when I get to heaven."

"What else do you want to ask?"

"Well... Number one question on my list will definitely be..." I grabbed her up and started tickling her. "How did I get so lucky, to have two terrific gals like you for my daughters?"

Listening to her giggle, I realized I hadn't laughed and been silly like that with my girls for a long time. The thick heaviness of grief was slowly lifting, and I could feel my heart growing a little lighter. The pain was still there, but putting it aside became easier, especially when I saw how much the girls had missed me. Their eyes told me they had been waiting to see if their mother was coming back. That was reason enough for me.

Since Pa had his radio in the front room, I put mine in the bedroom I shared with the girls. Fairy had opened my eyes to the importance of being informed, and of course, the safety and wellbeing of our military were now very personal to me. I continued to write Ned every week, usually on Sunday afternoon. His letters came less often, maybe once every two or three weeks, or sometimes several at a time, but he did do a little better than when he was in West Virginia. For the most part, he wrote about his buddies, the food, and his socks.

The soldiers weren't allowed to say much about where they were or what they were doing, but we did know that he was with the First Army Infantry Division, "The Big Red," and that they'd been sent to north Africa. It was hard for me to imagine such faraway places as we began to hear of in the news, and to know that my husband and so many others were in mortal danger in these exotic locations was hard to grasp. It was like the little world we'd always lived in was gone, replaced by one where the other side of the world was now thrust into our everyday lives. It was a strange time.

After Labor Day, the girls went back to school and the farmhouse was far too quiet without them. Or maybe it left us three women too much on top of each other. I loved my momma and my sister, but Flo especially could rankle my nerves, with her need to always be the main attraction. She was actually starting to flirt with Lumpy, and though I tried to subtly discourage her, she wasn't one to listen to advice from anybody.

I wondered from time to time if, in her mind, I was to blame for the episode with Gerald. Perhaps she never thought of it anymore, something which I thought was quite possible, as her thoughts were generally centered on herself, with the exception of her undisputed love for Gerry. I knew for certain she never doubted that she and Gerald were his parents, and for that I was thankful.

One Saturday in September, the girls and I caught a ride to Deckler Springs with our neighbors, the Robertsons. Part of Ned's monthly pay came to me, so I had a bit of money saved, enough for us to buy some pretty hair bows and indulge in a milkshake at the drugstore.

Sitting on our stools at the counter, the three of us were intent on slurping up the delicious treat, when I heard a familiar voice. "Birdie? Oh, my goodness, is that you?"

I spun around on my stool, and there was Gloria. I jumped off the stool and hugged her. "Gloria Smith, how are you?" Detecting a little bump, I held her out from me. "You're expecting?"

"Yes, ma'am, I sure am," she said, grinning and patting her tummy.

"I didn't even know you were married. Who..?"

"Marty Martin. It's been a year now."

"Smarty Marty? Oh, that's wonderful. And a baby..."

Gloria smiled, but then knitted her brows. "I heard about your baby, Birdie. I'm so sorry." She hugged me again. "And these are your two girls?"

"Yes, this one's Sally, and this is Susie."

"Well, they look mighty sweet."

I raised my eyebrow at the girls. "Hmm, sometimes, anyway."

"So, Birdie, what are you doing these days?"

Gloria took the stool beside me and we chatted, catching up on the years since we'd seen each other.

"Will you stay with your parents until Ned comes home?"

I squinched my eyes shut, then opened them. "I guess so. Ned's pay is enough, as long as I stay at the farm."

"You don't want to stay there?"

"You know how it is, moving back after you've lived on your own. And Flo's there, too, with her baby."

"Too many cooks in the kitchen?"

"Exactly," I laughed.

"What if you got a job? The mill's hiring again. They've got all these orders from the government for socks and undergarments for the military."

I considered the idea. "I hadn't heard. I thought the mills and the furniture factory were all still on half-capacity or less."

"Not anymore. Go down there and talk to them. You've got experience, so I bet they'd snap you right up."

She was right.

The only problem was, I didn't have a way to get back and forth to town every day. Before I accepted the job, I told the mill foreman, Mr. Ledbetter, about my dilemma. He scratched his head for a minute. "Where did you say you live?"

I told him, and he thought a bit more. "Wait here," he said and he left the office.

A few minutes later, he came back in with another gentleman, a few years older than me, whose hair had probably been bright orange when he was a child, but had now softened to a brownish-red, mixed with a bit of gray. He still had the freckles, though.

"Mrs. Parker, I'd like you to meet Danny O'Connell."

Mr. O'Connell held out his hand for me to shake. "Pleased to meet you, ma'am."

Mr. Ledbetter continued. "Danny here lives out just beyond you. He's the day shift manager for the sock floor, which is where I planned to use you. He said he'd be happy to give you a ride back and forth." Danny was nodding his head in agreement.

I was astonished at how easy they were making it for me. "I accept," I said.

When I told everyone at supper that evening, the only negative reactions, as I expected, were from Pa and Flo. Pa, because he was negative about pretty much everything, and Flo, because she knew I'd been doing all of the work that Momma wasn't able to do, and now she would have to do it. The girls didn't seem to mind, and actually, it would affect them very little. I'd continue to get them up and dressed in the morning, then I'd have to leave. Momma said she didn't mind fixing their breakfast and making sure they got on the bus. In the afternoon, they would get home about an hour before I did. The rest of the evening, until bedtime, would be as usual.

My first day of work, I made sure I was out at the road waiting for Danny in plenty of time. He was doing me a huge favor, giving me a ride every day, and I didn't want to inconvenience him in any way. Right at 7:15, a 1941 Special Deluxe Coupe pulled on to the shoulder of the road, and Danny reached across the passenger side to pop open the door for me.

"Good morning," he said, as he pulled back on to the road.

"Good morning," I replied. "Thanks again for giving me a ride." I tried to act nonchalant and sophisticated, as if I rode in a business coupe all the time.

"Don't mind a bit. Ten extra seconds in the morning, ten extra in the afternoon, let's see... How much time will that cost me every week?" He waited for me to answer.

I thought fast. "One minute and forty seconds?"

"You got it. I think I can afford to give you one minute and forty seconds a week."

I looked at this fellow out of the corner of my eye, and he caught me looking.

He laughed. "You'll have to forgive me. I like numbers and brain teasers. It's sort of a hobby."

"That's okay. I like to find animals in the clouds."

"Good for you. I've done that a few times myself."

We rode a few minutes in silence.

I asked him, "Isn't this a 1941 Special Deluxe Chevrolet model?"

He smiled again. "I'm impressed you know that. Yes, it is. I was fortunate to buy it when I did."

"When did you buy it?"

"The week before Thanksgiving, 1941. And of course, then two weeks later…"

"Pearl Harbor," I finished for him.

"Yes. With the immediate ban on any further new car production until the war is over."

"You were very lucky."

"I agree. I started to wait until after New Year's Day, but thank goodness, I didn't."

"We used to have a Ford Tudor. I loved that car. Of course, I threw a fit when my husband bought it without asking me, but it grew on me."

"Do you drive?"

"I'm crazy about driving."

"I'll let you drive sometime."

I looked at him in surprise.

He said, "If you want to…"

Oh, boy, did I want to.

Sock production covered the entire second floor of the building, with around eighty workers. When I worked in a mill before, I ran a sewing machine. This time, my first assignment was on the knitting cylinders. To start with, the giant spools of thread were loaded up onto the spindles and threaded into the cylinder. Then the cylinder's moving parts pulled the thread out and knitted it into a continuous sleeve of woven sock material. The sleeve was then cut off into the desired length, and passed on to the seamstresses. The work was fairly easy, but as with any type of machinery, you had to be alert and on your guard for danger.

Most of my fellow workers had done this all their lives. A few of them I knew from school, but there were also several close to my age I didn't know, and I looked forward to making some new friends. At the end of the week, getting my first paycheck gave me a great feeling. With what I earned, plus Ned's pay, there might come a time soon when the girls and I could move into town.

Between my new job, taking care of my girls, and helping out at home, my days were adequately filled, busy enough to keep me from thinking too much about things I didn't want to think about. Things like where my husband was, and whether he was dead or hurt. Things like the anniversary of Tommy's death.

Near the end of October, I got home from work and Momma pointed to the kitchen table, where a large package sat. "You got something in the mail today," she said. "It doesn't say who it's from."

I looked at the large, flat box. "I wasn't expecting anything. I didn't order anything…" I wondered what it could be. The girls must have heard me come in, for they raced into the kitchen, yelling, "Open it, Momma! Open it!"

Flo came in with Gerry. "Well, Birdie, don't just stand there. We're all on pins and needles. Open the dang thing!"

I got some scissors and cut the string, then pulled the brown paper away. Underneath, there was a wooden box of sorts, maybe about twenty inches square, but only five inches high. It was nailed shut all around, but the wood looked rather flimsy, so I got a kitchen knife and pried the boards apart until I could lift the top off. Inside there was something wrapped up in muslin cloth. I lifted it out and unwrapped it.

I knew who it was from. It was a painting. A painting of Tommy. I felt my legs going out from under me, so I slid into the nearest chair. My hand went to cover my mouth, as my body jerked with ragged sobs. My momma, my sister, and my daughters all gathered around me and touched me, comforting me in the best way they knew how. I absorbed their comfort and their love and it soothed me.

Fairy had painted Tommy as he looked on the morning of the mine disaster, when we were out in the woods picking blueberries. He was sitting in the grass, among the wildflowers, with the sun shining on his blond locks and a basket of blueberries sitting in front of him. He had a handful of berries in each hand, and the smile on his face was pure joy. It looked just like him, just like my bonny boy Tommy.

CHAPTER 30

The end of 1942 drew near. The mill continued to run at full capacity, which suited me just fine. The busier I was, the less time I had to think about Tommy or Ned. I hung the painting of Tommy in the bedroom I shared with the girls, not yet ready to openly share my grief. I probably should have talked more about Tommy and how I felt—they say it helps to talk about it—but I just couldn't.

The news from the war was scarce, and most of it was not good. At the mill, on our lunch break, it was a frequent topic of conversation, second only to the shortage of nylon stockings. Almost everyone there had a family member or a friend fighting in the military.

Gas rationing began on the first of December that year, and even though there was some grousing about it, for the most part we were all willing to do whatever it took to help our boys overseas. The big news lately was the invasion of Guadalcanal in the Pacific. Back in April, the newspapers had reported that we'd lost Bataan, and as the months passed and more eyewitness reports came in, we were told of the horrors of what they called the Death March, where so many of our soldiers died a miserable death. I couldn't help but feel some satisfaction that we were back in there at Guadalcanal, fighting our way back in the Pacific. To do less would mean those boys had died for nothing.

There was one very heavy woman, Bertha, who always wore bright red lipstick and shared her opinion loud and often, whether we wanted to hear it or not. She wasn't the kind of person I would normally become friendly with, but she was a fanatic about reading and listening to the news, so we often compared notes.

Around the middle of December, a group of us were having our lunch in the breakroom when Bertha spoke up. "Have any of you heard about those camps?"

"You mean the Japanese prisoner of war camps?" someone asked.

"No, not them, though they're bad enough, so they say. No, I'm talking about those rumors from Europe—well, not so much a rumor anymore—that the Germans are killing tens of thousands, maybe hundreds of thousands of civilians. The ones they don't like. Jews and political prisoners."

One sweet older woman said, "Well, they're not supposed to be killing anyone except other soldiers, are they?"

"What do you think those bombings in London are for, huh?" said Bertha, rolling her eyes.

Minnie, a young girl whose husband was in the Air Force, said, "Benny didn't come right out and say it in his letters, but he thinks it's true, too."

"From what I've read..." I paused. I had noticed that the others had begun looking to me as an authority on these matters, so I tried to be careful that what I told them was accurate. "From what I've read, the first report came from an underground paper in Poland. This young fellow escaped while he was burying bodies. He said the Germans were using a big van, loading it with people, and then pumping it full of poison gas. The place was called Chelmno."

I looked around the silent room. Everyone had been listening. I knew what they were thinking, because I was thinking it, too. If this is what Germany and Japan were capable of, what might be in store for our boys? Or maybe even for us?

Ned didn't forget the girls' Christmas presents. He'd taken the trouble of mailing the package in October, which was a smart move, since it didn't arrive until the week before Christmas. The package also included a letter, marked on the outside, "Read this on Christmas morning."

Sally and Susie were excited that morning, for they knew their daddy had sent them something and of course, at two years old, Gerry was old enough this year to share in their excitement. The night before, Flo had spread out all of Gerry's gifts under the tree, for him to discover as soon as he entered the room. On Christmas morning, he couldn't decide what to play with first, going from one toy to the other, dropping one only to pick something else up.

The girls' gifts were waiting to be unwrapped, and they wasted no time tearing into them. I had gotten them each a board game, a nice cardigan sweater, a game of jacks, and some paper dolls, all of which they seemed to like. But they were eyeing the boxes from Ned. They looked at me expectantly.

"Okay, go ahead." I hadn't even gotten the words out of my mouth before they had the paper off. Ned had chosen well. He gave each of them a beautiful hand beaded necklace and a colorful set of nesting dolls. They were occupied with their gifts as I picked up the box that had my name on it.

I opened it carefully. Inside, cushioned in crushed papers, was a bottle of perfume. "Night on the Nile." Hmm. Opening the bottle,

I took a sniff. Wonderful, light and flowery. Maybe Ned would be home soon and I could wear it for him.

But I was more interested in the letter. "Girls, here's the letter from your daddy." They stopped what they were doing to listen as I read aloud.

October 14, 1942

To my three dear girls,

No matter where I am or what I'm doing on Christmas morning, I will be thinking of you. We might or might not have a big Christmas dinner here, it just depends. Sometimes we have to eat K-rations, which are meals in a flat tin can. Imagine that, girls.

I keep your photos in my pocket all the time, so I can take them out and look at you every day. I've showed them to my buddies and they all agree, you three are beautiful.

I never thought I would see the world, especially not like this. When I get back, I'm going to tell you all about it. Maybe someday, when things are back to normal, we can all come back here and see the sights. I'd really like that.

Please give my best Christmas wishes to the rest of the family. Girls, be good for your momma, and do what she says. Birdie, take care of yourself and the girls. I'm always thinking of you and missing you. I love you all and I can't wait to see you again.

Daddy

"Well, that was sweet," commented Flo, breaking the mood of the moment. "What did you say you sent Ned?"

Sally said, "Socks. Mostly socks."

"He said his feet were always getting wet," added Susie.

"Ten pairs of socks, some cigars, and Susie and Sally's new school pictures." I said, hoping he got it in time. It wasn't much, as far as Christmas presents went, but at least he would know we were remembering him. It made my heart ache, thinking of him over there at Christmas, separated from everyone he loved.

With the war in full swing, the New Year of 1943 bore little celebrating. A year and a half before this, I would never have dreamed I'd be back at the farm, without Tommy, and with Ned halfway around the world, fighting a war. You never know what life is going to serve up.

Danny continued to be a sport, picking me up every day, and we grew to become good friends. He'd been to college, but he wasn't uppity about it, as some folks are. After he knew me for a while, he commented that I would have done well if I'd attended college. I didn't know about all that, but it certainly made me feel good that he thought so. Occasionally, I heard one of the girls at work make a smart aleck comment about me being such good friends with the boss and getting special treatment. I learned to ignore them.

After being there only a few months, I got quite proficient at my job. Most of the time, I could even fix the machine myself if it broke down, instead of calling the maintenance man, which usually involved a long wait. Sometimes the other ladies asked me to come and help them with their own machine, which I was happy to do.

One day, I left my station to go get some more spools of thread. The stock supply lads couldn't always keep up, so we sometimes had to get it ourselves. As I was walking to the supply room, I noticed that Ruth, two places down from me, was working on her machine.

"Do you need some help?" I asked.

She smiled at me, "Thanks, I think I've got it," she said, pushing her hair away from her face and trying to tuck it back under her hairnet. I waved and went on by.

After I got my thread, I was coming back and noticed Ruth jerk forward. I knew right away what had happened. She was leaning over that machine and her loose hair had gotten caught. Yelling for help, she tried to reach for the switch, but the machine was pulling her hair down into the gears and knitting prongs, so she transferred all her effort into grasping her hair. Dropping the spools I was carrying, I ran over and flipped the switch, but nothing happened. The machine didn't stop. Her head was now bent down into the opening, and some strands had already been pulled from her head. She was crying and spouting some choice words that don't bear repeating. Without thinking, I took the scissors from my pocket and cut that chunk of hair off close to the scalp. Then someone threw the main switch, and her machine ground to a halt as did all the others on her row. People were crowding around now, stretching their necks to see what was going on.

Leaning over with her hands on her knees, panting, she managed to squeak out, "Thank you. Thanks, Birdie."

I nodded and smiled apologetically. "Sorry about your hair..."

She reached up and felt of it, then, where I had whacked it off. Keeping her hand over the almost bald spot, she smiled. "Hey, that's okay. Hair grows back. Scalps don't."

Folks all around us clapped, then we all got back to work.

On the way home that day, Danny said, "You did a good thing today, helping Ruth the way you did."

I shrugged. "Anybody could have done it. Common sense, you know?"

"Maybe," he said. "Anyway, Sylvia Jenkins was standing right there at my desk when it all happened. Her husband owns the mill, and she's running it while he's overseas with the Army Air Corps. She commented about how quick you were to take action. Then she asked me about how you were doing at your job."

"And... what did you tell her?"

"I told her the truth."

"Uh-oh, am I in trouble now?"

He gave me a look. "Seriously, now. I told her you were a fast learner, efficient, highest production on the floor, and a smart cookie. Sassy, too."

I huffed at that last remark. "Well, thanks for the mostly good recommendation, I guess."

"Actually, I think she's looking for a production assistant."

"A secretary? I'm no good at typing."

"No, she's got a secretary for the office work. I think she wants someone to help her communicate with the various floor managers, stay on top of workflow and production status, and keep her informed of everything."

"Why would she be interested in me?"

Danny pulled over to the side of the road to let me out. "Beats me, kiddo. I only know I'm gonna be pretty upset if she steals you away from me."

I forgot all about that conversation until a few months later, when Mrs. Jenkins called me in to her office for an interview. When I walked out, I had a new job and a new title, Production Assistant to the Chief Executive Officer. P.A. for short. With the new responsibilities came a substantial increase in pay. Visions of automobiles danced before my eyes, and I knew what my first major purchase would be.

That first day in my new office, I wasn't sure how to act. I finally decided I should just be the same as I always was. When Mrs. Jenkins called me in to discuss my duties, the first thing I asked her was whether I needed to dress like a secretary.

"No, no. You dress just as you would on the production floor, without the hairnet, of course. You'll actually be down on the floors a lot during the day, so office attire would be too confining." That was a relief.

She seemed to want to get to know me better. She asked me what I'd been doing the past few years, how old the girls were, where my husband was stationed. Since she had opened that door, I thought it would be all right to ask about her husband, too. "Danny said Mr. Jenkins is overseas, too? Where is he?"

"He's in the Pacific, on an aircraft carrier."

"That sounds dangerous," I commented.

"Yes, but no more so than any service man. They're all in danger, all the time." She bit her lip and looked out the window. "It's nerve-wracking, isn't it?"

I nodded in agreement. "It sure is."

"Birdie. May I call you Birdie?"

"I'd like it if you did," I replied.

"Well, then, 'Birdie' it is. And I'd also appreciate it, when we're in private, if you would call me Sylvia. Unfortunately, in public, around other people, I need you to call me Mrs. Jenkins."

"Of course."

"It's hard enough being a business woman," she explained. "I have to use every means available to maintain an aura of authority. That's the only reason I insist on the formality. Otherwise," she leaned forward conspiratorially, "I wouldn't give a damn."

I knew right then I was going to like this woman.

CHAPTER 31

With the cash crop profits from the year before, Pa did the unthinkable, that spring of 1943. He bought a used tractor. So now with the three men—Pa, Gus, and Lumpy—and a tractor, he was counting on another good year. We had our own land, and now we had twenty acres of the Jamison's, too.

It did turn out to be another strong year for the farm, but not for Pa. He was over across the property line on the Jamison's land harvesting corn when he fell off of the tractor. Lumpy rushed to get him in the wagon, which was full of corn, but it was already too late. His heart had given out.

We buried him the next day in the cemetery at the church. My head couldn't get around all of my thoughts that day. I thought the most about little Tommy, all alone in that cemetery in West Virginia. Fairy had promised to look after the grave, and I knew she would, but it would have been a comfort to be able to visit him from time to time.

And then I thought of Ned, and his sweet voice singing at so many funerals. It would have been right and proper to have him sing at Pa's funeral, but he was far away. I wondered if he ever sang for his buddies over there.

Pa, and the bitter life he lived, was in my mind, too. What a waste of a good life. Being hateful and mean to your family. Abusing a child who was as good as yours. He'd been passable decent to me and to Carl and Luther, but that didn't excuse his treatment of Flo, and I'd never forgive him for it. On the good side, of which there was precious little, he was a good provider and a hard worker. We never went hungry and we always had clothes to wear and a roof over our head. That was the best I could say for him.

Lumpy and Gus said they could finish out the season, get the crops in and get them sold. Momma tried to oversee everything, with my help and with Flo's, but it was a hardship for her, adding to the misery she suffered with her hip. Before the leaves started to turn, she took to her bed, and except for a few good days here and there, she pretty much stayed there.

For quite a while, Lumpy and Flo had been thick as thieves, so it was no surprise to Momma and me when Flo announced that they were getting married at the county courthouse on the first Saturday in October. After that big event, Lumpy became a part of our family, and I have to say, he was a big improvement over Gerald. He was a little on the quiet side, more or less did whatever Flo told him to do, but he was gentle and kind with my girls and with Gerry, which told me more than any words he might say.

Together, Lumpy and Flo took over the running of the farm. You might say he was the muscle and she was the brains. Surprisingly enough, my little sister had a head for such things, and it turned her from a slightly lazy whiner to an industrious moneymaker. I guess finding something she was interested in, and good at, made all the difference. Whatever the reason, it was a relief to me to leave the farming to them.

In the evenings and on the weekends, I spent as much time with Momma as I could. She didn't get up much, but her mind was still sharp and her hands were always busy. She spent most of her time quilting and making rag rugs, so I sat and worked with her and we just talked.

One evening, everyone was gone, so I knew I could speak freely without fear that someone might overhear. I leaned my head close and said, "Momma, you probably don't know this, but one night, right after you first broke your hip, you took some pain medicine, and it made you get a little loopy."

Curious now, she said, "How so?"

"Well, you thought I was Flo, and you told me who her real father was. A preacher named Jim." I waited for her response.

"My goodness, Birdie. You been holding this inside of you for that long?" She almost looked amused.

"Yes, ma'am, I have."

Momma looked off into space and smiled. "It's been so long ago, it hardly seems to matter now. I was a married woman with a two-year-old daughter—you—and yet I couldn't stop myself."

"And Pa found out?"

She nodded. "He did. The day Jim left, your Pa beat me black and blue. Made me stay in the house for two weeks, so nobody would see me looking that way. Wasn't long before I knew I was expecting, and I knew whose it was. Couldn't have been your Pa's because I wouldn't let him touch me after he beat me. Not for about five years." I looked at my momma in wonder. She'd had her own life, with its own drama and mistakes and heartaches. Who would have guessed such as this? Not me. All I knew was that she was my momma, hardworking and caring. I'd never thought of her any other way.

I hated to ask the next question, but it had to be done. "Momma, did Flo ever tell you about what Pa did to her?"

She looked puzzled. "No. He was always harsh with her, but...what are you talking about?"

I told her what Flo had told me. Her face got sadder and more broken with each word I spoke.

"I didn't know," she said, her face crinkling with unshed tears. "I swear I didn't know, or I would have killed him myself." She shook her head. "My poor baby girl. And I didn't protect her. But Birdie, I didn't know..." The tears were falling now. She caught them with the rag rug she was working on.

I rubbed her shoulder. "I know you didn't know. It's all over now. Someday, when you get the chance, you might want to talk to Flo about it. Tell her about what her real daddy was like. I bet she'd like that. She might even want to find him someday. Quiet like," I assured her, at the look of panic on her face, "without stirring up a ruckus. You might want to tell her, too, that I knocked Pa up side of the head with a two-by-four when she told me what he did to her. She might like to know that."

Ma gasped. "Birdie, you didn't?" I could tell I had shocked her. Nobody ever messed with Pa - he was too dadgum mean.

"Yes, ma'am, I did. He had to be taught a lesson. You remember when he said he fell out of the hayloft and got banged up on the harrow?"

"That was you?" Momma looked at me real funny. "I always wondered about that." She shot me another sideways glance, as if she wasn't quite sure who I was, then picked up her rug again and looked at it as if she wasn't sure how to start. "I'll talk to Flo tomorrow. That'll give me time to think about it, what I'm gonna say to her." Momma turned to me, a look of dread in her eyes. "I'm afraid she'll hate me. I guess I did the wrong thing, not telling her before."

I tried to calm her. "She won't hate you. And as far as telling her, that wasn't the kind of thing you could have told her while she was still a child."

"Guess not."

We fell silent, each in our own thoughts. My momma was probably thinking about what to say to Flo. I was thinking about my own complicated lies, and how so many lives were now twisted up in the deceit.

While we worked on our rag rugs, I brought up another subject, as this seemed to be a good night for confidences and clearing the air.

"Momma?"

"Birdie?"

"Do you know why I did what I did, the night the boys were born?"

Momma thought a minute. "Partly." She lowered her voice, even though no one was there to hear. "Gerald was the father of your baby, too?"

"Yes."

"So Tommy was Flo and Gerald's child?"

"Yes."

"And Gerry is yours and Gerald's?"

"That's right."

Momma shook her head. "You know, you weren't the only one responsible for switching those babies. I let you do it. It's on my head, too. I...I just remembered how hard it was...when your pa found out..."

"I know, Momma. I know why you let me do it."

"And you know you can never in this life tell Flo what you did?"

"Yes'm. That goes without saying. Gerry belongs to Flo, always will. Tommy was my baby." I closed my eyes and said the hard part. "I had no business switching those babies. It was wrong. But it's done, and I have to live with the consequences." I bent my head, picking at the rags in my hand. "I admit, sometimes I wish I could... But then I know what's right. I'll never try to claim him, Momma. You don't have to worry about that."

Momma nodded her head slowly in agreement. "What I don't understand is how that came about to begin with, as crazy in love as you've always been for Ned. Did Gerald take you by force?"

I sighed. "Yes, and no. That's what made it so hard."

"What does that mean?"

"Remember that time I was so sick with the influenza, right after the hog killing, when the weather was so nasty?"

"I remember. Right after that is when Gerald got sick with it and passed."

"Right. Well, my fever was real high, so high that I was out of my head most of the time. You know how that is? You're freezing, then on fire, then you have fever dreams, that are so real and strange..."

"Yes?"

I found myself telling it, and the words were coming out like I was talking about somebody else. "All of you had gone to church, all except Gerald. My fever went back up again, and I was dreaming. I dreamed that Ned was home and we were...well, you know. When I broke free of the dream for a second, I saw that it was Gerald, not Ned, and we were already in the midst of things, so to speak. Gerald had snuck in my room and started touching me, and I truly didn't know it at first. When I realized it was him, I tried to push him away, but my dreams kept pulling me back in, and I missed being with Ned so much…" I sighed again. "I might could have stopped him. I don't know. I can't remember the hours after that, when I had the seizure. When I finally did come out of it, I wasn't even sure if it really happened. Not until I saw that smug look on Gerald's face."

I could feel a weight lifting off of me, the weight of carrying around this disturbing story for so long. It was a relief to finally let it out, the whole true story, the way it really happened. Why didn't I ever sit down with Ned and tell him the truth like this? I realized I knew why. I was afraid he wouldn't believe me. The same way he didn't believe me when Jerry Johnson made a pass at me at the Christmas party. He blamed me without even asking me what had happened.

I pulled myself back to the present where Momma was talking to me. "Birdie, don't blame yourself. You're not the one that did wrong." She reached over and took my hand in hers, all knotty and gnarled now, but still my momma's hand.

"Maybe not. But there was a second or two when I knew it wasn't Ned, but I just wasn't strong enough, or righteous enough, to push him away." I was ashamed of that, but I had to be honest and admit that it might be the truth.

"Birdie." Momma's voice had that old authority from when I was a little girl. "Birdie, you listen to me. If you had not been near dead yourself, this would never, ever have happened. Gerald is the one you should blame. Not yourself. I don't care if you did have a moment where your mind was clear. The rest of the time it was not clear, and you are not to blame yourself, d'you hear me? Now, you just get that out of your head, once and for all."

Could it be true? I took in a breath and let it out in a sob. "You're sure it's not my fault, Momma?" I wanted to hear her say it again.

"It's not your fault."

That heaviness was floating away again, this time for good. My momma had said it, so it must be true. "All right." I wiped my eyes. "I'm gonna let that burden go and never pick it up again." I took her hand in both of mine. "There's one more thing, and it's all connected, so bear with me, Momma."

"Go on, Birdie. This talk has been coming for a long time."

"Yes, ma'am. The thing is, do you understand now, now that we've talked about all these things, why I needed to switch the babies?"

"Not really, except that Gerry looked like Gerald, and Tommy could more easily pass for Ned's offspring."

"That's part of it, but not all."

"What do you mean?"

"Do you remember a long, long time ago, I asked you why Pa was never happy, and you said something like… sometimes a bad thing happens and some people can't get over it and be happy again? They live the rest of their lives bitter and unhappy?"

"I don't actually remember that… but it sounds more or less true, particularly where your Pa was concerned."

"After you told me that Flo wasn't Pa's, and how mad he was when he found out about you and Jim, I figured that was what made Pa bitter and mean. And I was afraid that if Ned knew that the child I birthed was not his, then he would turn bitter, too. Can you imagine all that sweetness and love that's inside of Ned turning to bitterness and hate? I would have done anything to save us from that."

"Oh, Birdie, child." She looked at me with sadness and love, as only a mother could. "You were trying to play God."

I was glad we had that cleansing talk when we did, because my good mother went to be with Jesus soon after. She made some mistakes in her life, just as I have made some mistakes in mine. She always drew back to God, though, and that's what kept her good and kept her true. I watched her spirit move with grace when she was old, even though her body was by then bent and frail and could hardly move at all. She was wise in the advice she gave me, when I was a child and then when I was grown. After she was gone, I remembered her words from our last long talk. I took them all to heart and I did my best to follow her advice. From then forward, I no longer blamed myself for what happened with Gerald. And I did my best to keep my hands out of the Almighty's business.

CHAPTER 32

With Pa and Momma both gone, the hierarchy of the household began to change. Flo ran the house now, and she acted like she owned everything, despite the fact that all four of us siblings had equal ownership of the house and farm. Christmas came and went, with hardly a ripple on the water. Lumpy was the only one who seemed to have any Christmas cheer, and I was glad to see it, for the children's sake.

Ned's division was in England for an extended break, so the package we received from him that year was bursting with goodies for Sally and Susie. His gift to me was a real silk scarf and a ruby brooch to pin it. Naturally, we sent him yet more socks, plus some books and magazines, cans of nuts, and some praline coated pecans that the girls and I had made. He sent two letters that year, one for me to read aloud to the girls and one for my eyes alone. The second one read:

November 28, 1943
My dear Birdie,

There are some things I need to say to you. To your face would be better, but I guess this will have to do. The last few months have been hard, and I've seen things I hope to never see again, but probably will, as long as this war continues. I'm a lucky son of a gun, to still be alive. I may not be so lucky next time.

We're taking a break from the front for a short while, so I've had time to think about a lot of things. I think I'd better say them now, in case I don't get another chance.

From the time I set eyes on you, I knew you would be the love of my life. I've always loved you, more than my own life. I hope you know that. You are the best part of me. Some things have happened over the last few years. There's no denying how hurt and angry I've been with you. I kept a distance between us, and wouldn't let you back in. I'm sorry for that.

When Tommy died, I thought things would go back to how they were before. That was stupid of me to think that. You wanted me to love Tommy, but every time I looked at him, I thought of what you'd done. I should have forgiven you, and loved him anyway. I admit that I never was able to do that either. At least, not in time for it to make any difference.

I don't know if we can ever put things right between us. We've both done some things wrong. Maybe we just need to talk it out, or maybe we need to think about splitting up, when this is all over.

You'll have plenty of time to think it over. I think we're going to be here in Europe a lot longer. The enemy has a strong hold and won't be moved out of the way easily.

I do love you, Birdie, and want the best for you. Take care of our girls and yourself, too.

Ned

I couldn't read everything at the end for the tears in my eyes. Everyone else was busy with Christmas, so they didn't notice when I tucked the letter in my pocket and snuck quietly out of the room. My jacket was in the bedroom, but I wasn't going back for it. I had to get out of the house right then.

On the way to the creek, I shook from the cold and from being upset and crying. I read the letter again as I stumbled along. I couldn't believe he was saying it. Saying that we might separate. I had thought it myself, and wondered if he was thinking it, but now he'd actually written it down on paper. That made it real.

At the creek, I leaned against a tree and hollered out my frustration in between sobs. How could I fix this if he wasn't here? Even if I had him right here beside me, could it ever be fixed?

When you lose someone, you can see with clarity the things that were previously obscure. I saw my lies for what they were. I saw what I'd done to all of us when I switched the babies. I saw how stupid I'd been to think that Ned should just follow along with me and pretend that things were the same as they'd always been.

His reaction was justified. I was the one who'd abandoned our true and honest relationship in favor of chasing after one based on pretense. Now it was over and I knew it. Despair, deep and bottomless, overtook me and I gave myself up to it willingly to escape the blinding glare of truth that pierced my heart and sickened me.

Sally found me there an hour later, near frozen. Taking off her own jacket, she put it around my shoulders and led me back to the house. I took a hot bath, then stayed in the bed the rest of Christmas Day. Nobody bothered me, not even Flo. They thought I had lost my mind.

By New Year's Day, I was over the shock of it, and set my feet firmly back on the ground. I had overreacted. All he really said was that maybe we needed to talk it out. I was going to deal with whatever each day brought. I was going to carry on just as before, as the wife of an American soldier and as a mother to our two girls. When the war was over, we could sort everything out then.

"Have you had lunch yet?" asked Danny, poking his head around the corner of my office door.

I looked up from the papers I was sorting. "Not yet."

"Come on, then. My treat. You've been working too hard lately."

It was tempting. I was putting in extra hours, trying to make sure that our government contracts would be going out on time. Still, I was a married woman, and it just wasn't done. "Mmm, I probably shouldn't," I said.

"Oh, come on. You ride to work with me every day," he reminded me.

He had a point there. "Okay. But it'll have to be quick. Mrs. Jenkins needs these reports pronto."

It was after one, so the diner's lunch crowd had dwindled, and we got a booth right away. Though we rode together every day, sharing a booth for lunch seemed different and awkward. That is, until we started talking, and then it was just my friend Danny, same as always.

We both ordered the Blue Plate Special, then Danny said, "Mrs. Jenkins is keeping you busy, huh?"

"Oh, yeah. Very. But I like it that way."

"To tell you the truth—and this is just between you and me—I wasn't sure how I'd feel about a lady for a boss. I mean, Mr. Jenkins is such a great guy, and a heck of a businessman. But taking orders from his wife? I didn't know about that."

"So? You changed your mind now?"

"You bet. She runs the company just like he would, if he were here. In some ways, maybe even better."

"Well, she does have a business degree. That alone would be credential enough for a man," I pointed out.

"Hey. You're right. Like I said, I'm behind her one hundred percent." He stopped to drink some of his soda. "Does she say anything about Mr. Jenkins? Or I guess I should say, Lieutenant Jenkins?"

"Not much, just that he's in the Pacific somewhere. And that may be all she knows herself. You know, loose lips sink ships. Evidently, my brothers take that slogan very seriously, since we've only gotten four letters from them since they signed up. Thank goodness, Bertha keeps an eye on the news for any mention of their ship."

"How about Ned?"

"As far as I know, he's still in England, but from things he's said, they're getting ready for something big in the spring." They brought our food and we began to eat. "This war. It's just horrible, the stories we're hearing." I looked up at him. "I know you told me you tried to sign up, and I'm sorry your heart has that thing, whatever it is, that made them turn you down, but be grateful you're here, instead of there."

He shrugged. "I am. I know I've got it easy here, but I try to do what I can."

"Oh, no. I didn't mean you weren't." I was afraid I'd offended him. "You do all those paper drives, and other things. That's just as important and necessary. I admit I'm selfishly glad you're here to be my friend."

"I'm glad, too." He smiled at me.

Twisting my fork in my cream potatoes, I said, "And speaking of being friends, didn't you say, a long time ago, that you were going to let me drive your car sometime?"

"Drive my car? Are you serious?" he teased me.

"Yes, you know you said it. So when can I drive?"

"How about today on the way home?"

"Today is great. Speaking of cars, I've been thinking of buying one for myself. Would you help me find one?"

"Sure. But you know they're hard to find since production is banned until after the war," he warned me.

"I know. But do you think we can find one?"

"We may have to go to Raleigh one Saturday, but yes, I think we can."

As it turned out, we found one in Deckler Springs. An older woman whose husband had been dead for a number of years was moving to Asheville to live with her daughter and would no longer need the automobile. She didn't remember me, but I recognized her as the rich lady who'd bought the smocked outfits from me, insisting that she could buy the same thing elsewhere for a cheaper price. I'd naively let her have them for a very low price, a lesson I'd never forgotten.

Addressing Danny, she said, "You know, it's quite a find, in the middle of the war as we are. When your wife called me, I wasn't really sure I wanted to let this automobile go."

Danny hastened to correct her. "Oh, no. We're not…"

"I'm the one buying the car," I interrupted. "Mr. O'Connell is my friend."

She gave me a disapproving look, as if she suspected there was more to it than that. Had I not wanted the auto badly, I would have let her keep it, war or not. But I did want it, so I held my tongue and stayed.

Danny and I had already determined the value of the 1935 Fordor, so when she asked almost twice that much, I politely declined and we started walking away.

A second later, she snapped, "Wait."

I turned back to her.

"How about five hundred?" she said.

"No, ma'am, I'm sorry, I can't give that much for it. The price was five seventy-five when it was new." I glanced at Danny, who gave a slight nod. "We think the car's value is three fifty, and that's what I'm willing to give for it."

She took the offer and I got my car.

Having a car again was wonderful. I missed riding with Danny every day, but we made up for it by having lunch together at least once a week. Sally and Susie were thrilled with the Fordor, because we could take the occasional trip to town without having to drive the wagon, which had become a bit of an embarrassment to them. Gas was strictly rationed, of course, but we were very frugal, and managed a couple of extra trips a month. We were used to the ration coupons for various necessities such as sugar, cooking oil, and canned goods, and by that time, we hardly missed them at all.

One Friday in April, Sylvia asked me to step into her office. I gave her an update on the production schedule, and then asked her if she needed anything else.

Tapping her pencil on the pad in front of her, she said, "No, not really." Then she sat up straight and leaned toward me. "Nobody knows, but today is my birthday," she said, as if she was telling a big secret.

I perked up and smiled. "Well, happy birthday, Sylvia."

"I know it is a completely useless idea, but I'd like to recognize it in some way. Roland always did something special. He'd take me to dinner, buy me a nice gift."

"Well." I wasn't sure how to respond. I considered Sylvia a friend, but she was also my boss. I didn't want to appear to be taking advantage in any way. Deciding quickly on the side of friendship, I said, "I could take you out to dinner, if you like."

"Oh, no. I wasn't meaning to suggest anything like that." She leaned back in her chair. "All of my relatives live in Pennsylvania. Roland has two sisters here in town, but they're the silly, simpering kind of southern belles. You know, like Suellen and Carreen, Scarlett O'Hara's sisters."

I giggled then, because that sounded so funny coming out of Sylvia's mouth, but I knew just what she meant. She continued, "Anyway, I certainly don't want to spend my birthday with those lovely ladies. I was wondering if you might like to come to my home this evening. I'll whip up something light and simple for our supper... I think I need a girls' night, Birdie, and I think you're more the Scarlett O'Hara type. Strong when it counts, ready to have fun when the occasion presents itself. Am I right?"

A girls' night. I couldn't remember the last time I'd had fun with my girlfriends. A momentary feeling of guilt crossed my mind, about actually having a good time in the middle of the war, but then I thought, if Ned had a chance to kick up his heels and have some fun for a few hours, wouldn't I want him to grab the opportunity?

I gave her my answer. "I'm not sure I can adequately fill Miss Scarlett's shoes, but I'm ready to give it a whirl."

Her house, as I expected, was gorgeous, the kind you see in magazines. She made me feel comfortable right away, saying, "You're here as my friend, not my employee, all right? And don't you dare treat me as better than you, just because I grew up with certain advantages and have a college degree. Tonight, we're just two women whose husbands have been overseas for much too long, trying to have some laughs and forget about the war for an hour or two." She handed me a glass of wine, and we clinked our glasses together.

She told me about her childhood, growing up the only daughter of a successful Philadelphia attorney, then her college years at Penn State, where she met Roland. She shared their attempts to have a child, and I realized that her sorrow over that was no different than any woman's would have been, rich or poor. Thinking that she couldn't possibly be interested in my story, I avoided speaking of it, then, before I knew it, she had wheedled first one tale, then another from me, until she had me spilling all the rest of it out.

By the time I left, I'd learned of Roland's love of football, and she had heard all about Ned's proficiency at building furniture. Best of all, we laughed. It did us both good, and I was sorry when the evening ended.

As I was leaving, she asked a question that took me by surprise. "What about Danny?"

I couldn't imagine what she meant. "Danny...?"

She crossed her arms and tilted her head, studying me a moment. "You don't know, do you?"

"What?"

She seemed to change course then. "Oh, nothing, really. He's just a great guy, isn't he?"

I nodded in agreement. "He sure is. He's been a good friend to me, carrying me to work and back every day, until I got my car." I stepped out the door.

"Be careful driving home."

"See you tomorrow," I said, as she closed the door. I wondered what she'd been going to say about Danny, before she changed her mind.

When I got to the house, all the lights were off, and I assumed everyone was asleep. I turned on the kitchen light to get a glass of water before going to bed. While the water was running, Flo came up beside me, saying, "Just where have you been until all hours of the night?"

Surprised, I said, "I told you where I was going, remember? I came home after work and changed clothes, gave the girls their instructions for the evening, and I told you I was going to have supper with Sylvia." I wondered what she could possibly be fuming about.

"Well, I was stuck here, watching your children, while you were out partying until almost midnight. And is that liquor I smell on your breath?"

I was beginning to get a little angry myself now. "No, it is not liquor, but even if it was, that would be none of your business. And as for watching the girls, Sally is eleven and Susie is ten, so I don't think they required much looking after. In fact, if the truth was said, they probably spent the evening watching your child for you."

"I take care of my own boy, as you well know. Now, we're not going to have folks coming in and out of this house late at night anymore. Do I make myself clear?"

I heard her loud and clear. She was saying this was her house now and I had to obey her rules. I just raised my eyebrow at her and walked past her on my way to bed. It was time to move. It might take me a while to find a place that we could afford on my salary, but we would definitely be moving out.

CHAPTER 33

That spring, there were rumors flying all over the place that the Allies were planning to mount a major offensive move in Europe, most likely in France. Bertha, my number one source for news, was of the opinion that it was true, the only question being when. She thought the first of June was likely.

Sitting quietly in England for months now, the Big Red was due for some action. It was all very logical that they would be in the thick of any battle in France, but I didn't care about logic. I cared about my husband. Though he could never be specific in any of his letters, the last one I received in May gave me the shivers. He said, "When you hear that my buddies and me are on the move, pray for us. Pray like you've never prayed before." For weeks after that, I prayed every moment of every day, with each breath I took.

The first of June arrived, and there was daily speculation that we'd be hearing that day that the Allies were on the move. Finally, on the sixth, the news reports began. The bigger newspapers had time to switch their front page stories, to report that the Allies were invading Europe from the west. But the radio had the latest, up-to-the-minute reports, as more and more details came in over the course of the next few days.

It was shattering and heartbreaking and glorious, all at the same time. The number of lives lost was stunning, but the tenacity and determination of our boys was just as impressive. The mill was in a frenzy for several days as newspapers were passed around and radios blared from every room. Sylvia didn't try to stop it. She understood our need to know.

Ned was in the middle of what was going on over there. I knew that one fact, and yet I knew nothing beyond that. The first day I was frantic for news, soaking up every tidbit I could find. The second day I was numb. The third day I was trembling, and Sylvia made me go home.

Back home, I crawled into bed with the radio on. When the girls got home from school, I called them to me and gave them the edited version of what was going on, and where their daddy was. They cried with me for a while, but then, with no urging from me, they seemed to find some strength within themselves. They straightened up and went about their business. How could I do less? So I dried my tears and got myself up out of that bed. The next time I had the urge to succumb to my fears, I thought of my daughters and how brave they were. Then I pulled myself together and carried on with the business of life, just as they did.

We lived in fear for six more weeks. It was the middle of July before we heard from Ned. Somehow, miraculously, he was alive and unharmed.

When the final casualty numbers were available, the nation was shocked and grieving. But as we waited and watched, the tide slowly turned.

Danny remained, as ever, my most stalwart friend. Sometimes it seemed his most important function was to help me take care of my automobile. Finding used car parts was hit or miss throughout the war years, and he helped me track down whatever was needed. I always wondered why such an eligible bachelor as himself was still on the loose, so one day I got brave enough to ask him.

"Okay, tell me the truth, now. Why haven't you ever gotten married?"

He looked at me with a chiding look. "Now, that's an intrusive question."

I made a face at him. "You never know, I might have a girlfriend who's interested in you."

"Hogwash. None of your friends would be interested in me. I'm too old and too intellectual."

"Well, okay, then. I admit I'm just curious. You're my friend, and I wondered, that's all."

He looked at me thoughtfully for a moment, then shrugged. "There's nothing to tell. I've had a few girlfriends through the years, but there wasn't any magic there."

"Magic?"

He stared deep into my eyes then. "When you know that the feeling you have for the other person is true and deep and unstoppable. The kind of love my parents have. I don't want to settle for less."

I couldn't get that out of my head. True. Deep. Unstoppable. Those words described my love for Ned, but it was overshadowed by the damage we'd done to that love. Some things, once broken, can never be fixed.

I slowly prepared myself to lose Ned. Though he hadn't again brought up the subject of separation, neither had he given me any encouragement in any of his letters throughout the year. Of course, we still cared about each other, for we had two beautiful daughters and years of history together, but that wasn't enough. There should be trust and forgiveness, passion and commitment. I feared our marriage was in danger of dying out, like a candle when the wick is used up and there's nothing left but a soft, warm pool of melted wax.

Just before Thanksgiving, I was working in my office when Sylvia's secretary threw open the door. "You need to go see about Mrs. Jenkins," she said, her chest heaving. I got up immediately and ran down the hall. Through the open doorways, I could see through the secretary's alcove into the inner office. Sylvia stood by the window, her back to me, and her shoulders were shaking. I feared the worst. I went in and shut the door.

Going to her, I placed my hand gently on her shoulder. "Sylvia? Is it Roland?"

Wordlessly she nodded, and turned to me, her face twisted with the torment of her sobs. I put my arms around her, and let the waves of her grief flow across me and through me. There was no way to change the tragic truth, but I went through the familiar motions of a mother comforting her child, hoping that the ritual would somehow ease my friend's pain.

After some time, the wrenching sobs tapered off, and she pulled away from me, wiping her cheeks.

"Is he...?" I didn't want to say the word.

She nodded and handed me a telegram from her desk.

Despite her recent loss, Sylvia decided to carry on with the company's Christmas party. It was always quite a tame affair, held in the afternoon, with absolutely no alcohol tolerated, the main attraction being the handing out of Christmas bonuses. I was aware that the mill had actually had a very good year, mostly due to the war, so I guessed that most of us would be pleased with our bonuses. Sylvia was a trooper, keeping a determined smile on her face most of the time, shaking each employee's hand and thanking them for another year of service. Mine was one of the last names she called.

When I heard my name, I went to the table where she was sitting. "Mrs. Jenkins. You're doing great. Roland would be proud of you. And soon, maybe you can go home and relax."

"Don't I wish. I've got dinner with the sisters tonight. Simper, simper." She smiled wryly, and I thought, that's good, she's making a joke.

In my best southern drawl, I replied in a low voice, "Now, Miss Scarlett, you know you shouldn't be makin' fun of the other ladies."

She laughed. "Go on home, Birdie. Have a good Christmas with your family." She waved to the next person to come forward.

I walked away, looking for Danny. I hadn't seen him in several days, and wanted to wish him a merry Christmas. I found him near the door, about to leave. Cold air was rushing in, and I didn't have my coat on.

"You leaving?" I asked.

"Yeah. Wanna go get some coffee?"

"Sure. Let me get my coat."

A minute later, all bundled up, we walked briskly down the street to the diner. Once inside, it was nice and warm, and it smelled like cinnamon. As it was Christmas Eve, most of the shops in town had already closed, and the diner was almost empty.

Looking around at the few customers, I said, "I bet these waitresses are ready to close up and get home to their families. Let's only stay a few minutes."

"That's fine," said Danny, motioning to the girl behind the counter to bring us some coffee. "Just one cup, and we'll go."

As the waitress poured our cups full, I asked Danny what his plans were for the holidays.

"I'll be driving to Raleigh in the morning. You know, my parents and my sister's family are there. I enjoy being around my nieces and nephews at Christmas, hardened bachelor though I am," he joked. "What about you?"

"I'll be at the farm. With the girls. And Flo's family."

"You don't sound too excited."

"I'm not. I know I need to be cheerful for the girls' sake." I took a sip of my coffee. "This is the first year we haven't received a package from Ned for Christmas, and that worries me. A lot. I don't want to upset the girls, so I've just said that he's been so busy, he hasn't had time, which is probably precisely the truth. Just the last couple of days though, I've been reading in the paper that something is going on where France and Belgium meet, almost at the German border, in a forest. The Ardennes. They say the fighting is heavy." I let out a shaky breath. "I think that's where Ned is."

Danny held his hand out, and I took it. "He's made it this far. He'll make it through to the end of the war. You've got to keep believing that, for the sake of your daughters."

I tried to smile through unshed tears. "I know." Taking my napkin, I blotted my eyes. "Ned and I... Well, let's just say it this way. I hope and pray that Ned will survive the war. But our marriage may not."

Danny was perfectly still. "I see." He waited a minute, seeming to gather his thoughts. "You never mentioned this before."

"I wasn't sure that it couldn't be fixed."

From the corner of my eye, I saw that the diner had emptied, and the staff was waiting on us to leave.

"We need to go," I said, picking up my coat.

"One minute." Danny held up his hand for me to wait. "I've been very careful to keep our friendship just that, and nothing more... because I had no reason to think that your marriage was anything but solid." He paused. "I want to say something, not to try to sway you either way, but just to give you a clear picture of your options."

What was he talking about? I was puzzled.

"For quite some time, I've felt that our friendship could, if given the opportunity, grow into something more. The feelings are already there, on my part. So, what I'm saying is, if you and Ned decide to part ways, I'd like a chance with you, Birdie."

I sat there, not knowing what to say, just staring at my good friend, wondering if he was going to burst out laughing and say, "Gotcha! Just kidding!" But he didn't. He was serious.

He jerked his head toward the door. "We'd better get out of here, before they beat us out the door with a stick."

I scooted out of the booth, putting on my coat as we walked to the door. Out in the cold wind, he placed his arm around my shoulder, something he'd never done before. I hadn't felt the security of a man's protection for a long time, and I admit, it felt good. So good I wanted to lean into the crook of his shoulder and lay my head down.

Suddenly, as if a door was flung open into a different world, I was aware of Danny as a man, not as a friend, but as a virile male who was attracted to me, and who could, if our fates converged, be a potential lover. I don't know if he felt it, too, but the air around us seemed to be charged with unseen energy, tingling and making my skin grow warm.

The walk back to our cars seemed an eternity, and yet, only a flicker of time. The parking lot was dark, with only the light of a waning moon to outline a few shadowy shapes here and there. As I fumbled in my purse for the car key, he took my elbow and turned me around. I didn't stop him. Slowly he raised his hands and cupped my face. He lowered his lips to mine, with a gentle whisper of a kiss. No more. With his face still close to mine, he searched my eyes. I don't know what he saw there, but he drew back.

Then he hugged me for a long time, a comforting, strengthening hug that went on and on, rocking me gently back and forth. I hugged him back. There was something good to be said about being close to another person, feeling them near you, touching you. Knowing that someone in this world knew who you were, and where you were, and that you needed a hug.

CHAPTER 34

1945 It was hard to believe that three years had passed since Ned signed up. The only time we'd seen him since then had been right after basic training. The Air Corps and the Navy sometimes let their men have home leave, but the Army infantry served for the duration of the war. Three years without my husband, three years for the girls to be without their father. And the war wasn't over yet. Improving, but not over.

The news from the Ardennes was harsh. The Battle of the Bulge, as they were starting to call it, had caught the Allies with their guard down, as they tried to take a breather from the last six months of almost continuous fighting. Our side had regrouped and eventually pushed the Germans back, but not without heavy casualties. We spent those six weeks praying and worrying and hoping. And once again, God saw fit to spare my husband.

When we finally heard from him, the second week in February, I felt like I could finally breathe again. It wasn't that he wasn't in constant danger anyway, but when those major offensives and battles were all over the news, and I knew his division was involved, it was so much harder to keep a calm head about it. For nine months, ever since D-Day, the action had been intense, and we were all ready for some relief.

The next weekend, Sally and Susie spent the night with a friend, and it seemed a grand opportunity for Sylvia and me to have another girls' night. She had hardly had time to mourn, with the mill still running full throttle, but I thought a night of relaxing conversation might be something she could use about now.

With that in mind, I fully intended to be the ear she could bend and the shoulder she could cry on. Maybe I was, to some extent, but in the end, it seemed that I was the one receiving her wisdom, instead of the other way around.

"You know what bothers me the most?" said Sylvia. "About losing Roland, I mean. Aside from the loss of a future together?"

"No, what?"

"It's all the time I wasted. All the times that could have been great, if I had only let them be." She'd been staring at the rug on the floor, wineglass in her hand. She looked up at me then. "Do you know what I mean?"

I knew exactly what she meant. I nodded slowly. "You fall in love and get married, and everything is like a storybook. The man is perfect and your life together is wonderful," I said. "Then things happen, and..."

"And all of a sudden, one of you is bitter," she finished. "I was so angry at Roland when he joined up. I gave him the silent treatment for weeks."

"What made him decide to join?"

Sylvia rolled her eyes. "It was James Stewart. That pilot recruiting film he did, 'Winning Your Wings,' that came out in forty-two."

"Oh, mercy. Hard to win an argument when it's Jimmy Stewart for the other side."

"Yeah, you said it, sister. I hardly gave him the time of day until right before he left. I wasted all that time…"

"Don't feel bad. I did almost the same thing to Ned. When he said he was signing up, I told him I hated him."

Sylvia shook her head. "I'm sure he knew you didn't mean it."

I shrugged.

She went on. "There are so many things I'd do differently, if I had the chance."

"Like what? Tell me. I really want to know."

"Yes. And I want to tell you, because you've still got time." She stood and walked about the room as she talked. "After we moved back here to Roland's home town, I got my first real taste of his family. His father was all right, although he was very demanding and couldn't stand even the suggestion of fun. But his mother and his sisters were quick to let me know they didn't approve of a woman with a degree in business, much less a woman who wanted to work."

"Sounds uncomfortable."

"It was. But, of course, here is where we had to live, because of the mill. Roland was in line to take over, which he did, when his father died in thirty-nine, much sooner than anyone had planned on. The ownership of the mill passed directly to Roland, and now that Roland is gone, it has passed to me."

"Will you stay here and run it?"

"I don't know yet. I'll definitely be here until the war is over. After that, who knows?"

Getting her back on track, I said, "You never said what you would do differently."

"Right. Let's see. Where was I?" She stopped to pour herself some more wine. "We had other problems, too. They were big to me at the time, but looking back, they seem mostly petty and small. Not that they weren't important issues in their own way, but they shouldn't have caused us to drift away from each other. We wanted children, but that didn't happen. I wanted to adopt, he wouldn't consider it. He wanted to go on weekend trips. I was always too busy. He wanted to go out in the cold, wet snow and play and build a snowman. But I was tired from working and didn't feel like it. There was always something creating a division between us. Or maybe it was both of us, letting it happen, not trying hard enough. Looking back, I think that's probably it."

"But how do you keep from doing that, especially when you don't even know it's happening?"

"I'm not sure," she groaned. "For one thing, we shouldn't have let things fester. We should have made sure that at the end of the day, when we went to bed, there was nothing coming between us."

My mind traveled back. How many nights did Ned and I not touch each other because of resentment or stubbornness?

"Half-truths and lies, instead of trusting the other person to be able to handle the truth." Sylvia twirled her glass in her fingers. "Wanting him to do things my way and agree with me all the time, instead of seeing his point of view. Expecting perfection, instead of understanding that he was only human, too, and needed me to see that he was doing the best he could." She sat back down on the other end of the sofa and looked at me.

"So much time wasted. You don't know what I would give to have another chance with him." She stared back down at the rug with her thoughts. "Don't let it happen this way with you, Birdie. Be grateful for what you have and forgive him when he needs forgiving. If you have the kind of love with Ned that I think you do, hold on to it and never let go."

As occasionally happens in the South, at the end of February, we had a couple of days that were just like springtime. That Sunday afternoon after church, I walked down to the creek to sit a while by myself and do some thinking. It's not in my nature to think I'm in the wrong, so some of it wasn't easy for me.

Sylvia's words had been thundering through my head all week, kicking up clods of doubts and sending clouds of questions to float around in my brain.

Was I guilty of such things as she regretted? I knew I was.

Was I brave enough to examine my faults and then—an even worse thought—strong enough to make an attempt to correct them?

I didn't know.

Listening to the waters gurgling downstream, I leaned back against the warm rock and looked up at the sky. I didn't know the answer, but I was sure God did.

I'd watched my momma and my pa live a desperate married life, with lies and meanness covered up with indecent normalcy. Flo's and Gerald's marriage was full of tawdriness and deceit, though my sister seemed now to have chanced upon a kind soul in Lumpy. In West Virginia, poor widowed Martha, for the sake of her children, had married a drunken boor. Within my circle of acquaintance, truly good marriages seemed to be few in number, though I would count Fairy and Samuel, and maybe Sylvia and Roland, among those few.

Distance and time had changed my perspective on our marriage. Things that had once seemed immense and insurmountable now were simply a part of the people and moments that were woven together into the fabric of my life. Those things were all in the past. What would I do with them now?

While sunlight dappled through the branches above me, I closed my eyes, remembering Ned the first time he came to visit me. Hot and red-faced from his long walk, fanning his face with a straw hat, taking off his shoes to stick his feet in the cooling water. That same summer, he'd come back to the brush arbor meeting, only because he hoped to see me again. In my head, I could hear his voice, singing clear and true. Trickling through the dust on my face, I felt a tear run down each side of my face and drip on to the rock.

Where was that innocent boy now? Over in Europe, fighting as a soldier. Part of the reason he signed up, he admitted, was because he was unhappy. What did that say about me? My husband was unhappy, and I'd barely noticed, so wrapped up was I in my own pain and my own purposes. He would most certainly have gone to war anyway, being the man that he was, but he wouldn't have had to go in order to escape his own unhappy life.

During our girls' night, Sylvia had said something about trusting the other person enough to tell them the truth. I hadn't trusted Ned with the truth, for I'd never told him everything about Gerald. He'd only heard parts of it, when Flo and I were fighting in the wash house. I was afraid to tell him because I thought that he would blame me. I could see now that he deserved to know the whole truth. While it took my Momma's words to convince me of it, I knew now that I had nothing to be ashamed of where Gerald was concerned. And though the truth about Gerry and Tommy was a more delicate matter, Ned deserved to know that, also. As a kindness to Flo, I would ask him never to tell her, as it would serve no purpose other than hurting her, and I had no doubt that he would take the secret to his grave. But between the two of us, I resolved right there and then, there would be no more lies.

Standing up, I dusted my clothes off then leaned down to the creek, to let the water run through my fingers. For the first time in a very great while, I felt at peace. My mind felt clear, like the water flowing around my hand.

From the very beginning, Ned and I had known something precious and rare. A love that was true, deep, unstoppable. Both of us were guilty of allowing our love to grow tarnished and battered. We should have protected it and nurtured it.

Now I was beginning to feel a flicker of hope burning, brightening, down deep inside of me. Ned hadn't said yet what he wanted to do; he'd been in continuous fighting for almost a year, so his letters had been short and few. It was my most fervent hope that he would want to work things out, but as for me, I was going to take Sylvia's words to heart. Our love was worth saving, and I was not going to let it go without a damn good fight.

CHAPTER 35

"Momma, I can't find Sally."

A bag of groceries in each arm, I walked through the back door into the kitchen, to find Susie standing by the stove, her arms crossed in front of her and a worried look on her face. I set the bags down on the table. "What do you mean, you can't find her?"

"I can't find her. She's not in the house, or on the porch. Not in the barn, or anywhere else in the yard. She's gone."

I began to put the groceries up. "Well, when's the last time you saw her? She got off the bus with you, didn't she?"

"Yes. And then we got something to drink, and went to our room to do our homework. Then, I went outside to swing on the tire. When I came back in, she was gone."

"Where's your Aunt Flo? Did you ask her about Sally?"

"She said she didn't know."

I started down the hall, calling my sister.

Susie stopped me. "She's not here. She and Uncle Lumpy and Gerry rode the tractor off toward the Jamison's."

I turned back around. "Well, your sister's got to be here somewhere. She didn't just disappear. Maybe she wanted to be by herself for a while." I noticed there was nothing on the stove for supper. "Aunt Flo didn't cook supper yet?"

"I guess not. When she got on the tractor, I heard her say she wasn't cooking supper for everybody in the world from now on."

I stopped short. I didn't like the sound of that, but there was no need to involve the girls. "Then how about an egg sandwich for supper?"

"That's fine," she muttered.

"Okay. I'll fix your sandwich in just a minute. I'm going to take a look outside for Sally first."

I walked out on the porch and looked around. Where would my child go, if she wanted to get away from her sister and the rest of the family for a while? I knew where I used to go. Down to the orchard, to hide out behind the tree trunks. I took off in that direction.

Fifty feet away, I saw the corner of her skirt sticking out from behind the trunk of the cherry tree. When I reached her, I plopped down on the ground next to her.

"You all right?"

She nodded.

"Your sister's worried about you."

She nodded again.

"Did something happen?"

She shrugged. Which meant something did happen.

"Tell me about it."

She let out a loud breath. "I was finishing up my homework in my bedroom. Aunt Flo went outside with Uncle Lumpy. She said, 'Gerry's in the front room playing.' I only had three more problems to do, so I sat there and did them. Then I heard a chair hit the floor in the kitchen. When I got there, Gerry was on the floor crying. He had used the chair to climb up on the counter, and open the cabinet to get a cookie. When he was climbing back down. he fell and busted his lip open, and it was bleeding. Aunt Flo came in while I was cleaning him up. She said I should have been watching him. She said we ought to be doing a little something for the free room and board we get."

My blood was boiling by that time, but the most important thing at the moment was comforting my daughter. "Oh, Sally. Sweet child of mine. You didn't do anything wrong, so don't you be crying about that. I'm sure Aunt Flo was just upset because she saw the blood—she's a bit squeamish about blood. You've always been a great babysitter for Gerry, even when you were a little thing yourself. And now look at you, twelve years old, and almost a young lady." I tipped her chin up to look at me. "Little boys are going to get into mischief sometimes."

"Especially Gerry," she grumbled.

"Especially Gerry," I laughed, as I stood up. "Let's go in now, so Susie can stop worrying. It's almost dark anyway."

Later that night, after the children were in bed, I asked Flo to walk outside with me. I told her that her remark was uncalled for, since the house and the farm were one quarter owned by me anyway, and that I always bought half the groceries and paid half the light bill. I told her she wouldn't be bothered with us much longer, because we'd be moving out just as soon as I could find a place.

That was all I said. What I didn't say, but was thinking, was that when Carl and Luther came back, we'd be going to see a lawyer, so if Flo and Lumpy wanted this place, they'd better be saving up some money to buy me out.

Though I had planned to look for a place to rent in town almost a year ago, I'd gotten sidetracked by D-Day and the Battle of the Bulge, so I never really got serious about my search. Now I did. I put up a notice on the bulletin board at the mill, and had several suggestions given to me, but nothing panned out. Sylvia had a friend in real estate who was keeping his eyes peeled for me, too.

The first week in April, I took a long lunch one day and went to look at a run-down shack of a house on the outskirts of town. Since the owner took the trouble to meet me there, I went inside and looked, just to be fair, but it was even worse inside than outside. I thanked him for his time and got back in my car. On the way back, I decided to take a different route, down the road that our first little house was on. Slowing down as it came into view, I have to admit that, like many things in life, it did look smaller than I remembered. But it was still a great little house. As I went past, I craned my head to look right at it, and was surprised to see that the windows had no curtains and the house looked empty. I turned my car around and went back by, turned around again and pulled into the yard. I got out and peeked into the windows. Empty.

As soon as I got back to my office, I called information for the number for Mr. Bartow, our old landlord. I was so excited I was dancing around my desk while the connection was being made. When a woman's voice answered, I asked for Mr. Bartow.

"Would you be wanting old Mr. Bartow, or his son, the younger?"

"Uh...I would be wanting the Mr. Bartow who would be around sixty years old, who owns the house on Hickory Lane?"

"Well, I guess you don't know. That Mr. Bartow passed away about two months ago. I'm his daughter-in-law. Would you like to speak to my husband?"

"Yes, please." A polite gentleman picked up the phone, and I explained why I was calling.

"Mrs. Parker, unfortunately, we're in the midst of disposing of my father's estate. You see, we live in Georgia, so we're not interested in retaining ownership of any of his property here. We're only interested in selling."

"Oh, I see. Well, I... uh, I'm very sorry for your loss, and thank you for your time."

"Not at all. Sorry we can't be of any help."

I was so disappointed. "Foot!" I blurted out.

Later in the day, I was in Sylvia's office giving her a production schedule update. When I was done, I mentioned my unlucky news about the little house.

She said immediately, "Well, why don't you just buy it?"

Stunned, I didn't answer right away. I'd never even considered it. "Me? I don't ... I don't think I could. Could I?"

"I don't see why not. Didn't you say that you've saved most of Ned's pay during the war?"

"Well... yes."

"You'd probably need a loan for the rest of it, but I can help you with the paperwork."

I felt a smile tugging at the corners of my lips. Maybe I could do this.

The thought went through my mind then of how pleased my momma would be to see me taking charge of my destiny like this. She always said that things would be different for me and Flora, that we would have choices and opportunities that she'd never had. Well, here I was, an independent woman with a good job, my own automobile, and, soon, my own home. My momma was a pretty smart cookie, huh?

Ever since our encounter at Christmas, Danny had been hanging back, allowing me time to resolve my personal feelings, and I appreciated the respect and consideration he showed me by doing that. Now I was certain where my heart would always be, so it was time to let Danny off the hook. He was a true friend, one who'd watched out for me for the last couple of years. I'd never forget that, but I wanted him to have a full-scale version of the love he envisioned, the unstoppable kind. He deserved it.

I stopped by his desk one morning. "Hi. Wanna get some lunch today?" I asked.

"Sure," he said, with the same wide open smile as always.

"One o'clock?"

"See ya' then," he said.

When we arrived at the diner, the lunch crowd was beginning to leave, so we managed to snag a booth.

"Two blue plate specials," said Danny, when the waitress came. He knew what I wanted, we'd been doing this so long.

"How've you been, Danny?" I asked.

"Pretty good, actually. I'm thinking about going back to school. Getting my doctorate. I think I might like to teach at a college or university."

This was surprising. "Wow. That's great. I didn't know you had any interest in doing that." This didn't seem like the plans of a man who was sitting around waiting for an answer from a girl.

He shrugged. "I guess it's always been in the back of my mind." He smiled. "Just never could get up the nerve to do it."

"Well, I'm happy for you."

The waitress clunked our plates down in front of us, then left.

Danny answered, "I knew you would be." He took a bite of his meatloaf. "Because you're a good friend. You see, Birdie, I never really thought that you'd be interested in me any other way, I just wanted to put it out there on the table. Just in case."

I opened my mouth to speak, but he went on.

"You love Ned, that lucky devil. I've always known that, even if you didn't. There's a bright sparkle comes into your eyes when you say his name. I'd have to be a fool to not see it, and believe me, I'm no fool." He looked at me, then, with all his attention. "Be happy, Birdie. When that man gets home, love him to pieces."

I grinned then. "I will. If he'll let me, I will."

CHAPTER 36

Following the Battle of the Bulge, Ned's division continued to push across Germany, taking towns, rivers, and trains, as they came to them. All through April, we read the stories and saw the pictures of the concentration camps. The atrocities committed were beyond our comprehension here in our safe, orderly, generally kind and decent world. How did the Germans come to this? How did they ever justify what they had done to millions of human beings? Those revelations made our purpose all the more urgent.

By the first of May, The Big Red One was heading into Czechoslovakia. Then on the eighth of May, 1945, Germany surrendered. The war in Europe was over.

It would be three more months before the war in the Pacific would end, with the bombing of Hiroshima and Nagasaki. We kept our vigil and our prayers going for those boys until the war in the Pacific ended, too. Then finally, it was over, and they could all come home.

The last letter I received from Ned before the war in Europe ended was dated the thirtieth of March, and I didn't receive it until a month later. I tried not to worry—I knew Big Red was constantly on the move—but I was so afraid that our luck was going to run out. We were so close to making it to the end without Ned being killed or hurt, and I desperately wanted the assurance his letters gave me that he was still alive.

But there were no more letters. So I prayed and I hoped.

During those last months, while the war was always foremost in our minds, we had other, more personal, victories to celebrate at the same time. The house loan came through without a hitch, thanks to Sylvia's help, and I signed the papers on the first day of May. I wrote Ned the next day, to tell him the good news about the house.

The day we moved in was May the eighth, VE Day, so we had two big things to celebrate that day. And celebrate we did, the girls and I, dancing and singing with the radio blasting away, eating popcorn and drinking Dr. Pepper. The only thing that would have made it more perfect was if Ned had been there with us.

Living on our own, away from the farm, was a relief to all three of us. However, as the days grew hotter, on into the month of June, the girls did miss the respite provided by the creek at the farm. So the last Saturday in June, I drove them out to the farm to spend the day. And just to avoid any snippy remarks from my sister about having to feed my daughters, I sent with them a picnic basket crammed with enough food and drinks to last them a week.

Driving back to the house, I couldn't decide what I wanted to do. I had the whole afternoon to myself, to do whatever I chose. After discarding several ideas as too hot, too boring, or too much trouble, I finally decided to go downtown to the garden center in the hardware store and purchase some more bedding plants for my flower garden.

I was paying for my selections when I heard the train whistle. It was already three o'clock; I had spent almost an hour picking out the flowers. The clerk helped me carry all the trays out to the car, and I shifted them around in the floorboard of the back seat until I had them all fitted in. As I was going around the car to get in, I looked toward the train station, across the street and two blocks up. There was a fellow in uniform coming out, a duffel bag slung over his shoulder. I should give him a ride, I thought.

Backing out of the parking space, I made a U-turn and drove toward the station. As I grew close, my breath started coming faster, and my vision started to blur. I feared I was going to have a sinking spell. This fellow looked a lot like Ned, but I just knew it couldn't be him.

Trying to pull up close so that I could see him, I ran the car up on the sidewalk, just a little. Okay, more than just a little. The soldier turned around and jumped back, probably afraid I was going to run right over him. I got a good look at him then. It wasn't Ned.

I quickly came to my senses, and stuck my head out the window. "Sorry if I scared you. Can I give you a ride, soldier?"

"Gee, that's awfully kind of you, ma'am. But I see my sister's here to pick me up." He pointed to a truck, a couple of parking spaces ahead of us. "Thanks anyway." He tipped his head and smiled, then headed toward his ride.

I put the car in reverse so I could back it off of the sidewalk. I hoped nobody had seen me do that. Facing backward, I had my arm resting along on the back of the seat. I gave the car a little gas, just enough to *floomp* back on to the road, when someone tapped on my window, and liked to have made me jump out of my seat.

Whoever it was, I was going to bless them out for scaring me like that. I whirled around and looked through the window.

I thought I must have been seeing things that day, because I could have sworn I was looking again at a soldier who reminded me of Ned. The car was still in reverse, but I was so addled I let my foot slip off the brake, and it began to move. So I jammed my foot down hard on the brake and my head jerked backward. Grinding the gear knob up into neutral, I pulled up the brake handle. I looked to my left and the face was still there. And it still looked like Ned.

"Birdie," he said. "Do you think maybe you ought to let me drive home?"

I couldn't breathe and my hands were all fumble-fingered, trying to get the car door open so I could get to him. He had to open it for me. When we embraced, if I'd gotten any closer against him, I'd have been inside him. I don't know how long we stood there in each other's arms, rocking, swaying, laughing, crying. It had been so long, so long, so very, very long. But now it was over.

He did have to drive, though, because I couldn't stop shaking, not for a long time.

While he drove, my eyes feasted on the sight of him. I paid no attention at all to the direction we were going, so we almost missed the turn to our house.

"Turn!" I yelled, and pointed to the right.

"Aren't we going home?" he asked, slamming on the brakes

"Yes," I answered, still so giddy that he was sitting there beside me, that I could barely think or speak.

He pointed further down the road we'd been on. "To the farm?"

I smiled then. He didn't know. He must not have gotten my letter. "No, to the house. Our house on Hickory Lane. We bought it."

He looked confused. "Who bought it?"

"We did. You and I. I used the money from your pay, and I borrowed the rest."

"When did this happen? Why didn't you ask me first?"

"Less than two months ago. I wrote you but...I guess the mail was slow. We had to move away from the farm. Flo was...well, she was being Flo. We had to get out of there."

We reached the house and pulled into the yard.

Ned looked at the familiar place, then at me. "Well, I guess you had to do what was best for you. Let's go in. I can't wait to see my girls." He closed his eyes for a moment. "They're going to be so much bigger, I won't recognize them. I've missed so much."

"The girls are at the creek. Why don't we take your things in, and I'll get these flowers unloaded. Then we'll go get the girls. They're probably going to scream when they see you, so don't be alarmed. They're at that age, that's just what they do." I was chattering and blathering, and so full of nerves, I didn't know what I was saying.

The rest of the day was a crazy whirlwind. The girls did scream, but we finally got them to tone it down to squeals and giggles. We decided to stop at the farm, too, so Ned could see Flo and Gerry and meet Lumpy. Then Flo insisted on feeding us supper, so it was nearly nine o'clock before we got back home.

Those first hours and the next few days were intense with feeling. It's hard to put the words together to explain how strong and deep was the joy coursing through me. It was all warm and white and bright. It glowed from the inside out and covered me so that drops of happiness were slung out whenever I moved.

Even the fear of something bad happening, which had never left us, not for all these years, was swept away, as if it were nothing, in the face of such intense happiness.

At some point, when all the hullaballoo died down, we would need to talk, Ned and I. But it could wait. For now, it was enough to look at my husband and say over and over to myself, "Thank you, Lord. Thank you, Lord. Thank you for bringing him home."

CHAPTER 37

For a week or two, Sally and Susie and I had a hard time letting Ned out of our sight. I think he felt the same way, too. I took two weeks off from work, and we spent our days in each other's company, mostly puttering around the house or splashing in the creek. We even went on a family trip. We drove to the ocean, spent the night in a motel, and drove back the next day. It was the most relaxing time I think we'd ever spent as a family.

When it came time for me to return to work, I asked Ned how he felt about it.

"That's fine, Birdie. You need to do whatever makes you happy."

"I do enjoy working. But now that you're home, if you'd rather I didn't, I'll quit." I have to admit, I was sure hoping he wouldn't ask me to.

"No, I don't think you should make a change like that, at least not until I've been home awhile, and we can figure things out."

So he was waiting for us to have our talk. I guess, like me, he didn't want to mar his homecoming with any conflict. I was grateful we'd had this time of peace between us, whatever changes the future might bring.

Ned began to putter in his shop again. One day I walked out to see what he was working on and he showed me some new furniture designs he'd drawn up, based on pieces he'd seen while he was overseas. They were quite beautiful, mostly clean simple lines, but with elegant shapes. I told him I thought they would sell, and suggested he make a sample of each one. A week later, as we were finishing supper, he told me he'd finished the first piece.

"May I come see it?" I asked.

"Sure. I'd like your opinion."

Pushing my chair back, I got up from the table. "Come on, then. Sally, I believe it's your turn to do the dishes. Susie sweeps tonight." I went to the back door and held the screen open for Ned, who was just getting up from the table. He was humming as he went out the door.

The door and windows of the shop were open, to let the breeze flow through. The interior was shadowed compared to the brightness of the late afternoon sun outside, making it hard to see at first.

Then I saw it. In the center of the open space in the middle of the shop was the chair. It was a simple design with no intricate carvings, but the normal lines were just slightly stretched and curved and smoothed into a comfortable elegance. I touched the arm and ran my hand up and down the polished wood. He'd not stained or shellacked it yet, but the grain of the oak wood itself was perfect. My hand still on the wood, I looked up at Ned. "It's wonderful."

He stopped humming and said, "Try it out." So I sat down. It was like molded satin.

"This is the best piece you've ever made," I said. "You were very good before, but this is a whole new level."

I could tell he was trying not to show too much emotion, but he couldn't entirely hold back his smile. He shrugged. "I got to see a lot of beautiful furniture and woodworking while I was there..." He seemed lost in thought, perhaps seeing it all in his mind again. "Northern Africa, Greece, England, France, Belgium, Germany... I thought, if I ever got back home, I could make something beautiful, you know?" When he looked at me again, his eyes begged for understanding. The need went beyond our relationship. It was one human being needing assurance from another human being, that even in the chaos that confounded us, beauty could still be found.

"You did, darling. You made something beautiful." Somehow, in the midst of all that ugliness he'd seen, he'd managed to find the beauty and bring it home with him. That's why I loved this man.

Ned hadn't mentioned going back to the furniture factory, which surprised me a little, because I assumed he would want to do that. Somehow, despite my tendency to say what I thought, I managed to keep my mouth shut about that issue. It seemed only fair that I should wait on him to figure that out for himself, just as he was leaving my decision to work up to me. After all, I was making enough for us to live on, as long as we weren't too extravagant. He had spent the last three years in strange places, killing other men, watching other men die, seeing things that no one should ever have to see. As far as I was concerned, he could do whatever he wanted to do from now on. He had earned it.

Within a couple of months, he had ten pieces ready to show. I described his work to Sylvia and she was eager to see it. When I introduced them right after Ned got home, they seemed to hit if off right away. So I invited her over to take a look.

The shop was rather crowded with all the furniture, so Ned had built another small building to house the finished work. He appeared a little shy and anxious when he opened the door to the building so she could go in, but all that nervousness disappeared when he saw her honest admiration.

"This is incredible, Ned. Are you saying you created these designs yourself?"

"Well, yes, but they're based on the shapes and designs I saw overseas. See, this table here is based on a Moroccan style." He moved to the other side. "And this chair over here has a definite Scandinavian feel."

"Well, they're marvelous." She was running her hand across the smooth arms of the chair.

"I told her they were really special," I said to Ned.

"I'm going to want this low table here, and two chairs like this one. And this bench. I have some pillows that will be perfect with that."

"Are you sure you want all that?" He said in disbelief.

"Yes, I really do, and I'm not just ordering because you're my friends. I really like the furniture. Now, I'm in no hurry, so there's no need to give me these samples. I can wait for you to build more. You're going to need these to show the other buyers."

"What other buyers?" he asked.

"The buyers from the fancy furniture stores. I have some connections, and I'm going to put your name out there. Do you think you could get a photographer over here to take some pictures next week? If we hurry, you might get some orders for the Christmas season."

With Sylvia's guidance, things moved fast. So fast, that Ned had to hire some help in order to get all the orders completed in time to ship before Thanksgiving. That success did a lot for him. I could see it in his step, and in his renewed confidence. Once he became known among the buyers, he never lacked for work.

We still hadn't had our talk. I didn't want to be the one to bring it up, but I didn't want to live the rest of my life in limbo either, married but yet not totally committed to each other. It's not that things were bad between us. We weren't fighting or even disagreeing. We were cordial and kind to each other, and as always, things went without a hitch in the bedroom, but we never shared the really serious things, the things that made us afraid, or ashamed, or angry. In the early years of our marriage, we'd been more than polite friends who made love and shared children. Back then, we had more, and I wanted us to have more again.

The last Christmas we'd spent together as a family had been in West Virginia. I'd just lost Tommy, then the Japanese bombed Pearl Harbor and the war began. It was a fairly wretched Christmas that year. With all its polite cheer and shallow good wishes, this year was just as sad to me.

Geographically, we were together for the first time in years, but emotionally, we were still thousands of miles apart. Soon enough, there would be anger and resentment and it would fester, because in our new politeness, we would never deal with it.

Both of us had secrets. For me, it began with Gerald and spiraled into a complicated mess. With Ned, I think he didn't want the pain that might come with keeping nothing back. He rarely spoke of the years he'd been away, but I sometimes saw glimpses of the horrors in his eyes. At those times, he would withdraw into himself, hiding his feelings from me. I wanted to lighten his burden by sharing it with him, but only he could open that door.

As Sylvia had said, we were wasting so much time. We had all these moments in our life that could be great, but we were settling for so much less.

Christmas morning was one of those times. We managed to keep our faces cheerful for the girls, but when they left to visit friends after lunch, there was only a careful politeness between us. Sylvia had given us a bottle of wine, so I opened it and poured two glasses, handing one to Ned, who was listening to the radio. I walked by and turned it off.

"Drink the wine. You may need it," I said, taking a sip from my own glass. He wasn't the only one who might need it. I was starting this. I only hoped I would be able to finish it.

"What's this about?" he asked.

"Do you remember the letter you sent me last Christmas?"

He looked wary. "Yes. Why?"

"Do you remember all the anger between us before we left West Virginia?"

"Yes," he answered.

"Last Christmas, in your letter, you said you hadn't decided if you wanted to try to work things out between us. You said you weren't sure if we should even stay together."

"Yes. I did say that."

"Well, honey, have you made up your mind yet?"

He raised an eyebrow. "Have you made yours up?"

"Yes. I have."

"What did you decide?"

I took the plunge. I would hang myself out to dry, take the bullet, whatever it took. I was ready to strip my heart naked, and hope that he would do the same for me. I wanted to be one with this man again, body, soul, mind, and spirit, and I was willing to die a little in order to get there. If he didn't want to take the plunge with me, so be it. There were worse things than being alone.

"I have to tell you some things first," I said.

Then I told him everything. About Gerald. About Pa and my momma and Flo. About Gerry and Tommy. About my own part in the deceptions and half-truths. I hid nothing. He sat silently and listened. I couldn't tell what he was thinking, for his face showed no expression. Only his eyes seemed alive, focused intently on me as I spoke.

Finally, all the layers of lies were stripped away, and still he said nothing. I tried to smile and made a mess of it, but it was all right that he saw it. I had nothing left to hide and everything to hope for.

He leaned forward in the chair, and held his head in his hands. I waited a long time, and still he didn't move and didn't say anything. Doubts assailed me. What had I done? What was I thinking? I'd lied to him and kept things from him for years. Did I think I'd get off that easy? Just confess and he'd forgive me?

Though your sins be as scarlet, they shall be as white as snow... Not *my* sins. Oh, no. Not *my* sins. To Ned, the person I loved most in this world, my sins would remain ever scarlet, like gashes of blood across our lives.

He spoke. "Tommy wasn't your son? Gerry is your son?" His eyes remained fixed on the floor, his head down, as his hands rubbed back and forth through his hair, back and forth, over and over. He looked to be in anguish. Why hadn't I left it alone? He'd just returned from years of violence and horrors, with barely time to feel normal again, and now I'd taken away any sense of security he might have felt in our relationship. All because I was selfish and impatient and thoughtless of my husband's needs.

My throat was clogged with the effort of holding back my emotions. But he deserved an answer. I cleared my throat. "Yes. Gerry is my son. And Gerald's. Tommy was Flo's baby. And Gerald's." I watched as his shoulders began to shake, knowing I was the cause of his pain. I couldn't stand it, that I was hurting him again.

I had to get out of there. I grabbed my purse and ran out the door.

I didn't know where I was going when I got in the car, but somehow I knew where I needed to go. I headed for the creek.

I had walked out without a coat again, but I had a blanket in the boot of the car this time. Wrapped up in it, I listened to the gurgle of the water. The rock I sat on held no summer heat. It was cold and dead and unforgiving.

What was the matter with me? Where had I lost my way? I searched my mind for the beginning of the tangle, pulling this thread loose, untying another, slipping the knots undone. Did it even matter anymore? What was done, was done. I couldn't undo it. All I had control over was now, and even that was tenuous and subject to being tossed around by the winds of life.

Unbidden, something the old preacher in the mountains had said came to my mind. I could hear his old, shaky, raspy voice. "My children, you get yourself straight with God, and it won't matter how hard this life tries to defeat you and knock you down and cheat you. This life can't take away from you what you've got with your God. So you hold fast to that. He's strong enough to carry you through."

And then I knew. I needed to get straight with God. How had I not seen this before?

I stood and let the blanket fall. Piece by piece, I removed my outer clothes, leaving just the undergarments. I wanted to be clean. I stepped into the water.

The icy coldness of it stole my breath away and I gasped. I took another step, then another. The water was higher than normal, and our bathing pool was up to my chest. I grabbed hold of a tree branch hanging over, and lowered myself deeper, until the water was over my shoulders.

Wash me clean. Please. Take my sins off of me. Make me pure and whole and strong. Hold fast to me, Jesus.

I dipped below the surface and stayed there. My skin was growing numb, but I wanted to feel the water rushing past, scrubbing me clean, purifying me.

I stayed under until I felt it. They were gone. My sins were gone. He took them away.

I stood with a smile on my face. And shivered. I needed to get out of this water; I was freezing.

Sloshing through the water to the creek bank, I heard something crashing through the trees and looked up. It was Ned, and he was out of breath. When he saw me in the water, he stopped with a strange look on his face. "Birdie? What the... What the heck are you doing in the creek?" He hurried to help me step up onto the bank. "Get out of there. And get some clothes on, you crazy woman."

I was shivering so hard my teeth were chattering against each other. He picked up the blanket and wrapped it around me. "Why did you leave like that?" he said.

"H-H-How'd you know where I was?" I countered.

He rubbed my arms and my shoulders and my back, trying to warm me up. "Well, where else would you go if you were upset?"

I smiled at him. He knew me well.

My fingers were so cold and stiff, I had trouble holding on to my clothes to get them on. He pushed my hands aside and began to dress me.

Ned was buttoning up my shirt when I asked him, "Can you ever forgive me?"

He kept buttoning. "I could ask you the same thing."

"But you didn't do anything..."

"Didn't I?" Draping the blanket around me, he pushed me down to sit on the rock, so he could put my socks on me. "I never gave you a chance to explain. I just assumed the worst, and left you to handle everything all alone."

"But I..."

"What else were you supposed to do?" He reached for my shoes and slipped them on me. Sitting cross-legged in front of me, he took my hands in his. Putting them next to his mouth, he blew his warm breath, over and over, until I felt the coldness fading, to be replaced by his warmth.

I hadn't expected this. Tears coursed down my cheeks, but I didn't care. Tears were unimportant. I wanted to reach for him, wrap my arms around him tight, and never let go, but I needed an answer first. I pulled my hands from his, and folded them in my lap.

"I love you. With everything I am, I love you." I sniffed and wiped my eyes. "And I'm sorry. For everything. Can you forgive me? Can we start over?"

"Ah. Birdie, my love. Yes, I forgive you. And will you forgive me?"

I nodded. "We can start over?"

"We already have." He took my hands, and, turning them over, kissed each palm tenderly. "I've loved you from the first moment I saw you, there in the brush arbor."

Then he smiled, and in his face I saw the boy I'd loved from the beginning of it all. My beloved gave me a promise to last all the years to come. "You have my heart. Forever."

THE END

COMING IN 2017!

FROM THE AUTHOR OF
HEAVEN'S MOUNTAIN TRILOGY

THE READER

A SCI-FI NOVEL

&

THE ANGEL'S PEN

A CHRISTMAS ANTHOLOGY

Turn the Page

For a Special Preview

of Both Books!

~ Coming in 2017 ~

THE READER
A Sci-Fi Novel

In the year 3725, only the Readers practiced the ancient art of translating letter symbols into words. Centuries earlier, when all computers converted to telepathic function, recognizing the written word became unnecessary for the masses. But every ten years, an infant would be selected from each pod-group as a Reader In Training, or "Rit", as they were commonly called.

Chapter 1

"There has to be another solution!" The desperate plea was shouted from the back of the chamber, accompanied by nodding heads and murmurs of agreement.

The answer was swift and decisive. "There could be. *If* we had another week to produce the antiviral. *If* the virus didn't work so fast. *If* we only needed one hundred doses instead of four hundred. *If! If! If!"*

Standing now, Captain Shader leaned forward, bracing himself on his forearms. His head and shoulders fell, indicating his anguish.

The crowded compartment was silent, as the group, consisting of all the key decision makers from every sector of the galleon's self-contained community, considered the implications of the captain's statement. The lull lasted only a few seconds, followed by low rumblings then a cacophony of shouted outbursts.

The captain raised his eyes to his companions, then stood upright, commanding their respect and attention. The room again grew quiet.

"I am willing to hear any suggestions you have. I welcome them." He waited for a response, but there was none. He continued. "Let's go over the facts again. You have heard the reports and opinions of our experts. Medical, biological, chemical, agrarian. This virus is previously unknown to us. Similar strains, of which we have knowledge, are not usually life-threatening, but from our experience today, we can assume that this particular virus is fatal within six hours of exposure. An effective antiviral is available and reproducible, but not within six hours. It takes a minimum of one week to grow and process the key ingredient, Aprozel. In our pharmacy we have sufficient serum for ninety-eight inoculations. There are four hundred twenty seven souls on board this ship."

First Officer Hathaway rose from his chair to the right of the captain. "Captain. What are your orders, sir?"

"Since we were all exposed to the virus just under two hours ago, we have approximately four hours left. For the next two hours, our minds and bodies should be able to function at almost normal levels." The captain's expression grew even more somber. "Let us use those two hours well.

"Our highest priority will be to prepare our young ones for their new responsibilities. We are twenty-one months into our twenty-seven month journey, so returning to New Earth is not an option. Planet 237 has been prepared for our arrival. Our young ones will be safe there. Consistent with colonization procedures, they have been mentally and physically nurtured and trained from an early age. We can have every confidence that they are prepared to assume leadership. Barring any unforeseen complications, the galleon will arrive at our destination in just under six months. As we are all well aware, the ship's systems require very little human intervention. For times such as this, we have made sure that multiple redundancies exist in both systems and human expertise."

Captain Shader turned to his first officer. "Mr. Hathaway, I'd like you to determine from the manifest which of the younger crew members will be assuming all key positions. Do this as quickly as possible, then meet with them and their current counterparts. Take no more than an hour for this. We have very little time."

The captain turned to his left. "Dr. Switt. Administer the inoculations immediately, starting with the youngest on board." With knitted brow, he closed his eyes as if in pain. Opening his eyes, he added, "We should be able to ensure the survival of everyone under twenty five."

Turning to the rest of the room, he continued. "Those of you needing to pass on specific vocational instructions, use your TOC and make it available to your successor. Beyond that, I remind parents that protocol requires that you record instructions, encouragement, and final words for your children. You have already prepared all other family matters as a prerequisite prior to embarkation. Beyond this, you should spend every moment with your family and, as best you can, prepare them for your imminent demise."

No one moved, as the eyes of all present remained fixed on their beloved captain and friend.

"Dismissed," came the order. One by one, they left the chamber.

****

It was an honor to be chosen as a Reader, Lissy reminded herself. Mom and Dad had been so proud to have a Reader in the family. The thought of her parents caused another outburst of sobs, choking their way out of Lissy's chest.

She still couldn't believe they were gone. Along with every other adult on the space galleon, they had fallen victim to a deadly virus. The disease had hit so quickly, there was no time to quarantine the virus or prepare enough inoculations. The devastation was complete in a matter of hours.

Their pod, consisting of the required 300 adults and their families, had volunteered to spearhead the colonization of Planet 237. Having left New Earth more than nine months ago, they were scheduled to reach their new home in just six months. Now, here they were in deep space, with less than one hundred souls remaining on board, and all of them young, too young for the responsibility that was being laid upon their shoulders.

Someone was buzzing at the entrance to her family's quarters. Wiping her cheeks with the tail of her shift, she squared her shoulders and opened the door.

"Lissy O'Connor?" A young officer stood uncomfortably at ease, hands behind his back.

"Yes."

"I'm Cameron." He ducked his head as if embarrassed, then looked at her apologetically. "I'm the new captain. May I come in?"

She motioned for him to enter and sit.

Obviously nervous, he began, "I..uh... I can't believe I'm doing this, talking to anybody as the captain of this ship, but...I'm the highest ranking officer left to take the job." He ran his hand across the short hair on top of his head, then stared at her, a strange expression in his eyes. "I'm twenty-three." He took a deep breath and sat up straight.

He continued, "You're the oldest Rit we have. The only other one is six-year-old Jaden. So, it's you, Lissy O'Connor. You are The Reader of the pod now."

Lissy sat numbly as he briefed her on their situation. She had known for a long time that the reading itself was not the only task that fell to the Reader. The pod counted on their Reader to be intuitive and wise, interpreting the words so that the correct meaning was applied. She was only sixteen and she knew she was not ready.

When Cameron left, Lissy walked to the door of her parents' bedroom, where her younger brother and sister were sleeping. Climbing up on the bed, she cuddled up against them and tried to sleep, but there were too many important questions demanding her attention.

With a wisdom born of necessity, Lissy pondered the possibilities for the years ahead. The remainder of the pod, young as they were, were to proceed to Planet 237 where facilities and provisions awaited. For the next two years, the older ones would manage the colony with the help of the Custodians, the one couple who had remained behind when the planetary preparation force departed.

And she, Lissy O'Connor, would be their Reader. This had always been her destiny, but she must embrace it *now*, though thrust upon her suddenly and prematurely. She resolved she would lead the young colony with calmness, integrity and wisdom, in the tradition of all the Readers who had come before her. With the certainty of this decision now inscribed on her heart, she slept.

~ Coming in 2017 ~

THE ANGEL'S PEN

A Christmas Anthology

Chapter 1 - Maggie's World

What a waste of time. A mandatory faculty meeting on the last day before Christmas break. Did they think some of the professors might slip away early? There was little enough pressing business to discuss, so maybe someone was in the back of the room counting heads. Maggie wouldn't have minded being somewhere else herself, maybe on a beach somewhere with a pina colada in hand. She could almost smell the coconut when the sound of the Dean slamming his notebook shut whisked her away from the white sand and back to the reality of the present.

"So, that's it for today, ladies and gentlemen. We're all done for the semester, except for those of you who still need to get your grades entered online." The dean of Wilson-Street College gave a mock salute, then dashed out the door, briefcase in hand, his last words echoing from the hall, "See you all next year. On January sixth. Ho, ho, ho."

Maggie heard one of the younger professors commenting to anyone nearby, "He certainly didn't waste any time getting out of here, did he?"

Maggie shrugged. After ten years heading the English Department, she'd seen it all. "Ignore him. Ignore all of us. We tend to get a little strung out at the end of the semester." Rising, she situated her purse strap on her shoulder and grasped the handle of her satchel. "See you in a few weeks." She joined the queue of faculty members at the double doors, their exit slowed by the student aides handing out holiday gift bags.

Waiting in the back of the crowd, she made a mental list of the stops she needed to make on the way home, the most important of which was the paint store. "The Plan" was to repaint her dining room and kitchen over the Christmas break. Beyond that, she'd made no other definite commitments--to herself or anyone else.

Maybe she'd stop at the coffee shop first. It would be nice to sit there as long as she liked--get the free refill on the coffee for once. There was a comfortable seating area in the back that she'd always wanted to try out. Yeah, now that she thought about it, she could finally start reading the new book that was in her satchel--the one she'd been carrying around with her since before Thanksgiving.

Lost in her thoughts, she didn't notice the attractive older man sidle up next to her. "Maggie. So glad I caught you. How've you been?"

Jim. She caught the voice as soon as he said her name, in that low drawl. Such a nice guy. If she were in the market for a beau, he would be at the top of her list. She turned to greet him. "Hey.. I'm doing great, now that I have this five week hiatus starting today. How about you?" Yes, it was a shame she had no interest in getting involved with anyone. Even though his hair was mostly gray, his genuine smile and fit physique gave him the look of someone younger.

"My son and his wife are coming for a visit this week. Then, the week before Christmas, I'll be skiing with a group of friends. Sure you wouldn't like to go with us?"

Maggie shook her head. Much too uncomfortable to be around a big group of strangers for a whole week, especially at Christmas. You never knew what might be dredged up. "Thanks, anyway. I've got too many things I need to do at home over the holidays."

"Well, do you have plans for Christmas Day?" He was persistent, she'd give him that. "I know you said you don't have any family around. I wish you'd join me at the Salvation Army, to help cook and serve Christmas dinner. Believe it or not, it's always a blast. Will you think about it?"

She shrugged. Easier to say she'd think about it, than to try to explain why she wasn't coming. "I'll think about it."

The look he gave her could only be interpreted as disappointed, as if he knew what her answer really was. He gestured for her to precede him through the door. "I'll still hope to see you there."

Slipping in front of him, she was handed a red gift bag of Christmas goodies by one of the staffers. She waited on him to get his, then they walked together to the faculty parking lot, not speaking until they said goodbye at her car.

At this hour, midway between the breakfast rush and the lunch crowd, only a few patrons were scattered around the coffee shop. After paying for her pastry and coffee, she made a beeline for that beckoning chair in front of the fireplace.

Breathing in the scent of the burning logs, peace descended on her. The smell took her back to her grandparents' old farmhouse, a long time ago, when she was a little girl. Leaning back into the big, soft cushions, both hands wrapped around the hot coffee, she sighed. Tension and troubles, real or imagined, evaporated into nothing. Her new book lay forgotten in the satchel as she relaxed into the moment.

Her head jerked up. Almost asleep there. Coffee would not match well, if spilled onto her cream sweater. She set it aside and took out her book. She was well into the first chapter and took only vague note when a young man took the seat opposite her, on the far side of the hearth.

Turning the page for chapter two, she was aware of being watched. It was the young man. When he saw her look up and their eyes met, he smiled at her. It seemed natural to Maggie to smile back. Evidently he took that as acceptance on her part. He spoke.

"Dr. Jones?"

She realized he must be one of her students. Funny, he didn't look familiar. "Yes?"

"I'm Gabe Lowery. I'd like to talk to you for a moment. But if this is not a good time, maybe I could set up an appointment?" The picture of politeness, this one. Which only made her less inclined to shut him up, spit-spot. Thing is, as of this very minute, she was totally relaxed, so talking with this lovely young fellow while she sipped on a refill of her coffee actually seemed like a pleasant way to spend the morning.

"If you would be so kind as to take my cup to the counter for a refill - just tell the barista it's for me - I think I could spare a few minutes for you." She held her cup out to him, and he immediately rose to do her bidding.

"I'll be right back," he said.

While he was gone, she marked her place in the new book and put it away, then slipping off her ankle boots, she tucked her feet up beside her in the roomy chair.

With two cups in hand, Gabe returned. He handed Maggie her cup, then drug his chair closer, to a more intimate distance.

"Do I know you? Gabe, was it? Were you in one of my classes?"

"No, I've never had the pleasure." He raised his forefinger for emphasis. "We do, however, have a mutual acquaintance, who recommended to me that I contact you as soon as possible."

Intriguing. "Who might that be?"

"Kitty Cantrell."

"Ah! Have you seen her recently, then?"

"Last week, as a matter of fact, at the publishing company office in New York."

"How is she?"

Gabe grinned. "Smart and feisty as ever."

"I'm glad to hear it. I always wish I could see her more often, but she doesn't return to her old hometown so much anymore."

"She said you were friends from way back? High school?"

"That's correct." Enough of the digging into her past. Maggie shifted to get more comfortable. "Now, then. Why has she sent you to me?"

"She told me you were a part-time editor, and that you sometimes agreed to help her out when they get overloaded."

"I think I did that once, about fifteen years ago...." She knew what was coming, and she was not going to dismantle all her holiday plans to save someone else's hide.

"She says you're the best."

Maggie shook her head. No way was she going to get lassoed into this.

Gabe began talking a little faster, as if he knew he was losing ground. "I know it's quite an imposition, and will probably disrupt all your Christmas plans, but I'd very much appreciate it if you would hear me out." His dark curly locks shimmered with the reflected glow from the fire, and his eyes were luminous with an ancient purity. Against her will and her better judgment, she felt drawn to him. What harm to hear him?

"Very well. I'm listening."

"Great." His smile made her want to keep him smiling. "Here's what I need. I need someone to edit my book. Kitty says if it's edited in time, it will be on the short list when the company chooses the offerings for next Christmas season. I have to have the first revision copy on her desk by the first of March." He stopped, waiting for her response.

She couldn't believe she was actually going to allow this to go any further. And then she did. "Tell me about your book."

Scooting to the edge of his seat, he used both hands as he talked. "Christmas anthology. Four novelettes. Real people, a shot of romance, family, missed chances, second chances... and, of course, Christmas."

"I could say it's all been done and said before."

"You're right. It has." He raised an eyebrow. "But never with these exact stories. And never with myself as the author." He sipped his coffee and set the cup back down. "Dr. Maggie Jones. Would you do me the honor of marking up my manuscript with as much red pencil as it takes?"

What a line. Still, if he told his stories as well as he presented himself, the book would be a delight. And as far as the Christmas break was concerned, her top priority was actually to keep herself busy. So busy that she would not have a minute to think about how empty her life was and how lonely she sometimes felt. Painting would only take a week of her time. She needed another major project, and this might well fit the bill.

It only remained to negotiate the fee. "Will the publisher be paying the fee?"

"No, that would be me. I'll pay whatever you ask."

Impressive. He hadn't even asked how much. "Very well. I'll consider the job." She took a card from her purse and handed it to him. "My email. Send me the manuscript as soon as you can. I'll take a look at it and let you know if I would be the right person to edit your book."

He had already taken the card, but when she finished speaking, he corrected her assumption. "Oh, no. It's not on a computer."

She cocked her head, as might a bird. Not on a computer? Surely, the manuscript wasn't... ?

"It's handwritten. All by my own hand." He looked quite pleased with his admission.

"You're kidding." How could it be that a young man of his age - twenty-five at the most, possibly younger - would not avail himself of the convenience and speed of a word processing program?

He shook his head quickly. "Not kidding. Oh, I know how to use a computer. I just found that when I was writing, the words flowed so much more smoothly and effortlessly when I wrote them out by longhand." He leaned over and pulled out a manila portfolio. "Here it is. You're welcome to take it with you today."

She hesitated, then held out her hand. What difference did it make? "Give it to me."

A NOTE FROM THE AUTHOR

I hope you enjoyed reading Birdie's story. I couldn't have completed what was, for me, a quite ambitious project, without the assistance, support and guidance of many people. Jan Ackerson, my wonderful editor, pushed me in new directions and helped me make the final product so much better than my first effort. Thank you, Jan!

My thanks also go to the brave souls who read the rough draft, Rena, Gail, Donna, but especially my daughter, Laura, who (poor thing!) patiently listened and gave me feedback whenever I asked for it, and my daughter, Rebecca, who is a constant source of marketing ideas.

I'm very blessed to have the support of my children, my parents, my grandchildren, my siblings, and many wonderful friends. If I don't say it often enough, thank you and I love you.

Jackie Wilson

BOOKS BY JACALYN WILSON

HEAVEN'S MOUNTAIN TRILOGY:

(Inspirational Romance with a Touch of Suspense!)

Heaven's Mountain

Mountain Song

Mountain Girl

SHORT & SWEET

(Three short stories – A little Southern and a little Sassy!)

WHAT WE HAD

(The Story of Birdie – 1929 to 1945)

COMING IN 2017

THE READER

(A Sci-Fi Novel)

THE ANGEL'S PEN

(A Christmas Anthology)